THE LION'S PATH

GIDEON WOLF BOOK 4

ERNEST DEMPSEY

138 PUBLISHING

CHAPTER 1

I heard them before I saw them. It shouldn't have been difficult for professionals to keep quiet down here in the catacombs beneath the city of Lisbon, but with a team that size approaching me, not everyone could stay perfectly silent. Maybe not every one of them was a pro.

A slight swish of fabric, a subtle click of metal. Easy to miss for a normal person.

But I was anything but normal.

Vero must have heard it too. Her head twitched to the left just slightly, as if listening more intently to hear it again.

We didn't say anything to each other. We didn't need to.

We figured someone had followed us here. Since my transformation, I just assumed that was always going to be the case. It had been ever since I discovered the medallion around my neck in the jungles of Mexico. People with evil intentions had sought my medallion—still did—and the one that dangled from Vero's neck.

I flicked my head to the side—a silent order for us to keep moving.

She gave a curt nod, and we continued ahead, faster this time.

We picked our way through the darkness, our flashlight beams dancing off the rows of skulls and skeletons lining the musty corridor. We'd passed several stone coffins along the way, tombs for the dead who'd had more wealth in life than those whose remains had been stacked so close to, and on top of, one another.

The hard, rocky ground underneath made it easier to keep from making too much noise. Vero and I also carried small day packs strapped over our shoulders, and we'd made sure before descending into the underground passages that they were tight against our backs, both for mobility and for stealth.

We'd come to Lisbon to hunt for the remains of a late fifteenth-century sailor—the first mate of the famous Portuguese explorer Diogo Cão.

I glanced back over my shoulder, allowing Vero to take the lead. At the end of a long straight portion of the passage up ahead, the pale circles of our hunters' lamps bounced off the walls of bones at a corner. They were still out of sight, but they were moving quickly.

If they were a tactical unit—and everything so far suggested they might be—they'd slow down at the corner, send a guy around it to clear the next section of tunnel, and then allow the others to move ahead.

These little pauses would give Vero and me a little buffer, but not much.

I hurried forward and caught up to her. Neither of us dared speak. Even though the group behind us knew we were down here, there was no reason to make their job any easier.

We rounded a long bend in the corridor and reached another sarcophagus on the left side.

I slowed down to inspect the name on the top. I swiped the dust from the engraving, then shook my head at Vero.

That wasn't the one.

We sped up to a near sprint. The thick, cool air made breathing more difficult. It squeezed our lungs, only letting in so much at a time. The smell—a pungent, musty odor of decay—didn't help things.

My heart raced. I knew I shouldn't be afraid of whoever was behind us, but I was also keenly aware that our enemies would only keep trying the same useless tactics, like bullets, for a limited amount of time. Sooner or later, they would come up with something new, a new plan of killing me and Vero, and taking the Medallions of Power from us. Whether we were in our monster forms or not.

The passage stretched out before us in a long, straight line. At the end of this section, it cut back to the right.

I hoped our pursuers hadn't gained on us while I'd checked the last sarcophagus.

We'd nearly reached the end of the straightaway when the toe of my shoe caught on an irregular piece of the ground beneath us. I tripped and fell forward, rolling to a stop. For two seconds, Vero kept going, assuming I'd regained my balance. But when she looked back, she saw me on the ground.

I grimaced and motioned at her. "Keep going," I hissed. "I'll catch up."

She shook her head and started to retreat.

"No. Check the next sarcophagus. I'll be right behind you."

She hesitated, then turned and moved ahead.

I looked back again. Flashlights shimmered on the wall of the long, curved portion of the corridor. Simply from the size of the circles, I guessed they were still only halfway down the previous section of tunnel.

"You know, you could always—" the voice in my head started.

"No, I can't," I countered. The ceiling was only eight feet high—maybe. There were sections that looked lower than that.

I knew that if I shifted into the creature, movement in here would be difficult. Hence why Vero and I had remained our human selves up to this point. There wasn't enough room for one of us, much less both of us in monster form to maneuver at all in here.

"Not with that attitude," the voice said.

I shook my head, wishing he would shut up.

My knee throbbed as I stood. I'd hit it hard on the ground as I fell, and the joint had taken the brunt of the fall. My jeans were scuffed but not torn. There was that little silver lining.

The knee would heal shortly, but would be faster if...

I let the thought go and hurried forward at a limping gallop. The pain screamed from the kneecap, and I could barely put any weight on it.

Up ahead, Vero waited for me at the corner, disobeying my request. It was a funny thing to think—*disobey*. She wasn't my servant. She wasn't beholden to me. But still, my desire for her safety outweighed that logic at the moment.

She pointed her light down the next section of corridor while watching me approach. As I drew closer, she was also looking beyond me, to the other end of the passage.

I risked another glance back and saw the circles on the stacks of bones getting smaller. The men were almost there.

Vero motioned with her free hand, as if that would somehow coax me into moving faster. She held out her hand, and as I reached her, she looped it under my armpit and ushered me around the corner.

"You're hurt," she said.

"Yeah. I hadn't noticed." I smiled.

She rolled her eyes at me. "You know if—"

"We don't have room. Not in here. Come on. We have to get to the sarcophagus."

"And then what? They'll have us pinned."

"Maybe," I countered.

During the days that followed the events near Panama, I had discovered another clue regarding the possible location of the next medallion. At least, that's what I believed.

It could have been nothing, but the fact the team behind us was bent on stopping us from getting to it first only reinforced my theory.

In one of his old books, my friend Jack had discovered an interesting bit of information regarding Diogo Cão.

Cão had been a Portuguese explorer who made significant contributions to the exploration of the west coast of Africa in the late fifteenth century. He was known for discovering the mouth of the Congo River and exploring the coastline southward. His last voyage was around 1485-1486, and it was presumed that he died during this expedition. It was believed that he'd been buried somewhere along the way, and that his first mate continued on their quest, taking over as captain of the ship.

But there was no conclusive historical record pinpointing Cão's final resting place, and much of what was known about his death and burial was based on speculation and fragmented historical accounts. Historians generally believed that he was buried somewhere near the area he was exploring when he died, likely along the coast of present-day Angola or Namibia.

But I wasn't interested in any of that, other than out of historical curiosity.

What Jack had found in his library suggested that Cão had been searching for something hidden in Africa, something that could give him incredible power.

Along with the book in Jack's collection were notes from the captain himself, a sort of diary he'd recorded before leaving on his fateful expedition.

Then came the final piece to the puzzle, at least in my mind. Along with the book and the journal notes were a collection of writings in the hand of Cão's first mate, Marcelo Fernandez.

Contained within Fernandez's notes were references to a powerful relic. He said that he would take the secret to the grave with him—and that only one who didn't fear death would be able to find it.

I couldn't say I didn't fear death, but it had become an afterthought following the events in the jungle of Mexico.

I knew I wasn't immortal. But I had an edge that most humans didn't.

I felt the medallion around my neck warming against my skin. It was connected directly to the voice in my head, and I knew that subtle signal meant the wicked men chasing us were getting closer.

Up ahead, I saw another sarcophagus on the right side of the corridor. *Jeez, I hope that's the one.*

Adrenaline pumping through my body helped the knee pain slightly, but it still couldn't bear much weight.

We reached the stone coffin and stopped. I leaned over, bracing my hand on the edge of it while I swept the surface with my other hand.

Vero looked back at the other end of the passage. She and I both noticed no sign of our pursuers, but that wouldn't last.

I refocused my attention on the sarcophagus lid.

The image of a Portuguese ship was engraved near the head, with a cross above it. Underneath the vessel was the name of the coffin's occupant.

Marcelo Fernandez.

A wave of excitement and relief hit me. This was the place. The only question was, did it contain Diogo Cão's secret or merely the bones of his first mate?

CHAPTER 2

Vero and I quickly shifted to the head of the sarcophagus, positioned our hands on the back edge of the lid, and pushed. The heavy piece of stone barely budged. We shoved again, moving the top a few inches this time.

"One more," I said, noting the flashlight beams striking the wall at the corner seventy feet away.

We took a deep breath then pushed.

This time, the lid slid over the front edge of the sarcophagus. Gravity took over and pulled the entire thing down, crashing it to the hard floor, chipping off a corner.

Dust plumed into the dense air.

We shone our flashlights into the container, allowing the beams to pierce the swirling clouds. I waved my free hand to clear the dust in the air, but the result we saw with our eyes was still the same.

The sarcophagus was empty. No bones. No secret map or book or whatever it was Cão left behind with his first mate. Nothing.

"That's impossible," I said. "He has to be here." I looked back down the corridor at the dancing lights drawing ever closer.

"Where's the skeleton?" Vero asked, echoing my sentiment. "Grave robbers?"

"Of all the graves in here, why this one?" I wondered under my breath.

Then, as the dust cleared, I noticed something in the bottom of the coffin—a tiny hole in the bottom right corner.

"Wait a second," I said, slipping the day pack off my shoulders. I quickly removed a small hammer from a loop on the side, jumped into the sarcophagus, and raised the tool over my head.

"Gideon?" Vero asked, looking at me like I'd lost my mind. "What are you doing?"

I answered by smashing the hammer down onto the floor as hard as I could.

One second, I was crouching inside the coffin. The next, I was falling through shattered chunks of stone and onto a subfloor of the passage.

I hit the bottom with a thud but fortunately landed mostly on my feet. I looked back up, pointing my light through the opening. Vero was leaning over the edge of the sarcophagus, looking down.

"Come on. It's not bad."

She looked back over her shoulder then climbed over the edge of the coffin, clipped her flashlight to her belt, then lowered herself down until she clung to the lip with her fingers. For a second, she hesitated while I held my arms out, ready to brace her fall. Then she let go and dropped.

It was only eight feet from the bottom of her shoes to the floor below, but I still caught her to ease the landing, catching her at the hips.

She paused when her feet touched the ground and looked up at me in the peripheral glow of the flashlights.

"Thanks."

"Don't mention it."

Above, I didn't see any signs of our pursuers... yet.

I pointed my flashlight at the nearest wall then swung around in a circle. The walls reflected a faint glow of phosphorescent fungi clinging to the damp stone. The air was even thicker than in the catacombs above, reeking of decay and earth. As our eyes adjusted to the darkness, the layout of the tomb began to take shape.

The chamber was rectangular, approximately thirty by twenty feet, with a vaulted ceiling supported by four intricately carved stone pillars. Each pillar was adorned with faded, almost indistinguishable carvings and frescoes of nautical scenes—ships battling stormy seas, sea monsters, and mermaids luring sailors to their doom.

The intricate artwork portrayed both the adventures and the superstitions of the fifteenth century, when explorers ventured into unknown waters in hopes of finding undiscovered, and mysterious, lands.

Along the longer walls, there were three alcoves on each side, each deep enough to conceal a person. The recesses were shadowy, and as I noticed them, an idea formed rapidly: It would only be seconds, maybe a minute, before the men behind us discovered the empty sarcophagus and the hole within. The alcoves brimmed with old, crumbling artifacts—broken chests spilling ancient coins, rusted swords, and rotting books.

Ornately carved stone tiles made up the floor, but I could discern no pattern or hidden message in their placement. The amount of craftsmanship it had taken to build this hidden chamber . . . I marveled for the thousandth time at the skill and ingenuity of men in the so-called Middle Ages.

Being an archaeologist, I couldn't help but feel a knife of regret pierce my gut, making me wish I could collect everything in the room and take it to the surface for analysis.

But there was no time for that. Not right now, anyway.

At the far end of the chamber, on a raised dais, was the creepiest and most fascinating of the room's offerings. A skeleton sat atop a stone throne like an ancient, dead king. The seat was carved to resemble a ship captain's chair, the bones clad in tattered, once-regal clothing: a moth-eaten doublet of dark, velvety fabric, frayed lace cuffs, and a faded crimson sash draped across his chest. His skeletal feet were shod in what remained of leather boots, now almost disintegrated.

I knew immediately that the clothing was exactly what someone like Fernandez would have worn during the fifteenth century.

We hurried over to the dead man but stopped short of the lowest platform of the dais, running our flashlights over the remains, the clothes, and most importantly, what the skeleton held in its bony fingers.

In the sailor's right hand, he clutched a golden cylinder engraved with intricate patterns that glinted faintly in the dim light. His left hand rested on the armrest of the throne; the fingers curled as if once holding something important. Around his neck hung a silver disc on a tarnished chain, the disc engraved with characters, or glyphs, unlike any I'd ever seen. In the center of the symbols, a detailed image of a lion's head stared back.

I started to reach out to take the cylinder—and froze. A fine, almost invisible wire connected to the shaft. It snaked its way down the arm and disappeared into the base of the throne, suggesting a booby trap designed to protect the precious object.

The atmosphere in the tomb was tense, the silence only broken by the occasional drip of water from the ceiling.

"What?" Vero hissed, her expression seeming to tell me she wondered why I hadn't taken the cylinder.

"It's a trap," I breathed.

My eyes fell to the necklace again. There was something about it, an energy that radiated from it, almost as if it were calling me. Vero had no such compulsion.

I heard the shuffling of feet from the hole in the ceiling behind us and stole a fast look over my shoulder.

The floor lit up as the men above pointed their flashlights down into the cavity.

I turned back to the skeleton and carefully removed the worn, leather hat. Then I pulled the skull forward and looped the necklace up over the head before letting it rest against the stone backing behind it.

"What are you doing?" The tension in Vero's voice was rising as fast as my blood pressure.

"This is what we came here for." I held the little medallion by the necklace, shining my flashlight on it as I held it aloft. The disc spun slightly, and on the back I noticed a single word. It wasn't one I'd ever seen before, and I had no idea what it meant or what language it was. I couldn't even conjure an idea of its place of origin—not even the continent, much less whatever culture or nation it came from.

"Apedemak?" Vero said.

"No clue," I answered.

I heard the clank of carabiners through the hole in the ceiling.

The men were about to rappel down. At least their caution had bought us a few seconds.

"What do we do?" Vero asked. Her question didn't seem to carry an ounce of fear. Down here in the chamber, the ceiling was higher than in the catacombs, and the breadth of the room offered plenty of space to maneuver.

"Hide in that alcove over there," I said, pointing to a recess in the hall where a stone dais stood with a chest of coins spilling out of it. "Behind that plinth."

"And then what?"

"Then we wait for the opportune moment."

CHAPTER 3

Vero hurried across the room to the alcove I'd indicated, then I retreated to one on the opposite side and tucked into the shadows behind a collection of artifacts that filled another chest atop a stone altar.

Just before I dipped into the darkness, a black rope dropped to the floor. The men would begin descending in seconds.

I retreated farther into the alcove until I was engulfed by the shadows, then I ducked down and waited.

The silver medallion in my hand felt warm against my skin, as if it radiated some kind of energy. It wasn't like the amulet around my neck. This was less ornate, but just as mysterious.

I stuffed it into my left front pocket and tried to duck down farther behind the dais to wait.

The flashlight beams filled the room, spraying around in all directions as the tactical team checked the chamber.

Several voices shouted the word "Clear!"

"Where are they?" one man demanded. The voice was American; gruff, and sharp. I figured he was the one in charge. He sounded like a leader, probably an officer of some kind.

But they were American. What were they doing here in Portugal? These guys weren't Justice Department. They were something else, probably the Sector's pets from an agency I'd never heard of.

"Sir, look," another said.

All flashlights focused on the skeleton at the other side of the room as I peered out from behind the deep recesses of the alcove. Even if the men pointed their lights in my direction, I doubted they'd bother checking behind the dais once it appeared no one was here.

The first of the men came into view, and I ducked back behind my cover a second before he passed his weapon's flashlight across the alcove. The beam lingered there for two seconds before the man moved on with the others.

I shuffled forward until I could see around the dais. Eight men in black tactical gear loitered around the skeleton's throne.

Always with the black outfits. Don't get me wrong, I love black. I often wear it myself. I'm even a fan of Johnny Cash, the ultimate man in black. But these guys were wearing cargo pants.

What, they didn't have enough room on those utility belts and vests weighing them down? What could they possibly need to put in those pockets?

Then again, I wore cargo shorts, but those were different. They were camouflage, and sort of my comfort clothing—like a cozy sweater in winter, or some soft pajama pants while sitting next to a fire.

But it didn't matter what they were wearing. No one else was going to see them again anyway.

I crept back a little into the shadows.

"Are you going to do it, or what?" the voice in my head asked. He was almost begging me to do it.

Unlike him, I didn't have an insatiable bloodlust. After all, I was just an archaeologist. At least I had been.

Now, I was something else. Something terrible, but well, frankly, also pretty awesome.

I closed my eyes for a second and felt the power course through me. When I opened my eyes, I knew they glowed red, and that when the men by the skeleton throne saw them, they'd pretty much wet their drawers.

"Is that what we came here for, sir?" one of the men asked.

I noticed a pair of glowing eyes across the chamber in the opposite alcove. Vero had seen mine, and taken that as her cue to shift.

"It has to be," the commander said. I watched the man reach out his hand to grasp the golden tube.

I waited until the last second to interrupt him.

"I wouldn't do that if I were you," I warned, my voice booming through the chamber.

The men turned, pointing their weapons around the room. But I remained in the shadows, tucked behind the dais, holding back the full transformation until I was out in the open.

"Who's there?" a man shouted.

The team fanned out, each taking a ready stance to open fire at the first sign of the enemy.

"There's nowhere to run, Gideon," the commander said. "Come out with your hands up. Maybe we go easy on you."

"You shouldn't have come here," I growled. "You're meddling with things you can't possibly understand."

The men immediately snapped all their attention on me. I knew they saw my glowing red eyes in the shadows of the alcove, where even their flashlights seemed to veer away just a touch to avoid my face.

They shouldn't shoot. Not yet. Too much risk in this stone room that one of the rounds might bounce and hit them. Even with that problem, I knew their reluctance would only last so long.

"You should put those down," I suggested. "I thought you would have been warned that bullets can't kill me."

"Oh, I am well aware of that, Gideon," the leader opposed. He held a pistol away from his body, extended toward me along with all the other weapons.

"This should be good."

"It is. These aren't ordinary rounds."

"I don't know if you're aware of this, chief, but I'm not a were-wolf. I know I kinda look like one when I transform, but silver bullets won't do anything to me except make me angrier. And you gotta believe me when I say you really won't like me when I'm—"

"They're not silver either," he said, cutting me off before I could steal one of my favorite lines.

"Whew. That's a relief. I think I have some kind of an allergy to silver. You know? I can't even wear silver rings on my fingers or they break out in these little red spots like hives. It's weird."

"You don't know when to shut up, do you, boy?"

Boy? Did he just call me boy? That happened once at a poker table in North Carolina. A guy called me boy when he didn't appreciate the fact I just scooped all his chips from him. He was a moron, and drunk, and definitely a moron. Did I already mention that?

He ended up leaving broke an hour later. And I bought the table a round with his money.

"Are you going to kill this nitwit, or what?" the voice in my head asked me.

"Yep," I whispered.

"The tips of these rounds are filled with acid," the leader said. Neither he nor his men were paying any attention to Vero slipping out of the alcove behind them.

"Okay, you can't really expect me to believe that—"

The commander fired his pistol, and the round sank into my shoulder. I staggered back into the shadows and looked down at the black wound in my skin. It burned like someone had poured molten lava on it. I felt the acid burning through muscle, ligaments, tendon, and even the bone.

It took every ounce of energy inside me not to scream. I'd been shot, stabbed, virtually blown up, and experienced every other kind of near deadly attack humans could throw at me. But this. This was something new, and horrible, and I did not like it. Not one little bit.

"Hurts, don't it?" the commander said, a smug air in his voice.

"You see, we know regular bullets can't kill you. But these little babies; these can bring you to your knees. And when it does, we take your head off, and that medallion with it."

I didn't doubt what he was saying. A couple more rounds and I really would have been on the floor, writhing and screaming. The power of the medallion enabled my body to heal quickly, and while I could feel it starting to regenerate the damaged tissue and bone, it was slower than the times I'd been hit by regular bullets.

"So, you want to do this the easy way, Gideon? Or do you want some more pain?"

"Is there an option C?" I asked.

The man chuffed. "You don't know when to shut up, do you, son?"

"No," I said, emerging from the shadows. The red fog swirled around the men as they stared at me, ready to fire on command. "I don't. And my question was rhetorical. There is an option C."

All of the men puzzled over my statement, expecting me to say something else.

"Checkmate," I said.

"What?"

The leader noticed the direction of my gaze and turned just as the huge bear in gleaming battle armor roared. Vero swung a paw at the nearest gunman before he could turn his weapon at her. The blow knocked the man through the air, all the way across the room until he hit the far wall with a crunch before falling to the floor.

The second pivoted, but she slashed his throat with a sharp claw. The swipe spun the man into the guy behind him, who caught the bleeding gunman for a split second before she charged forward and snapped her open jaws down onto his neck.

The rest of the men shouted, panicking as they spread out to try to defend themselves.

I stepped forward, shifting into the ancient monster known as the Chupacabra, and grabbed the man closest to me by the neck. He yelped. Then I threw him up with enough force that when his head hit the rock ceiling, it crushed his skull and broke his neck instantly.

I kept moving as the body fell back to the floor at my side. A second later, the mist began snaking its way into his nostrils to consume what was left.

No matter how many times I'd seen that phenomenon, it still creeped me out. But it sure beat trying to hide bodies when you needed to.

I stepped ahead as the last three gunmen to the left of the leader tried to fire their weapons. One got off a shot, but panic diluted all those years of training he'd been through. Let's be real, there was no training for what that poor sap saw stalking toward him—a monstrous wolf-like creature with glowing red eyes that had just thrown one of his buddies into the ceiling with one arm.

The acid-filled round cracked as it whizzed by my ear. I grabbed him and his friend by the back of the skull, lifted them off the ground, and then slammed them headfirst into the stone floor.

A few of their muscles twitched, but they were gone.

I turned and found the leader backing toward the skeleton.

He brandished his pistol, switching back and forth between me and Vero, as if trying to figure out which monster to shoot first.

"How do you think this is going to end?" I asked in a deep, haunting baritone. "You gonna unload that magazine and then pray you have enough time to load another one?"

"Stay back," the leader demanded, almost pleading, his feet sliding back along the floor an inch at a time.

I noticed the golden cylinder still gripped in the skeleton's fingers.

"You're here for that, aren't you?"

He didn't dare risk taking his eyes off me or the huge, armored bear to my right.

"What did they tell you it would do?" I added.

"That's classified. I'm warning you."

I glanced over at Vero. "You hear that? He's warning us."

She snorted through her nostrils.

"If you want the cylinder," I said. "It's all yours."

A puzzled expression streaked across the commander's face, as if he didn't trust me. The look in his eyes only lasted a few seconds. Then he saw his men disappearing on the floor around us.

"What is this?" he asked. True fear seemed to rip through his heart now, and drew on every muscle in his face. "What's happening to them?"

The lone remaining henchmen took a step back, as if that would help him.

"The mist is taking them," I said. "It feeds off evil men like you. Each wicked soul is an offering, you see. It purges darkness from the world, and by doing so, brings to all a little more light."

"What are you talking about?" His tone shook from the terrible sight. "What is this?"

"You already asked that," I said. "I mean, I just told you a second ago. You see, our job is to fight evil, men like you, and the ones who sent you here. I don't suppose they told you that you and your group were expendable, huh."

"We're not ex—"

"Look around, chief. Your guys are expended. Spent?" I huffed a laugh. "I gotta be honest, I don't know if that's a word or not. But you get the idea."

"Shut up! Just... shut up! Whatever you are!"

I leveled my gaze and let him peer so deep into my eyes that I saw the reflection of the two glowing orbs in his dark, glossy pupils.

"Okay," I said, raising my paw-hands. Hand-paws. Whatever. They were hands with claws, but covered with fur. Not great for, say, working on a keyboard, but they came in handy in a fight.

I took a step back. "Come on," I said to Vero. "Let's get out of here."

We backed away several steps toward the opening in the ceiling.

"What are you doing?" the gunman snarled.

"You want that golden tube," I said. "It's yours. You're right, by the way. Those bullets really smart. Probably the worst pain I've ever been in in my entire life. Good job to whoever invented those little suckers. I don't ever want to be hit by one of those again."

Vero glanced over at me, making sure we were on the same page. I offered a subtle nod.

I knew there was no way the guy with the gun was that dim. He'd climbed the ladder through the military, or whatever organization he was working for now, and he didn't get there by being a total moron. Although I had a few military buddies who might have argued differently about their commanding officers.

I stopped underneath the hole in the ceiling and waited. Vero stood next to me.

Now, I couldn't exactly jump up through the opening overhead. Neither could Vero. We'd have to switch back to our human form.

Then there would be the issue of the darkness in the catacombs. Look, I knew I was a freak, a shape-shifting monster that shouldn't be afraid of anything, especially the dark. I mean, I'm the darkness shadows fear. But there was just something about being down in tunnels full of dead bodies that just creeped me out. Ironically, hunting for bones and artifacts was one of my routine jobs when I did normal archeology.

That life seemed so far away.

I shrank back into my human form. "I'm going to take his flash-light," I said, jerking my thumb at the crumpled, vanishing remains of the first guy Vero had taken out. "Doesn't look like he's going to need it anymore."

"Don't move," the leader barked. "You're not going anywhere."

"Maybe you should switch back," Vero suggested. She hadn't changed back into the beautiful, young Mexican woman I'd fallen for.

To be honest, I still hadn't gotten used to the idea of her being... well, a bear.

I wasn't even an animal. Not really. I was some other kind of weird thing.

"Yeah, okay," I said. "But it's really dark up there, and I would rather not try to feel my way back up to the surface, if you know what I mean."

"Shut up!" The guy's voice shrieked in a way that made me wonder if the manly, gruff sound from before was just a show.

I waited, watching him inch his way back toward the skeleton until his fingers hovered over the golden tube.

I kept my eyes on the gunman, but I spoke to Vero, keeping my voice quiet so the man wouldn't hear clearly.

"As soon as he grabs it, get up the rope."

"And you?"

"I'll be right behind you."

The gunman's fingers touched the cylinder and wrapped around it. He lifted it from the skeleton's grip, unaware of the wire that was connected to the bottom until it went taut.

A loud click echoed through the chamber, followed by an enormous trembling. The entire room vibrated, as if struck by an earthquake.

The gunman's eyes opened wide. He looked around at the floor shaking under his feet; his face full of apparent concern and confusion.

"Go!" I barked at Vero.

She didn't hesitate and immediately started ascending the rope, clasping one hand over the other just like in a 1980s gym class.

I darted to the dead man by the wall and scooped up the light, clipping it to my belt. The man with the gun struggled to keep his pistol aimed accurately at me as he fired a volley of shots as I rushed back to the rope.

Rounds sparked off the hard walls behind me. One struck the floor close to my right foot just as I jumped and grabbed the rope.

Vero was already at the top and pulling herself up over the edge of the sarcophagus.

Another bullet cracked the air near my head and severed the

rope, dropping me back to the floor. I landed on my feet and quickly regained my balance as the entire room rocked and shook.

The gunman charged at me, emptying the pistol's magazine with wild shots that ricocheted dangerously off the walls. That's when I noticed the first sections of floor disappear behind him. The enormous tiles fell into the darkness behind the gunman as he ran toward me.

His pistol empty, he stuffed it into a holster as he moved—such a useless gesture so close to his untimely end.

I bent my legs and jumped hard. Fortunately, I was still much stronger even in human form than most people due to the power flowing through me. I easily reached the bottom of the cut rope that dangled nearly eight feet above the floor and grabbed it with both hands.

The floor tiles continued dropping away, as if chasing the gunman running toward my feet.

He never looked back, instead keeping his focus on me—now his only hope for salvation.

I reached my right hand up higher and gripped the rope again. As I pulled myself toward the opening, the gunman leaped and wrapped his arms around my legs just below the knees.

Even with my strength, the added weight caused my fingers to slip on the rope, dropping us both a few precious inches toward the frayed end.

The floor collapsed beneath us, leaving a gaping blackness beneath. Dust clouds swirled around the gunman's feet as he desperately tried to keep a hold on my legs.

He looked down into the darkness and then back up at me, his face seemingly clenched in a menacing *If I go, you're coming with me* expression. The red mist danced around him like a vortex, ready to consume its next victim.

I tried to kick my legs around to free myself from his grasp, but he held on with a vise-like grip, desperate not to fall. My forearms burned from bearing the additional weight, and I felt my grip failing.

My hands slipped, and I nearly lost my grip on the rope as we dropped to the severed end. I tried desperately to reach higher, but with the added weight I couldn't manage it.

I was holding on by a thread, and not just in a figurative sense.

"Are you just going to hang around here," the voice in my head asked. "Or are you going to lose the dead weight?"

"Not helping," I answered.

"Fine. Do I have to do everything?"

"Seriously? You barely do anything."

The killer's eyes narrowed as he listened to me having a conversation with who he must have assumed to be myself.

"That hurts, Gideon," the voice said.

"You want to hurry up with an idea here? Because if I go, you go."

"True, but we don't know what's at the bottom of that. I doubt whatever it is will take your head off."

"But there's no way out of it."

"Good point. Look, just intertwine your fingers with the rope, then...."

He didn't need to finish.

I summoned the power of the medallion again as I twisted my fingers around the rope. My body morphed again, swelling into the Chupacabra.

The man's face twisted in panic as he began to lose his grip on my growing legs. He slipped several inches, now holding on by my ankles.

Normally, I would have fired off something clever just before I killed the bad guy, but nothing came to mind.

Nice hanging with you? No. That's terrible. Hang in there? No, also terrible.

Eh, screw it.

I pushed my right leg forward and pulled the left one back, spreading them apart. The man tried with all of his strength to hold on, but against my full power, there was no chance.

His face streaked with panic as his hold on my legs faltered. He fell, arms flailing as if to grasp something that wasn't there. He yelled as he dropped into the darkness, the red mist falling with him.

I quickly shifted back into human form and reached up, overlapping my left hand to ascend. Without the additional weight, the effort suddenly seemed much easier. As I neared the hole in the ceiling, the residual light from the flashlight touched Vero's face. She was leaning over the edge of the sarcophagus, looking down.

"You okay?"

"Yeah. I am now."

I continued climbing until I was through the hole. There, I grabbed the edge of the sarcophagus and pulled myself the rest of the way up, using my feet to ease the burden on my exhausted hands and arms.

I swung my legs over the top of the stone box, and landed on the hard floor next to Vero. I sat there for a full two minutes, trying to catch my breath. My forearms felt swollen and hot.

Vero crouched next to me, her hand on my shoulder as she stared at me, saying nothing while I recovered.

Fortunately, that didn't take long. I felt the warmth of the medallion's power radiate through me, and after a mere two minutes, I was reenergized and ready to go.

I stood and looked down into the darkness through the opening.

"That was close," Vero said, following my gaze.

"Aw, man."

"What?" She faced me as I kept peering through the hole.

"Thanks for dropping by."

"What?"

I shook my head. "I should have told him thanks for dropping by."

CHAPTER 4

I felt uneasy from the first moment I set foot on the sidewalk outside Nashville's international airport.

Amid the faces coming and going, the cars driving by picking up or dropping off travelers, none of them seemed like any kind of threat. Which meant absolutely nothing.

I tightened the bag hanging from my right shoulder and looked left at Vero, who stood there looking around at the passersby. She seemed to wear the same look of concern and mistrust smeared on my face.

"They should be here in a second."

"All good," Vero answered with what sounded like a hint of nerves in her voice.

"Relax. They'll love you."

"It's not them that bothers me. It's all the unknowns."

"I know. You live your life just assuming everything is going to go on as planned, with a few interruptions here and there. But once you've had the veil stripped away from your eyes, nothing will ever seem the same again."

"Did you think of that all on your own?" the voice in my mind asked. The spirit of the ancient god Xolotl had taken on quite the snarky nature after melding with my consciousness, and I often found myself wishing he would take a day off. Or a few years. But I knew that wasn't possible. And on top of that, I needed him.

Vero was dealing with her own adjustment to the same unusual circumstance, though the deity talking in her head was the spirit of Artemis.

The two gods had been humans of great power in ancient times, guardians of the earth for those who could not fight evil on their own.

We'd been told that something bad was coming, that the forces of evil were amassing to launch a massive assault on humanity.

I turned left toward the long line of cars wrapping around the terminal exterior. The sunlit morning cast a brilliant sheen on the sleek glass façades, making them shimmer like crystal under the clear blue sky. The modern design—an impressive blend of curves and sharp angles—gave the terminal a futuristic feel.

The expansive entryway had meticulously landscaped greenery that provided a striking natural contrast to the steel and glass. The neatly trimmed hedges and vibrant flower beds added a touch of warmth and hospitality to the otherwise contemporary structure. Overhead, towering flagpoles stood proudly, their flags gently fluttering in the warm afternoon breeze.

I couldn't help but appreciate the thoughtful architecture, even though I knew I needed to be on high alert.

The large transparent panels allowed glimpses of the bustling activity inside, bathed in natural light. It was a fitting gateway to the city, embodying both modern sophistication and Southern charm. As I waited, I felt a sense of anticipation, the airport's dynamic energy matching the vibrant pulse of Nashville itself, or what it used to be.

Over the years, more and more people had migrated to the city from other parts of the country, where their customs and traditions were different from the once-proud Southern culture that permeated the city.

Old honky-tonks with great music had been replaced by trendy bars with shareholders and pop music that somehow still fell under the category of country. Upscale shops and restaurants had invaded the town too, swooping in and scooping up local businesses that had been taxed into bankruptcy by bad local policy.

Still, there were some good places left in Nashville owned by locals who'd managed to scrape through the lean times to emerge on the other side.

I spotted the black Toyota Sequoia as it came around the bend and merged into the far-right lane.

"That's them."

She followed my gaze toward the approaching SUV and wrapped her fingers around the rolling suitcase at her side.

I did the same with my luggage but gave one last look across the lanes. Two men in black suits stood next to a metal column. They hadn't been there a moment before. I couldn't see their eyes behind the black sunglasses wrapped around their faces, but their jaws were set in a hard, menacing fashion.

"Great," I muttered loud enough for only Vero to hear.

"What?" she asked.

"I'll explain in the car."

"What do you mean? What's going on?"

She must have noticed me glance across the road again because she followed my eyes until she saw the two men.

"Do you know them?"

"In a manner of speaking."

"Is that what you're going to do?" Xolotl chimed. "Downplay a couple of fallen angels in suits to try to keep your girlfriend calm?"

"Sometimes I think maybe I got the wrong deity," I breathed so Vero couldn't hear me.

"What is that supposed to mean?" Vero asked.

She seemed pensive for a second, as if listening intently to something. Then her eyes widened. "Okay, never mind. Artemis just told me. So, okay. Those two are fallen angels posing as covert agents?"

"Yeah. That's exactly what they are. They work for an agency called the Sector. They can't touch us." I started moving toward the curb. The black Sequoia was nearly to us.

"What can they do?"

"They can influence the timeline, alter reality by manipulating people. Just like they always have. Temptation is one of their favorites, but they have other ways. These guys like to go direct. It's a good bet their minions are nearby. They must have known we were coming here."

Vero's eyes darted around as she walked to the curb, pulling her suitcase behind her. She didn't seem panicked, but not exactly calm either.

"Minions?" she asked.

"Yeah. Federal agents, cops, criminals. Doesn't matter to them. They'll use whoever they can."

"Why?"

"Same reason they always have, Vero," I said, leveling my gaze with hers. "Evil wants chaos. And they will destroy anything or anyone who might stand in the way of that."

The SUV pulled up to the curb, and Jack started to climb out of the driver's side door to welcome us and help with the luggage.

"Stay in the truck," I barked before he could exit the vehicle.

"Okay," Jack answered. "Great to see you too, buddy. Jeez."

"Is the back unlocked?"

"Yeah, of course."

I turned to Vero. "Get in. I'll load up our stuff."

She nodded and opened the back passenger side door while I hurried around to the back and popped open the rear. It took three seconds to stuff our luggage into the cargo area. With it secure, I closed the back door and shuffled around to the driver's side rear door. I opened it and took one last look at where the two agents had been standing. They were gone.

That bothered me just as much as seeing them there.

I scanned the area, searching the faces, the bodies, the vehicles passing by. The two Sector agents had simply disappeared.

I climbed into the truck, closed the door, and tapped on the back of the driver's seat.

"Get us out of here."

"What's going on, man?" Jack asked. "Are you okay?"

"I'm fine. But we have company."

"Company? I hope you don't mean the kind of company that destroyed my shop."

My expression remained hardened. "You should drive."

"Okay. Okay. Not sure if you noticed, but there's a lot of traffic here today."

"I did notice. Pretty unusual for this airport." I looked around at the hordes of people.

Jack accelerated away from the curb. I noticed his eyes darting from the road ahead to the mirror and back again, probably checking to see if we were being followed.

He and I weren't special agents, born of some government underground training program. I was just an archaeologist, more accustomed to dealing with trowels, shovels, and sifters, not deadly weapons or hand-to-hand combat.

Jack was a bookstore owner with a keen interest in rare and unusual books. His shop had been destroyed by government operatives under the influence of the Sector.

Vero, too, hadn't been trained for this life. Then again, there probably wasn't any kind of training for this.

We'd been plunged into a world that defied logic. Gods, monsters, angels, demons—all of it was so impossible to the human mind. And yet here it was, unfolding right before our eyes.

On top of that, Vero and I had become monsters ourselves, equipped with the powers of ancient gods, long dormant until—as I'd been told—the world needed guardians to rise again and stand against the forces of evil.

When I thought about it, the whole thing seemed like a movie, except I was playing a part.

I swiveled my head around and looked through the back window in case Jack had missed something.

"They aren't there," Xolotl said. "Not yet, anyway."

I hummed a quiet tone to let him know I'd heard what he said. Not that I could not hear him. Luckily for me, he didn't speak while I slept, and I wondered if that meant he was sleeping too, or if his power was connected to me in such a way that it was symbiotic in nature.

Those were questions that would have to wait for another day.

I faced forward again and relaxed a little. If there was a threat coming, I'd be warned.

"Anything?" Vero asked.

"No," I shook my head. "Not yet. But we both saw them. They were there, waiting for us."

"Those clandestine operatives that destroyed my place?" Jack interrupted.

"Only two of them," I said. "And those guys only oversaw the mayhem."

"How did they know when we would arrive in Nashville?" Vero asked.

I exhaled and rubbed my knees. "It's difficult to hide from them. They can access anything that's online at any time. A flight manifest is no problem for those creatures. That goes for news events, credit card purchases, you name it."

"So, if you go off grid, they can't find you?"

"Maybe," I said. "But I doubt it. I was told when I was young that when we're born, we're assigned a guardian angel. That angel of light also has a counter, an angel of darkness, a follower of the dark one. I always thought their job was just to tempt us, to lead us astray."

"It isn't that?" Jack wondered.

"I'm sure that's a big part of their assignment. But in our case,

I'm guessing they report back to the one in charge. But there are rules for us. This is just a hunch, but I don't think they always know where we are."

The realization gave me an idea, but it would have to wait.

Jack merged into the outbound lane and continued away from the airport.

"What makes you think that?" Vero asked.

"Because they weren't with us on the plane. We don't see them all the time. And they appear in human form, looking like government agents. I feel like with us, they have to play by a different set of rules. Otherwise, everything we've done up until now would have been compromised."

"So, you're saying they can only track you the way regular cops and feds would?" Jack clarified.

"Seems that way. Why were they waiting for us at the airport? Why not just try to take us out before we even got on the plane? Or after?"

No one had an answer, so I let the issue go and just assumed that they accepted the hypothesis.

"Where's Jesse?" I asked, suddenly aware that she wasn't here.

"Oh, she's at her warehouse."

I didn't say anything for ten seconds. My silence caused Jack to follow up the statement.

"Do... you want to go there?"

"No," I said after contemplating the decision. "I don't want the same thing to happen to her place that happened to yours."

"That's thoughtful," Jack chuffed.

"What happened to—" Vero started.

"Best not to ask," I answered quickly. "Sore subject."

"You could say that," Jack agreed. "So where to, then?"

"We need to meet somewhere neutral."

"Dude, her warehouse *is* neutral. It doesn't have any identifying signs on the outside. There's a fence around it, security cameras. The place is like the Fort Knox of weed."

"Weed?" Vero asked, suddenly sounding concerned. "I didn't think that was legal in this state."

"The 2018 Farm Bill changed that," Jack said. "It legalized nearly every form of cannabis except Delta-9 THC, but even that is legal in edibles. But it's not necessary. Jesse grows THCA cannabis, which qualifies as hemp, and is perfectly legal here in the great state of Tennessee. Farmers grow it all over the place here since we have terrific growing conditions for it."

"Sounds like you've been brushing up on that topic," I quipped. "Or spending a lot of time with Jesse."

I smirked at him in the mirror and caught him blushing.

"Ha, ha, ha," he returned. "Maybe I have. What does that matter?"

"Doesn't to me," I answered. "It's a good thing. I think you two make a great pair."

"Speaking of pair," Jack said. "Are you going to introduce me or not?"

I hadn't even thought about it since we entered the vehicle. Getting away from the airport and the potential threat there was the priority.

"Sorry. Yeah, this is Vero. Vero, Jack Morrow."

"Nice to meet you, Jack," she said in her sweet Mexican accent.

"Mucho gusto, Vero," Jack replied in her native tongue.

"Habla Español?" She sounded pleasantly surprised.

"Un poco."

"Mentiroso," I interjected, using the Spanish word for liar.

Vero laughed, but Jack didn't understand what I said.

"What?" he asked defensively. "What does that mean?"

"Exactly," I said.

Vero shook her head while still smiling. "I can see you two are going to be a lot of fun."

"Seriously," Jack whined. "What did he say?"

"Never mind that," I answered. "I guess we'll go to Jesse's place;

just call ahead and let her know we're coming. We have a lot to discuss."

"On it," Jack said, seeming to forget about the Spanish for the moment.

I was reluctant to go to Jesse's place, but a plan forming in my mind told me it was the perfect opportunity to strike back against the Sector and send them a message.

CHAPTER 5

J ack waited as the automated gate rolled out of our way. Once there was enough room, he drove the SUV through and around to the side of what looked like an abandoned building, save for the glow of lights through some of the front windows.

I peered through the SUV's windshield as we approached the old knitting warehouse. Unlike the surrounding abandoned buildings with their boarded-up windows and graffiti-covered walls, this structure pulsed with hidden life. Soft light seeped through gaps in the papered-over windows, hinting at activity within.

The knitting mill was a reminder of Nashville's past, its weathered red brick façade looming four stories high against the sky. As our SUV approached, I took in the details of the building's front. Large arched windows dominated the ground floor, their panes mostly intact but heavily tinted, offering no glimpse of the activity inside. Above them, rows of smaller rectangular windows lined the upper floors, their faded green frames peeling and cracked.

My eyes were drawn to the ornate cornice above the main entrance, where intricate brickwork spelled out Nashville Knitting Co.—Est. 1923 in faded gold lettering. The double doors below were solid oak, freshly painted a deep forest-green that contrasted sharply with the aged brick surrounding them. A modern keypad lock glinted in the fading light, an anachronistic addition to the vintage entrance.

To the left, I could just make out a ghost sign, its faded letters advertising Quality Woolens in a style that whispered of the 1950s. On the right, a newer but discreet sign warned Private Property—No Trespassing in bold red letters.

As we drove past, I noticed the roofline was punctuated by a series of dormers, their windows dark and seemingly unused. A tall brick chimney rose from the right side of the building, no longer in use but standing as a silent sentinel to its industrial heritage.

At street level, old loading docks had been converted into additional entryways, their original doors replaced with modern steel ones. The concrete steps leading up to these were cracked and worn, with weeds sprouting from the crevices, but I could see signs of recent foot traffic.

Despite the building's attempts to blend in with its abandoned neighbors, signs of current activity were evident: security cameras discreetly mounted at the corners, and the faint hum of industrial-grade air-conditioning units barely visible on the roof. As we turned the corner, I couldn't shake the feeling that this old mill was harboring secrets behind its historic façade.

As Jack steered the vehicle around the corner, my gaze swept over the stark contrast between the warehouse and its neglected neighbors. The narrow alley between the buildings was barely wide enough for the SUV, its sides nearly scraping the brick walls on either side. Shadows deepened as we entered this urban canyon, our headlights illuminating discarded trash and overgrown weeds that pushed through cracks in the pavement.

The alley opened into a small, secluded area behind the warehouse. Here, the signs of current use became more apparent. A steel door, freshly painted and equipped with a modern security system, stood out against the weathered brick. Above it, a new, bright LED light cast a harsh glow over the immediate area.

Jack eased the SUV into a spot next to another vehicle; a similar black SUV with tinted windows, its clean exterior at odds with the surrounding decay. The confined space was hemmed in by the looming walls of the warehouse and the adjacent abandoned facility, creating a sense of isolation from the outside world.

As the engine quieted, I became aware of a low hum emanating from the warehouse—the sound of powerful ventilation systems working overtime. The air carried a faint, skunky odor, barely noticeable but unmistakable to those who knew what to look for.

In this hidden pocket of activity, surrounded by the hollow shells of Nashville's industrial past, the old knitting warehouse stood as an island of clandestine industry, its true nature concealed from casual observation.

Just the way Jesse wants it, I thought.

Even with the proper growing license from the State of Tennessee, there were still threats to her production. Instead of police or DEA, now the problems hemp growers faced were of a criminal variety.

"So this is the joint, huh?" I asked.

"Did you just make that pun on purpose?"

I chuckled. "No. But now I kinda wish I had."

Jack shook his head. Vero giggled.

We stepped out of the vehicle and walked up to the back door. A keypad hung next to the frame.

Jack entered a six-digit code, and the door unlocked with a buzz.

He turned the latch and pulled it open to allow Vero and me to enter first, but I insisted he go in, and I held the edge of the door while I took a quick glance around the area behind the building.

I hadn't noticed anything suspicious. Yet. But as darkness overtook the light of day, I knew something sinister encroached with the shadows.

As I stepped through the heavy steel door, the musty scent of the alley gave way to a pungent, earthy aroma that filled my nostrils. The interior of the old knitting warehouse unfolded before me, a stark contrast to its weathered exterior.

The vast open space was bathed in an intense, purplish glow from rows of LED grow lights suspended from the high ceiling. These modern fixtures hung incongruously from old wooden beams, their cables snaking alongside remnants of the building's original electrical system.

Directly ahead, long tables stretched to the other end of the building, each supporting neat rows of cannabis plants in various stages of growth. The verdant leaves seemed to pulse with life under the artificial light, creating a sea of green that filled most of the floor space.

To the right was a section cordoned off with clear plastic sheeting. Inside, larger, more mature plants stood in individual pots, their distinctive seven-fingered leaves unmistakable. The air around this area felt thick and humid, controlled by a complex system of fans and ducts that hummed steadily.

On the left wall, the knitting mill's past blended with its present in surreal fashion. Old machinery—looms and spinners—stood silent, repurposed as makeshift shelving for fertilizers, soil bags, and various gardening tools. A vintage foreman's office had been converted into a modern control room, its walls now lined with monitors displaying temperature, humidity, and security-camera feeds.

Near the back was a processing area where harvested plants were being dried and prepared. The sweet, skunky odor was strongest here, mingling with the chemical smell of cleaning products used to maintain sterility.

Despite the industrial scale of the operation, there was an almost clinical precision to everything. The concrete floor, though old, had been scrubbed clean, and the air felt filtered and controlled. The surroundings were old, but nowhere was there even a dust bunny to be seen. This was one tight ship.

As my eyes adjusted to the unique lighting, I couldn't help but marvel at the juxtaposition of old and new, the way this relic of Nashville's textile industry had been reborn into a high-tech agricultural facility, hidden in plain sight.

"Hey, guys," a familiar voice said from behind the last plants in a row to the left.

Jesse stepped into sight, crossed her arms, and grinned. "Look who came crawling back," she said.

Jesse wore her calling-card black—a tight-fitting tank top that exposed the tattoos on her forearms and triceps, and a pair of matching skin-tight jeans with shiny black Doc Martens. A pair of sunglasses with green lenses rested on her nose. It was, in fact, the only part of her wardrobe that showed any color.

"Hey, Jesse." I waved.

Jack moved over to where she stood and wrapped his arm around her, planting a kiss on her neck.

The maneuver sent my eyebrows up an inch. "Hey, when did this happen?"

"While you were gone doing your thing," Jack answered then took a step away from Jesse.

"Don't act so surprised," she said.

"I'm not. Well, just that you would lower your standards like that."

"Hilarious," Jack said, shaking his head.

"This is Vero." I motioned to her with a smile.

"We've heard a lot about you, girl," Jesse said. "From what he tells me, you're a tough one. You and I are going to get along just fine."

"Nice to meet you," Vero said, smiling shyly.

"So," Jack said, "you've been gone a minute."

"Yeah," I answered, scratching the back of my head. "Bounced around some. Greece, Panama, and then a couple of days ago, Portugal."

"And did you find anything?"

I nodded and removed the necklace from my pocket. "We found this in the catacombs, in a hidden tomb."

"So, the lead was right?" Jack took the item from me and studied it.

"Yeah. You did good, kid."

Jack rolled his eyes at the statement, but I could tell he appreciated the sentiment. He'd discovered the lead regarding the Portuguese captain while searching through some of his rare books.

Jack's collection of tomes was exceedingly rare and esoteric, containing information about events and people in history that had long since been either forgotten or relegated to the files of legend.

Cão had been a notable Portuguese explorer in the late fifteenth century, credited with significant discoveries along the west coast of Africa.

Born around 1452 in Vila Real, Portugal, Cão embarked on his first major voyage in 1482 under the commission of King John II. During this expedition, he became the first European to navigate the mouth of the Congo River, which he called the Zaire River, and established contact with the Kingdom of Kongo.

Cão's second voyage, from 1485 to 1486, took him even farther south along the African coast, reaching present-day Namibia. On this voyage he continued mapping and claiming African coastal territories for Portugal. His explorations significantly expanded European knowledge of sub-Saharan Africa and laid the groundwork for future Portuguese expeditions, including those of Bartolomeu Dias and Vasco da Gama. Cão's contributions were recognized in his time by King John II, who granted him a coat of arms, among other riches and privileges. Despite the lack of detailed records about his later life and the exact location of his death, Diogo Cão's pioneering efforts in African exploration established him as a key figure in the Age of Discovery. Of course, modern-day Africans didn't think much of him or his exploits, but he was regarded as a serious, groundbreaking explorer among Western historians.

But something about the man had been left out of known

history. And those details were highlighted in the journal Jack had found in his library.

Marcelo Fernandez claimed that Cão had been scouring the African continent for something that he believed would make Portugal the uncontested superpower of the time.

And contained within the pages of the journal was a drawing of a medallion that looked eerily similar to the ones Vero and I wore.

But there'd been nothing else in the journal regarding where Fernandez or Cão believed the amulet to be hidden. It was unclear if the men had ever discovered it.

If they had, and if Fernandez had kept it after his captain died, then *it* should have been in the tomb instead of the necklace Jack now held in his hands.

"Apedemak," Jack said in a befuddled tone.

Jesse took a step closer to him and looked at it over his shoulder.

"Cool lion," she said, noticing the engraving on the front. "The detail is really good."

"Yeah," Vero agreed. "Do you guys know anything about that name?"

Jack and Jesse both shook their heads.

"You?" Jack asked.

"Not until we found that. Then we did some digging while waiting for our flight home. Turns out that Apedemak was an important deity in the pantheon of ancient Nubian religion, particularly worshipped in the Kingdom of Kush, which flourished in the region of present-day Sudan. Apedemak is often depicted as a lion-headed warrior-god, symbolizing strength, power, and protection."

"Interesting. So, one has to wonder why a Portuguese explorer had this in his tomb."

"Yeah, it was something right out of a movie, honestly," I said. "I had to take that off the skeleton of Fernandez himself."

Jack pulled back as if he might drop the necklace to the floor.

"I cleaned it, dude," I added. "Relax."

"Cool," Jesse said, seeming to be even more interested in the necklace.

"That's great and all," Jack started again, "but it doesn't tell us much. This could have just been a gift given to him by the people of the area they were exploring."

"Except that Apedemak was a god," I insisted, "just like Artemis and Xolotl."

"Thank you," the voice in my head chimed.

I resisted the urge to comment back at him.

"So, you think this Nubian deity could be the next guardian we're looking for?" Jack clarified.

"It seems to fit. And on top of that, there was a queen of Kush named Amanirenas, who fought against the Roman Empire, even won some significant battles that enabled her to negotiate terms with Rome. She went down as a legend in the annals of Kushite history. There are still statues and records honoring her achievements and triumphs."

"So, if you're going to start looking, I guess it would be in that area, huh?"

"Seems logical," Vero said. "But we need to know for sure where to look, and what we should expect to find."

"Which is why we're back," I added. "We need to look through your collection to see what we can find about all this."

"Yeah, sure," Jack said. "Of course. I had to move all of my rarest stuff after what happened at the bookstore."

"Where is it now?"

Jack turned his head and looked over at Jesse.

"It's here," she said. "Downstairs."

I looked around the huge room, scanning it for any sign of stairs that might lead to a lower level. Through the forest of plants, though, I couldn't make out anything. The floor was poured concrete, so I couldn't figure out how there was a basement unless there was something I was missing.

Jesse's voice turned conspiratorial. "There was a storage area over there," she pointed toward one of the old loading docks. "It isn't the size of the entire mill, but it's a good amount of space. Enough for him to securely store his things, and for me to work on new gear for you two."

"New gear?" Vero said.

Jesse's lips curled into a mischievous grin. "Oh yeah. Come on. I'll show you."

CHAPTER 6

J esse and Jack led us over to a concrete staircase that descended down into the bowels of the old knitting mill. At the bottom, a steel door blocked the way beyond. A red-and-white warning sign with a lightning bolt in the center warned us: Danger. High voltage.

"Electrical stuff down here?" I asked as we reached the landing.

"Nah. I just put that there to deter anyone in case they were able to slip through my security measures."

She fished out a set of keys from her pocket and inserted one into a deadbolt over a vertical door handle. Then she turned the key, removed it, and pulled the door open.

"Welcome to my secret lair," she said in a faux superhero voice.

Fluorescent lights flickered on automatically inside.

As I stepped through the heavy steel door, a rush of cool, dry air hit my face. The basement level of the old knitting mill opened up before me, a cavernous space that seemed to hold secrets from another world entirely.

To my immediate left, I saw Jesse's workshop. The fluorescent lights hummed overhead, illuminating long metal tables covered with an assortment of tools, wires, and half-finished projects. Some 3-D printers whirred quietly in one corner, slowly building components I couldn't begin to identify. The walls were lined with pegboards holding an array of tools, many of which I'd never seen before.

Directly ahead was a series of glass cases full of what must have been Jesse's finished pieces—sleek body armor that looked like it belonged in a sci-fi movie, helmets with advanced-looking visors, and weapons that defied easy categorization. One particularly eye-catching item looked like a gauntlet with a complex array of circuitry running along its surface.

To the right of the cases, a heavy vault door stood ajar, offering a glimpse into Jack's domain. As I approached, I felt the temperature drop further. Inside, floor-to-ceiling shelves were packed with books —their leather spines cracked with age, gilt lettering faded but still visible in the soft, ambient lighting. A faint scent of old paper and leather hung in the air, held in check by what I assumed was a sophisticated climate control system.

Back in the center of the main room, a large worktable dominated the space. Its surface was covered with blueprints, sketches, and notebooks filled with Jesse's cramped handwriting. Nearby, a powerful computer setup hummed, multiple screens displaying complex diagrams and lines of code.

The contrast between the sections was striking—Jesse's area spoke of cutting-edge technology and innovation, while Jack's space felt like stepping into a slice of history. Yet somehow, in this underground sanctuary, the two seemed to coexist in perfect harmony, much like Jack and Jesse themselves.

As I took it all in, I couldn't help but feel I really had stepped into a secret lair that melded history and the future, a hidden nexus of ancient knowledge and modern invention buried beneath an unassuming old knitting mill.

Jesse led us to a workbench in the center of the basement room, her eyes gleaming with excitement. "All right, you two, I've got some goodies I think you're really going to like," she said, pulling back a cloth to reveal her creations—a bow and quiver full of glimmering, translucent arrows and two spiral blades that looked like larger, more curved throwing stars.

Vero's eyes widened. "Is that... for me?" she asked, reaching out to touch an exquisitely crafted bow.

"Yep," Jesse nodded. "Figured the spirit of Artemis deserved something special. And since the goddess famously carried a bow, I thought this would be appropriate. This baby's got an unlimited quiver too—just draw, and boom, an arrow appears, courtesy of your medallion's mojo."

I whistled low. "Very nice. Ranged weapons. Will be good to take out the creeps from a distance now and then."

Jesse's grin widened as she handed me a pair of gleaming, spiral blades. "Uh-huh. And these beauties are for you." She lifted one of the spiraled blades. "They're like boomerangs with an attitude. They'll seek out your target and come right back to you. Bad guys won't know what hit 'em."

Jack, who'd been quietly observing, chimed in. "Just don't go throwing them in here."

We all chuckled, and I gave the blades an experimental twirl. "How do they work with the medallion?"

"Great question," Jesse said. "Your medallion's power will amp up these weapons, big-time. We're talking increased speed, accuracy, and impact. But beyond that, only you will be able to use them. If you were to drop them or lose them, they'll just come back to you. Same with the bow and quiver. Plus, when you shift back to human form, they'll vanish along with your monster selves. No need to worry about explaining why you're carrying around lethal projectiles at the grocery store."

Vero nocked an invisible arrow, getting a feel for the bow. "This is incredible, Jesse. But won't we need practice? I haven't shot an arrow since summer camp."

"That's the beauty of it," Jesse explained. "The medallion will guide you. It's like having Artemis herself steady your aim. You too, wolf-boy," she added, nodding at me. "Your throws will be supernaturally accurate. Then again, I guess since those two sort of reside in you now, they really will be guiding those things."

"Awesome," I said, grinning.

"Very cool," Vero echoed.

I nodded, suddenly serious. "Thanks, Jesse. Really. Will be nice to fire back at dudes shooting at us. Superhuman or not, those bullets really hurt."

"And it's worse now," Vero said, her voice turning solemn. "A team of men tried to beat us to the tomb in Portugal. They were armed with a new kind of round; bullets with some kind of acid in the tips."

"I have no idea how they managed that kind of engineering," I said. "But they did. I got hit by one, and it was the worst pain I think I've ever been in."

"Acid?" Jesse said. "That's new." She rubbed her chin as she considered the problem. "Your armor should have stopped that."

"It did. Most of them anyway. One slipped through a crease, I guess."

"Well, I can take a look at your armor, but there's only so much I can do. Too much, and you won't be agile enough to fight. Of course, there is one other option…"

We waited for her to say what she was thinking, but she left it hanging.

"I'll mull it over," she said after a moment of thought. "Right now, you have other things to tend to. Just think about the weapons vanishing as you hold them, and they'll disappear until you need them."

"Just don't go getting cocky," Jack warned. "New weapons don't make you invincible."

"Noted," Vero said, carefully setting down the bow. "So, when do we get to test these out?"

Jesse's expression turned thoughtful. "Whenever you're attacked."

"So, no practice run?"

"You won't need it. You already know what to do. Trust me."

"Okay," Vero surrendered but still sounded uncertain. "Just curious, how do you know all this stuff?"

Jesse shrugged. "Some of it I get from his books," she explained. "Some of it... I can't explain. I have weird ideas, then make things that probably no one else would."

"Right," I said. Her explanation didn't fill me with a ton of confidence, but I had to trust she knew something I didn't. Remembering why we were here, I turned to Jack. "The next medallion. We need to know where to look next."

Jack moved toward his book-filled sanctuary. "I have a book about legends and mythologies of Africa. It's really old, like most of the collection in here. Doesn't say who wrote it either."

"An anonymous author," I quipped.

"Yeah."

We followed Jack into the glass-encased library and over to a shelf in the near corner.

"Looks like you have a good system here," I noticed, unsurprised. Jack had always been organized. So it made sense that he was a keeper of books, in every sense of that word. Librarians and bookstore owners always had a method to their madness. If they didn't, they'd never find anything. Jack was surely no different.

"Alphabetical," Jack said. "Africa is over here."

"Are all those books from the African continent?" Vero asked, suddenly overwhelmed by the number of tomes.

It was a lot, especially for a continent whose ancient cultures were often either overlooked or simply unknown. But just like with most other, more well-read histories, records had been kept—and in the case of Nubia or Kush, scholars down through the ages had retained and preserved highly detailed information regarding the ruling dynasties, their achievements, religions, and culture.

"So, I guess we each take a stack and start looking?" I suggested.

"Probably a good idea," Jack agreed. "Although I would say we can eliminate most of the southern African folklore and legends if we're focusing on Kush."

"How many books does that remove?"

"Five," he answered with a smirk.

"Well, it's better than none."

Jack started on the top shelf and pulled out four books. He handed them to me and instructed that I could use the worktable in the center of the library to scan the pages. "You'll find a drawer full of white gloves in the table as well," he added. "Don't want to do any damage to these."

"Right."

I walked over to the table and set the books down carefully on the surface while Jack retrieved four more volumes and handed them to Vero.

I slipped on a pair of gloves from the drawer and began with the first book on the top of the stack.

I set it down next to the others and opened it. There wasn't a table of contents or an author name. Just the title, *Legends of North Africa.*

Vero plucked a pair of white gloves from the drawer, slid them onto her hands, and stood next to me while she began her own search.

Jesse and Jack joined us, each taking a corner of the table to pore through the old books in search of answers.

We toiled for half an hour, rifling through the stacks until we'd finished the first batch. Still, no answers to our question.

"Next," I said, gently setting the last book of my four on top of the others.

"Help yourself," Jack said, still turning through the pages of his last book.

I walked over to the shelf and replaced the four books where I'd seen Jack take them from, then removed four more from the third shelf from the top. I took the tomes and returned to the worktable as Vero finished the last of hers and collected the books to return to the shelf.

"Nothing, huh?" I asked.

"Nope. Nothing about Apedemak. Just a lot of stories about heroes and legends, monsters, but nothing about that one."

"If it's here, we'll find it," Jack insisted.

I kept scouring the pages, looking for anything about the lion god engraved on the necklace I'd found in the catacombs. Jack and Jesse continued their search, sifting through the books from the fourth shelf.

I started to worry there wasn't anything about Apedemak, or about the medallion that I assumed was associated with that deity. Doubts crept into my mind. I'd jumped to the conclusion when we were in the tomb back in Portugal, but now I wondered if there really was a connection between the ship's dead captain, and the location of the amulet we sought.

Of course, per the norm, the voice in my head had gone deafeningly silent. He could have lent a hand, told me which book to check, or if I was wrong about the necklace and its association. But he'd said nothing.

"God helps those who help themselves," the voice teased.

I know he does, I thought. *But there's nothing about the lesser gods in that text.*

The thought caused more to bubble to the surface of my mind. Everything I thought I knew about the universe—about religion, about science, about history—had been thrown in a meat grinder and extruded out the other side as something unrecognizable.

Based on what little I'd learned since the events in Mexico, there was still a Creator, the big boss, the one who—in a flash of energy and design—made it all start, added life, and continued to imagine new wonders throughout the cosmos.

The deities from ancient mythologies played into that hierarchy, which actually brought a great deal of clarity to the commandment from the Bible that says, "Thou shalt have no other gods before me." Turns out that hadn't been just an idle Old Testament warning from the Most High; there really were other deities out there fighting for market share.

They were created beings, just like humans and angels, but more powerful, more capable of using the power that flowed around us and through us.

I'd done a lot more reading on the subject in the last few months, learning about great masters who were capable of incredible things, what most would call miracles. One book in particular had forged a great deal of curiosity in my brain, a book about shifting from one reality to the next. The concept posited that all realities were already created, which is taught both in Judeo-Christian traditions and in quantum mechanics.

I shook off the train of distracting thoughts as I reached the end of the book at my fingertips. *Still nothing.*

"Oh," Vero said, stopping on a page in the middle of her current book.

We all looked over at her and then at the page.

A few seconds later, we were all gathered around Vero, looking down at the worn, frail material on the right side. An image of a lion's head was drawn near the top above lines of text.

I took the necklace out of my pocket again and held it up to compare. It and the image were an exact match. A single word separated the drawing from the rest of the page's content—*Apedemak.*

CHAPTER 7

"Looks like that's it," I said with confidence. My eyes were already poring over the text, written in a form of English that had been used centuries before. It made reading more difficult, but I could manage.

"It relays the mythos of the lion god, Apedemak," I noted, though I knew the others were reading the page too.

I kept going until I reached the end, then waited for everyone else to finish so Vero could turn the page.

When she did, the image at the top of the next page caused all of us to catch our collective breath.

"The medallion," Jack whispered.

There above the next rows of text was a drawing of a medallion. It was similar in some ways to the ones Vero and I wore, but there were a few distinctions in its design. The links that composed the chain featured animals from the African continent. Giraffes, zebras, elephants, hippos, exotic leggy birds, buffalo, and even a snake adorned the necklace. And in the center of the medallion that dangled from the chain, the image of a male lion head stared back at us, almost as if it were alive.

Vero checked to make sure we were all ready for the next page then flipped it gently.

The passage told of the history of Apedemak, and not as if it were some legend or myth but as though everything this deity did actually happened. Most mythologies had that in common. If they weren't believable to the masses, no one would have accepted them as truth.

The page also told the story of the Medallion of Power Apedemak bestowed to humanity. Included in this passage was the part I'd been waiting for to confirm our suspicions. It spoke of the guardians of old, those who stood against evil and performed wonders through the power of the amulet.

According to the book, the medallion was left by the last guardian, hidden in the Temple of Apedemak. It claimed that the next guardian must be a person of great humility and kindness but also of strength.

Wasn't anything out of the ordinary based on my experience so far. Except that I didn't really consider myself to be any of those things. I still struggled with that, with why I had been chosen to undertake this role. There were so many out there in the world better suited for it than me. I was just an archaeologist, a student of history. I didn't possess any special skills except what I'd honed during years of study both in the classroom and in the field. Hardly skills that were useful when it came to fighting back the forces of evil that seemed to be swarming.

Then again, maybe it took an archaeologist, someone like me, to break down these clues in order to locate the seven lost medallions.

I kept reading silently, pushing the thoughts aside for the moment.

Where the white and blue embrace, in the shadow of the sacred mountain of Amun, where ancient kings rest eternal, the lion guards the path.

I waited a minute until everyone was done. Then we exchanged looks, the other three focusing mostly on me as if I had all the answers.

"What do you think, Gideon?" Jesse asked.

"Well, I'm not sure, to be honest. There isn't much to that riddle."

I rubbed my chin and paced to the far wall, turned, and paused.

"Is the sacred mountain a reference to Sinai?" Jack theorized.

I shook my head. "No, I don't think so. It says the mountain of Amun. Plus, I can't think of anything white or blue there. And the Kingdom of Kush wasn't close to that area. It would have to be in Sudan."

"What do you know about Amun?" Jesse pressed.

"Amun was one of the most important deities in ancient Egyptian religion. Over time, Amun became a central figure in Egyptian mythology and religious practice, particularly during the New Kingdom period. His name was also pronounced Amen, which has caused many theologians and historians to consider that perhaps the ancient Egyptians worshipped the same deity as their Jewish and Christian contemporaries."

"Hence why we say Amen after a prayer?"

"Exactly. Amun was also the king of all the gods. He ruled over the entire universe, and was the source of all creation. Another interesting feature was his hidden nature. Sort of like the god that Jews, Muslims, and Christians worship."

The room fell silent for moment. I understood why. It was a fascinating topic—and not just to archaeologists.

"No other gods before me," Jack breathed.

"Right. Amun was above them all, just like Jehovah, the I Am, God the Father. You get the picture."

"And his name should always be revered," the voice in my head said. There was no snark to it, only blunt sincerity.

"Do you think the blue and white are references to the sky and clouds?" Vero asked. "Maybe, to the person who wrote this, it was talking about the mountain reaching high up."

"Could be," I managed. But I still wasn't sure that was the solution.

I took the phone out of my pocket and pulled up a map. "Obviously, Amun was worshipped heavily in ancient Egypt, as far back as the Old Kingdom, though his cult thrived more in the late Middle Kingdom and into the New Kingdom, mostly rooted in Thebes."

I entered a search into my phone to find the sacred mountain of Amun, and within seconds, the AI app responded with an answer.

I grinned as I read the text. "So Thebes, or Luxor, was originally the primary center of Amun's worship. That's where the great Temple of Karnak was dedicated to him. It became one of the most significant religious sites in Egypt. But no sacred mountain there."

"And the other?" Vero pressed.

"Khartoum, the capital of Sudan. There's a mountain two hundred and fifty miles north of there called Jebel Barkal, and it just so happens that this site was a major religious center during the rule of the Kingdom of Kush."

The air seemed to get sucked out of the room with the revelation.

"And the white and blue?" Jack asked.

I grinned. "There are two Niles that come together to form the great river of the Nile. A white one and a blue one. The White Nile's primary source is Lake Victoria in Uganda, although the river also has tributaries that begin farther south in Rwanda and Burundi."

I checked the screen again before continuing. "From Lake Victoria, the White Nile flows northward through Uganda and into South Sudan. It continues its journey northward through Sudan until it reaches the capital, Khartoum."

"The Blue Nile originates from Lake Tana in the Ethiopian Highlands. From there, it flows westward and then northwestward through Ethiopia and into Sudan, eventually joining the White Nile at Khartoum."

"So, the first place we look is this mountain two hundred and fifty miles north of Khartoum?" Vero asked.

"Seems that way."

"Whoa. Not to put a damper on things," Jack said, "but Sudan? Not the safest place in the world. Superpowers or not."

I knew he was right. Sudan had been ravaged for a long time by warlords, criminals, terrorists, and every known type of scum on the planet.

At the moment, the United States government had issued a Level-4 warning against traveling to Sudan due to armed conflict, civil unrest, terrorism, kidnapping, and general crime.

Still, with the power of the amulet, Vero and I would be fine. At least, that's what I told myself.

One thing the location did ensure was that Jesse and Jack couldn't come with us.

"We'll be fine," I reassured. "But you two definitely can't tag along."

"I couldn't anyway," Jesse said. "I have a business to run."

"Same," Jack said.

I felt a little relieved that neither of them tried to insist on coming with us.

"So," Vero crossed her arms, "back on another plane?"

I nodded. "Yeah. We can crash here in Nashville for the night but probably need to get back in the air as soon as possible."

Suddenly, I sensed something. It wasn't a sound, or any movement. It was just a feeling. For a second, I thought I was just being paranoid.

"You're not," Xolotl said in a voice only I could hear.

Two seconds later, Jesse reached for the phone in her front left pocket. She pulled it out and looked at the screen. A scowl crossed her face. "Oh great," she said. "Looks like we have trespassers. Coming from the back."

"Those aren't trespassers," I corrected. "It's worse."

"What's wrong?" she asked detecting something in my concerned expression.

I looked at Vero, who nodded. "She said they're here."

"Who said that? Who's she? Oh right. Artemis. You have the head thingy too now." He twirled a finger around to indicate both of us having the same "blessed" malady in common.

We didn't have time to elaborate.

"You two stay down here," I ordered. "Lock the door. We'll handle it."

"Handle what?" Jesse asked. "Who's here?"

"Jack can explain. Stay here," I reiterated.

Vero and I hurried out of the room, into the workspace where we scooped up our new weapons, and out the door. Once on the other side, I closed it behind us and continued up the steps.

When we reached the top, I paused and looked to Vero. "I guess there's no time like the present to test out these new tools."

Her lips curled into a wry grin. "You read my mind."

CHAPTER 8

Vero and I exited through one of the side doors of the old knitting mill and found ourselves in an alley next to an abandoned warehouse. Its crumbling brick walls looked like they might collapse at any second. The portion of the metal roof I could see was peppered with holes and rust.

I checked down toward the front of the mill first then peered into the darkness beyond the parking area in the back where Jack had left his SUV.

Several old shipping containers sat beyond the asphalt in a stretch of gravel that ran from the fence to the right all the way to the back of the property and presumably, to the other end of the industrial park.

"I don't see anything yet," Vero whispered.

"Me either. Which is good. That means we can circle around behind them. Come on," I said, motioning to the left.

We crept out of the shadows and behind the next building, then skirted farther that direction until we reached the far corner. There, I cut across the open area to one of the shipping containers. The run was twenty yards, and I hoped whoever was out there didn't see us.

Fortunately, none of the lights were on in any of the buildings, and the moon had hidden itself behind a series of black clouds.

Thunder crashed in the distance. A storm was coming.

For the people who'd followed us here, there would be two.

We looped around behind the shipping container and stopped at the corner, leaning out to get a look at the space between the fence at the rear of the property, the other containers, and Jesse's place.

Ten men in what looked like SWAT gear were creeping through the tall, uncut grass, making their way toward the knitting mill. They each held submachine guns braced against their shoulders as they moved ahead with knees bent to use the strands of grass for cover until they reached the shipping containers.

"Only ten?" I said, barely loud enough for Vero to hear.

"Only?" she questioned.

"The ones giving the orders know what we are, and what we can do. They would have sent a lot more firepower than this."

Something felt off.

"In here," I snapped, motioning to the shipping container door hanging ajar.

She didn't hesitate. Vero ducked into the shadows within, and I followed just in time to leave full view of another ten enemies approaching from the western side of the industrial park.

They wore night-vision goggles, which would have been a problem if we were going to approach them from the front. But that wasn't the plan.

"What do we do?" Vero whispered.

"We'll have to wait until they pass."

"If they're coming from the front too—"

"We can handle it."

This was what I'd planned on, an ambush from the underlings working for the Sector. I'd seen them at the airport, and they knew I had seen them. The only question here was, what were they really trying to do?

The Sector agents would surely know that these men with guns couldn't take us down, even if they were equipped with those terrible acid rounds. Then again, the more I thought about it, the more I worried they actually could bring us to our knees with those things.

I'd only been hit by one, but the burning pain in my arm had been nearly unbearable.

"As soon as these closest to us pass, we hit them hard and fast with everything we've got. Do it quietly."

Vero nodded and held her bow at the ready.

I noticed the residual red glow against the interior walls of the container, the scarlet hue radiating from my eyes.

My heart rate quickened as I felt the power radiate from the amulet around my neck all through my body.

I heard the sounds of movement just outside. Ordinary human hearing probably wouldn't have detected it. Animals would have heard the noise. That sense was adept at detecting sounds of danger, or of prey.

The footsteps in the grass, the gentle swish of their clothing, even the reeds of grass brushing against them as they passed, were all easy to hear no matter how stealthy they tried to be.

I breathed slowly, forcing myself to be patient. Typically, in a situation such as this, Xolotl started begging me to kill, to rush out and destroy.

But he was showing unusual signs of restraint.

"I'm not only a butcher," he whispered. "I can be tactical when I need to be."

I shook my head subtly so Vero wouldn't notice. I wondered what she must be hearing in her own head at that moment, what Artemis would be saying.

"Don't worry about her, kid," Xolotl cut off the thoughts. "She's probably just talking about spanakopita or olive oil."

I arched an eyebrow. *Wow. At least you don't just go straight to food-based stereotypes. What did your people even eat back then?*

"Maize, mostly. And whatever they could hunt."

It was a rhetorical question.

I saw movement beyond the crack in the container's door. The first intruder came into view, moving deliberately toward the knitting mill.

They were trying to surround the place, which meant they must have gotten through the front gate.

"Or cut their way through the fence. Let's be honest, it's not really a great barrier."

Can you shut up for a second? Just speak up if someone is about to hit me from behind or something. Okay?

"Fine. But when I'm gone, you're going to miss me."

I caught myself wondering if that meant I wouldn't have this power forever. Or if he was only alluding to the next few minutes.

I shook it off and nodded to Vero, then stepped out into the night.

Lighting flashed in the distance, followed by thunder four seconds away.

Storm is getting closer, I thought.

For a second, I figured Xolotl would offer some snarky remark, but he kept to his word and remained silent.

The instant the lightning pierced the sky, an idea hit me.

They would have to remove their night-vision goggles, otherwise if the storm got too close, the next flashes would blind them for a few seconds. Which was fine by me.

I opened my palms, and the spiral blades appeared as I transformed into the ancient creature. To my surprise, my hands remained mostly human to better grip the new weapons. I glanced at Vero as she shifted and noticed the same thing.

I have to admit, I wondered how she was going to pull that bow with bear paws. It was probably hard enough to even open a door or twist open a pickle jar.

I stepped out into the night, keeping my body mostly behind the open door in case one of the other guys saw me from a distance.

Lightning flashed again, and this time, the thunder only took three seconds to reach my ears. *Closing fast*, I thought.

I gripped the center of the bladed weapons where Jesse had cut two openings for my fingers.

Some of the approaching gunmen looked over at each other. They were probably wondering if they should take off their goggles, or if the storm was going to reach the industrial park or blow past to the south.

I imagined they were communicating with each other through radios in their ears. If they'd discussed removing their goggles, they must have decided against it because the men continued to press toward the building.

I looked back over my shoulder at Vero. "Keep one alive," I hissed. "We need answers."

The upright bear gave a curt nod.

The nearest gunman was thirty yards away now, and all of them were focused on the rear entrance to the building. They'd probably cut the power first. It's what I would have done if I were in their shoes. But they weren't going to get close enough to do that.

I extended my hands out, holding the blades wide and away from my body. The churning clouds overhead rolled by angrily. The accompanying wind blew the tall grass halfway over and spun debris and dust around in clouds.

Then lightning cracked through the sky in a brilliant white light.

Every one of the gunmen twitched their heads downward, and one grabbed at the goggles to relieve the burning in their eyes.

"Now," I said.

I took a step away from the container and flung the first blade, spun my body around, and threw the second.

The closest target to my right instantly lost his head and toppled over. The other blade flew toward the gunman nearest him and stuck him the same way. *Two for two.*

I rushed forward, knowing we had to clear the entire perimeter before anyone got inside.

The blades circled around and made their way back to me as if they were drawn to my hands. For a second, I worried they might cut off my fingers, but instead I caught them easily and clutched them again, ready for the next throw.

As I cut to the left to get directly behind the next victims, Vero ventured into the open, her bow drawn with a sparkling black arrow notched. She loosed it. Her first target fell as the arrow pierced through his upper back and stuck out of his chest. Before the man was down, she notched another and fired again. The second shot went through the side of another gunman's ear, just below his protective helmet.

Four dead in a matter of seconds.

Yeah, so to say I was liking these new tools would have been an understatement.

Vero took down another one with a shot through the neck. But the one beyond him saw him fall and turned toward us.

I was already charging at him when he opened fire. The shots were taken in a panic. I mean, I can't say I blamed him. If I saw a big monster running toward me as a normal human, I'd have freaked out too. There was no training for that.

The bullets whizzed by as I spun the blade in my right hand toward him. The sharp weapon sank deep into his chest, the power from the blow knocking him backward ten feet onto the ground. The blade dislodged and flew back toward me as I threw the other.

Vero moved slower behind me, but the arrows continued to fly at a devastating pace.

Within thirty seconds, we'd eliminated six men.

Reinforcements from around the front side of the building rushed to help their comrades. Weapons fired from three directions, and for a second, I hunkered down and covered my head, allowing the rounds to ping off my armor. Unlike in the catacombs, I did everything I could to avoid taking a bullet to the flesh. That wasn't the kind of pain I ever wanted to feel again, if there were a kind of pain I wanted to feel again.

The second blade hit one of the men in the leg and cut straight through it just above the knee. I could hear his screams over the sounds of suppressed gunfire and barked orders.

Both blades returned to my hands, and I waited for a second before acting again.

I looked back at Vero. She stood in the open, with multiple gunmen peppering her armor with bullets. But one by one, she took them down until the reinforcements concentrated their fire on her.

Then she stumbled backward toward the shipping container. I couldn't tell if she was hit or not, but the way she was moving suggested she'd taken at least one round.

I needed to distract them.

I sprang from my position and retreated to the left, toward the back of the property, to extend the distance between the gunmen and myself, circle around them, but also draw their attention.

The sound of bullets cracking through the air around me resumed. Then the rain hit.

Heavy drops started pelting down, their fat smacks audible as they hit the ground, the shipping container, the surrounding buildings. They came slowly at first, but rapidly what began as a sprinkle turned into a deluge.

Then the storm struck in full force, wind blasting across the industrial park with the intensity of a tropical storm. It was so strong, I felt myself working to run into it.

There hadn't been a tornado warning today, and it wasn't even that time of year. A thought occurred to me that maybe this storm wasn't natural after all. Had someone made it happen?

I kept running, perishing the thought for now. Whether the violent storm was purely natural or something else didn't matter. It was here, and I could use it to my advantage.

I dove behind a big tire to the sounds of thunder crashing and bullets thumping into the rubber. The rain continued, blasting across the area at a sharp angle, driven by the fierce wind.

I'd succeeded in dividing their attention and drawing some of the heat away from Vero. After four quick breaths, I popped and flung one blade then another at the first two gunmen I saw.

They were running toward me, their boots splashing in the puddles that had formed in seconds around the abandoned park.

The blades sliced through the first two on the right, ripping a hole in the chest of one, and cutting through the neck of the other.

I growled loudly enough for the remaining gunman to hear me over the storm around us.

They hesitated, slowing their speed to a near crawl. In the corner of my vision, I saw more of them dropping from the arrows Vero loosed.

The familiar red mist swirled around those who stood and lingered over the gunmen who'd already fallen.

I charged to the left while the men focusing on me renewed their fire. A round struck my helmet and bounced off; two more hit my shoulder armor as I continued to circle around their formation.

Then I stuck out my right hand as if to call for the first blade. Lightning flashed and glinted off the spinning metal a second before it tore through the wrists of one of the gunmen en route to my fingertips.

I passed it to the other hand and reached out for the second.

The next gunman spun around in time to catch the spiral edges in the face.

Look, I try not to be too gory when I talk about this stuff. Honestly, as a student of history and cultures, all this violence is really new to me—until my change, I'd only read about these things in primary sources. And sometimes, it's been a little much. So, I won't describe what happened to that guy's face. Or the top half of his head. I'll just say it was grotesque to the level that even the most battle-hardened soldier would probably lose their lunch.

The blade zipped through the air, back to my awaiting hand as the remaining guys took off in the other direction, desperately running toward the front of the facility.

Three more who were left from the assault on Vero tried to do the same, but that was a fool's errand. Not only were they without cover, but now they were simply turning their backs on the enemy, providing an easy target without the distractions of impotent gunfire on her position.

Vero could handle those three. I still had these four to deal with.

My powerful legs thrust me forward at immense, superhuman speed. I let the two blades fly, directing them at the two gunmen on the right, while I surged toward the other two.

I reached the first one as he fled. I snapped my jaws down onto his neck and squeezed. I didn't like the taste, or the feeling of the warm liquid gushing over my lips and tongue, but it was an effective way to take out a bad guy.

I leaped high into the air and landed right in front of another. The gunman nearly ran headlong into me. Instead, I reared back and punched him square in the face. I felt bones crunch under my fist before my arm stopped and retracted.

The blow knocked the gunman backward, his feet flailing in the air until he hit the ground. His face was unrecognizable, covered in blood. I'll spare you the other details. Again, I'm not a big gore guy.

But it really was bad. Bad enough that he didn't get up or move or breathe. Basically, the fight had two hits. I hit him. He hit the ground.

I held out my hands and waited until the blades returned, then I clipped them onto both hips and rounded on Vero.

Through the pillars of mist all over the area, I saw her walking toward me. I checked back down the alley on my side, but didn't see any other assailants.

I wondered if she'd left anyone alive. I was pretty sure I had.

"You okay?"

She nodded. "Yeah." There was a shudder in her voice, and a wince on her face as she shifted back into human form. "You?"

"I'm good. There's a guy missing his hands back over there. Check on him while I sweep around front and make sure that's all of them."

"Okay," she said, following the general direction I'd pointed.

I knew the interloper wouldn't be hard to find. He'd be the only one writhing around, moaning. Everyone else was dead.

"Quite the assault team," Xolotl said. It was the first time he'd spoken up since the attack began.

"Yeah." I trotted forward then picked up speed, concerned there would be more of them around the front of the building.

I slowed down when I reached the front corner and peeked around the building. Two gunmen stood on either side of the entrance, waiting in case anyone inside tried to go out through the front door.

I pulled back and looked down at the ground for something I could use to lure them over. A chunk of asphalt lay at my feet, and I picked it up. In my old life, it would have felt like a ten-pound rock, but now things were lighter thanks to my new strength. Oddly, my human form had remained somewhat slender and only looked a tad more ripped.

I tossed the chunk out in front of the corner and waited for the two men to react to the sound.

I heard them coming less than two seconds later. They moved clumsily, their gear jiggling and clinking as they rushed to check out the cause of the sound.

I could have taken them out with my new blades. But I didn't like the angle, and sometimes it was better to do things the old-fashioned way—by hand.

I heard the men stop at the corner just beyond.

"What was that?" one asked.

I stepped out and saw them both standing there with their weapons held at an angle, pointing down toward the chunk at their feet.

"Sorry, that was me," I said.

Before they could react, or even blink, I reached out and grabbed them by their collars, spun around in a circle like a discus thrower, and tossed them at the brick building next door.

They both hit headfirst. The sound of their helmets striking, bones cracking, and even some of the bricks breaking loose from the force, was both disturbing and a teeny bit satisfying.

These guys were here to kill us, and our friends. They got what they deserved.

"That's the attitude," Xolotl said.

"Whatever. That all of them? Or are you going to keep radio silence?"

"I seem to recall earlier you requested me to shut up. So I am."

"But not now?"

"The fight is done. There are no more immediate threats."

I didn't like the way he used the word *immediate*. It made me wonder if there were others lurking farther away but still within range of the knitting mill.

"You're safe at the moment," he reiterated. "I don't think there will be another attack tonight." He'd barely gotten the words out before he said, "Wait..."

"Wait?"

I felt a sting in the back of my shoulder in the narrow gap between my armor plating.

I grimaced and turned around to see where the shot had come from. It didn't feel like a bullet, though. It was something else. And it wasn't the acid rounds from before. I reached back and felt around until I discovered a small tube with a puffy end. I pulled it out and looked.

"A tranquilizer?"

No sooner had I said the words, the drug began doing its work.

The world blurred around me, and I struggled to see the shooter.

"Gideon?" a voice said. "Gideon, are you okay?"

It sounded familiar. I turned, but everything tilted. Darkness encroached around the corners of my eyes.

"Gideon?" This voice was in my head. I recognized it, but also felt like I didn't know who it was. "What is this? What's happening?"

I spun around in time to see the shape of an animal, huge and furry, stepping toward me with a bow in its... hands? A bear with human hands? It fired an arrow, but I didn't see where it went. I didn't see anything after that. Or feel anything.

CHAPTER 9

"Gideon?"

I heard a woman's voice, but I couldn't see where it was coming from. I tried opening my eyes, but they felt like they were sealed shut with vise grips.

"Gideon, can you hear me?"

The voice was clearer now. But it sounded weird, like it was coming through a tube.

"Yeah," I managed. My body felt heavy, as if gravity had tripled.

"Do you know where you are?" the woman asked.

How could I know where I was? I couldn't see anything. My eyes were glued shut, and the realization sent a ripple of panic through me.

I rolled a little onto my right side, but I felt hands press against me and force me to lie back.

"Don't try to move, man," another voice said from my left. "Just relax."

That voice I knew. "Jack? Jack, is that you?"

"Yeah, Gid. It's me. Just take it easy. You're going to be okay."

"Why can't I see anything?"

"Your vision should come back soon. Just give it a little while."

"A little while? What's that supposed to mean?"

I felt soft, smooth fingers touch the back of my right hand. At first, I started then instantly calmed.

"It's me, Gideon. It's Vero. I'm here."

"Vero? Were you hurt?"

"No. I'm fine. But there was a shooter. He was hidden beyond the gate. I didn't see him until he hit you with that tranquilizer dart. I took him out a second too late."

I furrowed my brow. "Tranquilizer?"

"Yeah," another female joined in. It had to be Jesse, but everyone still sounded weird, hollow. "He hit you hard with something. Had to be strong. Maybe a horse tranq."

"Or something else," Jack offered. "Something they've been working on."

"It's possible. I'll have to run some analysis on it. A friend of mine works at a lab where she can do that sort of thing."

"How long?" Vero asked.

"Couple of days. Maybe less if we're lucky?"

"Excuse me," I said, my eyes finally cracking a little. Blurry, dim light started creeping in. "Do you guys mind talking a little less? I feel like I'm gonna puke, and the conversation isn't helping."

"Sorry," they offered all of at once.

"Jeez," I complained. "What was in that thing?"

"We... were just talking about that," Jack answered.

"No, I know. It was rhetorical. How long have I been out?" My vision continued to gain slowly, but steadily. I could see I was in a room now. A pungent smell filled my nostrils. It was skunk and... Oh. Then it hit me. I was in the facility again, probably down in the basement.

"You were only out like half an hour," Jesse explained. "We dragged you into the office when we realized you weren't dead. Luckily, you shifted back into your human form. Otherwise, we would probably still be trying drag your monster rear through the alley."

If I had shifted when I passed out, that could only mean my subconscious awareness was connected to using the ability. There was still so much I had to learn about all this, even though it felt like I'd been in this bizarre new world for a lifetime.

"There's a lot more you don't know, kid," a new voice said, this time coming from inside my skull.

"And there it is," I muttered.

"What?" Vero asked.

"The voice. He's back. Sorry. Was talking to him."

"Yeah, that's still super weird right?" Jack asked, obviously pointing the question at Jesse.

"Yep."

"You don't know the half of it," Vero said. "At least Artemis is polite, kind, but also pretty savage when it comes to battle."

I felt a wave of nausea sweep over me again, and I felt my stomach tighten. I rolled over onto my side and curled my feet up to my gut.

"You okay?" Vero asked.

She put her hand on my arm and caressed it slowly.

"Just nauseated. Whatever was in that dart really messed me up."

"And they were a really good shot."

I blinked rapidly, which seemed to aid in my vision clearing. I pushed my palms into the hard surface beneath me and sat up.

"Did you get a look at the shooter?" I asked. My balance seemed okay. That was a good sign.

"No," Vero admitted. "I took him down, then I focused on you when I saw there were no others. His body will be gone by now. Like all the others."

"What about the guy with the missing hands?"

"He was dead when I found him. Bled out."

I'd worried that might have happened. What little I knew about losing limbs from a medical perspective came from military buddies. A person only had a few minutes before they bled out, which to me made it all the more remarkable people had survived that sort of thing in combat, or otherwise, for millennia.

"Great," I muttered. "I'd hoped we could get some information out of one of them. Who they worked for at least."

I knew the Sector was behind this, but not which of their umbrella agencies had led the attack.

It could have been any of them. The FBI was the first to come to mind. The Sector had used them before. My mind wandered back to the two incompetent but overzealous agents who'd interrogated me before. But the bureau wasn't the only resource they had at their fingertips. It could have been any of them, even the IRS for that matter.

Most people didn't realize that those tax collectors have millions of rounds of ammunition in reserve, along with more firearms than some small cities. Well, not a small Southern city. But like a small city in New England. Or definitely California.

It was always a mystery as to why seemingly benign agencies were so well armed. My friends who indulged in conspiracy theories had their own ideas as to that answer. Some speculated it was in case the laws were changed and violated the constitution. In such an instance, the military—at least the guys and gals I knew—wouldn't take action on their own people. But the agencies could be leveraged as a sort of gestapo to carry out executive or legislative orders.

I wasn't sure how true any of that was, but the more exposure I got to groups like the one who attacked tonight, the more plausible basically everything became.

"Did you guys check any of the bodies, or what's left of them, for identification?"

"No," Jack said. He and the other two shook their heads. "We were more worried about you."

"Thanks for that," I managed. "Seriously."

"I do think it's odd," Jesse started, "that they would send a huge team after you like that, all equipped with traditional firearms and rounds, but had one shooter with that tranquilizer dart."

"Almost as if they were leading you to the front, away from the fight out back," Jack said.

I could see the gears turning in his mind.

"There were only two gunmen stationed at the front," I recalled. "Seems like an unusually low number to leave there. Initially, I thought all of others went to the back as reinforcements. But now—"

"Now it seems like you were being corralled," Vero offered.

"Yeah."

I replayed the battle in my head. It hadn't lasted more than a few minutes at most. The visuals of the gunmen—their formations, how they split up and seemed to be pushing me one way but then retreating toward the main gate in the front—all flashed through my mind.

"That means they were trying to take me alive. They used that tranquilizer to knock me out. They must have had a truck or something nearby to take me away once I was unconscious."

"They did," Vero said. "It's still out there."

"Show me."

I followed her out of the office with Jesse and Jack close behind me. They were acting like they were afraid I might fall over and hurt myself. While I still felt woozy from the drug, that feeling was fading fast. I wasn't sure if it was because of the power of the medallion or because the stuff was just naturally working its way out of my system.

Any info you can share would be super helpful, by the way, I thought, focusing my statement at Xolotl.

"Hey, I'm just as confused as you. I'm still trying to figure out how I didn't detect the shooter in time."

I wasn't going to say anything.

"You didn't have to."

We exited the building through the front door, and each of us scanned the perimeter to make certain there were no more threats lingering on the property.

"I don't sense anyone," the voice said to me. "But I've been wrong before. Just the one time, but still."

I grinned at the statement.

Sometimes he drove me crazy, but now and then he made me laugh.

We walked across the asphalt to the gate, where Jesse pressed a button on a fob in her hand. The gate slowly rolled away, opening a path to the driveway leading to the street.

A tall oak tree on the left stood amid a patch of green fescue, and parked just behind it was the delivery truck Vero had seen before.

"You two," I said to Jesse and Jack, "hang here for a second until we know it's clear."

They both nodded and stopped where they were while Vero and I continued toward the truck.

I kept the monster on speed dial in case I needed to shift and take out more assassins, but I didn't detect movement anywhere inside or outside the vehicle.

"What is that?" Xolotl asked.

I frowned. *What do you mean?*

"That sound. It's... horrible. I can't think. It's almost as if it's disrupting my mind."

I considered offering a backhanded insult, but the unusual nature of the anomaly held me back.

I glanced at Vero, who also looked perplexed. She met my questioning gaze and shook her head. "It's Artemis. She's saying she hears some awful sound, like it's scrambling her circuits or something."

"My guy is saying something similar."

I looked through the window of the driver's side but didn't notice anything or anyone. I stepped closer then up onto the step to get a better look inside. The cab was empty. I climbed up onto the hood then scrambled onto the roof of the cargo area, where the shooter's clothes and gear lay—the body having already been consumed by the mist while I was unconscious.

The rifle rested just ahead of the clothing, along with a small black satchel. I opened the bag and found six more darts inside, all full of whatever toxin they'd injected into me before.

I closed it up and slung it over my shoulder.

Vero watched from below as I rifled through the clothing. As I suspected, no ID. These guys wouldn't be so stupid as to carry a driver's license to a hit like this.

I noticed a radio earpiece lying next to the rifle and picked it up, along with the transmitter. I stuffed the items in the bag then shimmied down the windshield, onto the hood and back down to the ground.

"Anything?" Vero asked.

"I found these," I said, holding out the satchel. "More darts. Should be easy enough to identify the drug with those. And I got his radio. It's possible we could isolate the agencies that use this one, but that's a stretch."

"Should we check in the back?"

"Yeah." I looked around. Jesse and Jack were still standing where we left them, both with pistols held by their hips.

We walked around to the back of the truck and paused at the gate.

"Be ready," I said. "No telling what's in there. And it could be a trap."

Vero nodded.

I grabbed the handle and stepped up onto the edge of the cargo hold, then pulled up the door in one quick movement. I braced myself for an onslaught of bullets I felt sure would follow, but instead I found the cargo bay unoccupied. In the center, bolted to the floor, stood a strange machine. A black metal box on the base propped up a matching cylinder on which sat a black cube. Wires stuck out of it in a couple of places. A control panel with one knob and one switch were fixed to the side of the base.

"Ah!" Xolotl nearly shouted. I clamped down on my ears as if that would help, but the only loud noise was coming from him.

"What?" I asked the voice. I saw Vero having the same kind of reaction just below me.

"It's some kind of... noise. It's... coming from that thing."

I hurried into the cargo hold and knelt down, inspecting the panel. All I heard was a faint whirring sound, like you might hear from a computer fan.

"What is this thing?" I asked.

"Turn it off. Please!" Xolotl begged. It was a strange tone to hear coming from the usually snarky deity.

I reached out and pressed the button switch down. The fan sound stopped, but that was all I could tell had changed.

"Oh. Oh thank you. Wow. That was terrible," the voice said.

I looked back at Vero. "Better?"

She nodded. "Yeah. I think so. What is that thing?"

I wondered the same. Crouching near the base, I shuffled around to the back then to where I started. There weren't any identifying marks or decals, which didn't entirely surprise me. This clandestine group who'd attacked us wouldn't be stupid enough to leave a brand label on any of their gear.

I moved back over to the open door, leaned out, and shouted at Jack and Jesse.

"Hey. Y'all come over here and look at this."

"What is it?" Jack said, already in stride next to Jesse.

"No idea. That's why I want you two to take a look at it."

They stopped outside the truck and looked in.

"What is that thing?" Jack said, seemingly unaware he had just repeated the question.

"There's a switch at the base of it," Vero said. "We turned it off. Something about it was driving our invisible friends crazy."

"Oh, so now we're invisible friends?" the voice in my head asked.

I ignored him.

"Once we turned it off," I said, "it stopped whatever was causing the problem."

Jesse grabbed a handle on the other side of the truck, planted her foot on the step, and pulled herself up. She turned on her phone light and approached the machine, panning the wide beam across it. She walked around to the other side and back, leaning closer to the contraption a few times.

"I've seen something like this before," she said.

"You have?" I asked. "Where? What is it?"

"I can't be sure. Not yet. But it looks like something Nikola Tesla developed more than a hundred years ago."

"Like an electricity machine?" Jack guessed.

"No. Tesla was obviously known for many of his inventions dealing with electricity, but he worked with other sciences too. One of those drew more criticism than others, which I believe had more to do with keeping the public in the dark than to retain scientific integrity."

"Which was?" I prodded.

"He did a lot of work with frequencies, or what he called subtle energy. He understood that frequencies could alter a person's mood, and even more incredibly, alter reality itself."

"Alter reality?" Vero said. "What do you mean?"

"There are only two things in this entire universe that compose all that we see and all that we are—energy and matter. Through quantum physics, we now understand that energy becomes matter, and matter becomes energy. They are two sides of the same coin. Also illustrated by the famous yin-and-yang symbol. Through the double-slit experiment, we learned that observation changes the form or behavior of energy or matter. But of even greater interest are frequencies. Each atom vibrates at a certain frequency. We vibrate at a frequency, or many. Those frequencies can be disrupted with the application of others, and new ones can be formed. The most famous search for powerful transmutative frequencies was through the ancient study of alchemy."

"The turning lead to gold thing," Jack realized.

"Yes. Interestingly, Jesus' first miracle was alchemical—turning water to wine. A miracle that was forbidden by the religion of the day, and still is by the Christian church."

I grinned, remembering discussions with my chaplain about how Jesus was a rebel. It was one of the things I liked most about him.

"Okay," I said, "all this is interesting and cool. But why would this group of hit men be using something like this?"

"If this is a frequency generator, like I think it is, due to the size of it I would say that it has a pretty big range. Impossible for me to guess how wide a perimeter it can affect. But why they would use it seems clear. They figured out that whatever is in your brains"—Jesse pointed at me then Vero—"operates at a different frequency. This thing probably didn't even affect you."

I shook my head. "It didn't. In fact, I didn't notice anything."

"I didn't either," Vero added.

"How did they know?" Jack wondered.

"That answer, I don't have," Jesse admitted. "But I would like to break this thing down and find out how it works. If they have it dialed into a specific frequency, it may be able to be tuned to other frequencies. I'd have to test it."

I didn't have to think long about Jack's question to come to a conclusion. "The Sector," I blurted. "They must have told whoever this team was, or who they work for, that using a specific frequency would disrupt the things in our heads."

"Things?" Xolotl spoke up after a longer than usual silence. "I am not a thing. I am an ancient and powerful—"

"Then we're lucky," Jesse realized, cutting off his rant that I felt certain would go on for at least two minutes. "If they had hit the right frequency..." She trailed off, leaving the thought unfinished.

"What would happen?" I pressed.

"In theory, it might be possible to make it so unbearable for those consciousnesses that they would have no choice but to break the bond."

"Break the bond?"

"Yeah," Xolotl echoed. "What does that—"

"The medallions' power could be broken, separated from you. Once that happens, whoever gets them—"

"Gets the power," Vero finished.

"Whoa," the voice in my head sighed. "Things were much simpler back in the old days. Well, not the old, old days. Before the great flood, the tech was way more advanced than what you have now. But between those ages, there wasn't much after the Egyptians."

"So," I said, ignoring him. "I guess we'll need to be even more careful from now on. If they're using this kind of tech, it's clear what they want to do—harness the medallions for themselves."

"But can't these... beings within our minds resist?"

"No," I said. "They must work with who bears the amulets. Like a genie with whoever rubs the lamp."

"That is an oversimplification, and if I might say, also demeaning," Xolotl chirped.

"I'll see if I can find anything about this in my library," Jack said.

"And while he's doing that, I'll see what I can find out about this machine, who made it, and who these guys were who were using it."

"Right," I agreed. "I guess we need to find a flight to Sudan. Not sure how many of those fly out of Nashville."

"I doubt any of them are nonstop," Jack joked.

"Yeah," I agreed with a chuckle.

But I hoped Vero shared my silent, unspoken concern. I didn't want to leave Jack and Jesse here alone. Maybe they could defend themselves, though I doubted they could handle a unit like the one Vero and I just took out.

"So, what are you going to do if they send another team like this one?" I asked. "It's probably not safe for you two to stay here. They may come back even if we're out of the country."

"Yeah," Jack conceded. "They left us a lot of guns, but even so, it might be best if we leave town for a bit."

Jesse seemed reluctant. "I have all those plants to worry about, but I guess my employees can handle it for a bit while I'm gone. They know what to do."

"Either way, we should scoop up all those guns, maybe put them down in the basement. But I'd keep a few on hand just in case."

"Where will you go?" Vero asked.

Jack and Jesse glanced at each other for a few seconds before Jesse responded.

"My parents have a cabin down in Sequatchie Valley near Chattanooga. We can lay low there until things die down."

"Sounds like a good plan," I said. "You're sure you'll be all right?"

They both nodded.

"We'll be fine," Jack said. "You two just be careful. Sudan is dangerous enough as it is without a bunch of covert operatives trying to kill you."

CHAPTER 10

I'd been in some crappy places before—Third World countries with little to no plumbing, spiking crime rates, poor to zero infrastructure, waves of poverty spilling over the streets. But I can honestly say this place was right up there in my ten worst. One-half star. Would not recommend.

The instant we stepped off the plane in Khartoum, the heat hit us like a physical force. It was as if we'd walked into the devil's sauna, the air shimmering with mirages even on the tarmac. I glanced at Vero, her dark hair already clinging to her forehead with sweat, and saw my own discomfort mirrored in her eyes.

"Well," I said, squinting against the glare, "welcome to Sudan."

Vero nodded, adjusting the strap of her bag. "Is it too much to hope for an easy trip here?"

I snorted a laugh and smiled at her. "Definitely."

We made our way through the airport, every sense on high alert. The bustling crowds, the mixture of languages, the unfamiliar scents —it all served to keep us on edge. It was tempting to think we'd come too far to be caught now, but the Sector had eyes everywhere.

For all we knew, they could have agents waiting for us right here in the airport just like back in Nashville.

As we reached the baggage claim, the familiar weight of Xolotl's medallion against my chest seemed heavier, as if responding to the proximity of whatever we were seeking in the Nubian Desert.

"You feel it too, don't you?" Xolotl's voice echoed in my mind.

I gave a slight nod, not wanting to speak aloud and draw attention.

I had no idea if it was the fact we were surrounded by elements of danger in every direction or if it was because we were close to the next medallion. I hadn't gotten that sort of feeling when we were near the Artemis Medallion that Vero now wore. So I had to assume it was my first instinct—that evil lurked nearby.

"Be on your toes, Gideon. Not just for trouble. The desert does not give up its secrets easily."

We collected our bags and made our way out of the airport and into the chaotic streets of Khartoum. The city was a jarring mix of old and new—ancient markets and mosques juxtaposed against modern high-rises and billboards. The air was thick with the scent of spices, vehicle exhaust, and the undercurrent of thousands of lives being lived nearly on top of one another.

"We need to meet our contact," I said, my eyes constantly scanning our surroundings. "He said he'd have a ride and supplies ready for us."

Vero nodded, remembering the brief conversation we'd had before leaving Nashville. As an archaeologist, I had connections around the world, even here in Sudan. Sometimes.

We hailed a taxi, a battered old Toyota that had seen better days. The driver, a wiry man with a neatly trimmed beard, eyed us curiously as we climbed in.

"Where to?" he asked in accented English.

I guess we really did stick out in this town.

I gave him the address to a small café in the older part of the city, and he stepped on the gas.

As we weaved through the traffic, I couldn't shake the feeling that we were being watched. Every face in every passing car, every pedestrian on the crowded sidewalks—any one of them could be an agent of the Sector.

"Relax," Vero whispered, placing a hand on my arm. "We're fine. We can handle anything."

I forced myself to lean back, to adopt a more casual posture. She was right, of course. The best way to blend in was to act like we belonged here, like we were just another pair of tourists exploring the city. And the fact we were basically demigods didn't hurt.

The taxi dropped us off in front of a small, unassuming building. The smell of coffee and freshly baked bread wafted from the open door, making my stomach rumble. We hadn't eaten since the plane, and the aroma was tempting.

We slipped on our backpacks and walked to the entrance. Vero's smile let me know she appreciated my pulling the door open and waiting for her to enter first, just like I was raised to do.

Inside, the café was dimly lit and sparsely populated. A few locals sat at small tables, sipping coffee and engaged in quiet conversation. I scanned the room, looking for the familiar face of my old colleague.

"There," I said softly, nodding toward a corner table.

Dr. Abdel Rahman sat hunched over a steaming cup of coffee, his salt-and-pepper beard neatly trimmed, his eyes hidden behind thick glasses. As we approached, he looked up, a smile breaking across his weathered face.

"Gideon, my friend," he said, standing to greet us. "It's been far too long." He looked at me as if I were a long-lost son finally returning home.

I clasped his hand, genuinely glad to see him. "Abdel, thank you for meeting us. This is Vero."

Vero shook his hand.

A mischievous glint sparkled in the man's eyes. "A diamond truly shines in the desert," he said, holding her hand a second longer before he glanced at me. "It seems you are doing well, my old friend." He winked at me as we sat.

I shook my head, smothering the laughter that tried to escape my lips.

A waiter appeared almost immediately, and Dr. Rahman ordered coffee for all of us in rapid-fire Arabic.

"So," he said, leaning in close once the waiter had left, "you're really going through with this expedition of yours? Into the heart of the Nubian Desert?"

I nodded, glancing around to make sure no one was listening. "It's important, Abdel. More important than you can imagine."

Dr. Rahman's expression turned serious. "You know, there have been... whispers. Rumors of other interested parties asking questions about the region you're planning to explore. Dangerous people, from what I hear."

I felt a chill run down my spine, despite the oppressive heat of the day. Was the Sector already here, already sniffing around? If so, our timeline just moved up. We'd have to move fast.

"What kind of questions?" Vero asked, her voice carefully neutral. I could tell she was holding back any emotion.

The old archaeologist shrugged. "Odd ones. About old legends, local myths. Things most serious researchers wouldn't bother with. They seemed particularly interested in stories about guardian spirits and hidden temples."

I exchanged a quick glance with Vero. We both assumed the same thing, what—or rather, who—these "interested parties" must be.

I decided to focus on what we could control. "Abdel," I said, leaning forward, "what do you know about the ancient Kushite god Apedemak?"

Dr. Rahman raised an eyebrow. "The lion god? Not much more than what's in the standard texts, I'm afraid. He was a warrior deity, associated with royal power. The 'Lion of the South,' they called him." He paused, studying my face. "Does what you're searching for have something to do with that ancient myth?"

I hesitated. Abdel was an old friend, and I hated lying to him. But the less he knew about our true purpose, the safer he'd be. "We're following up on some... unconventional leads," I said carefully. "Things that would be better not released to the public."

"Ah," Dr. Rahman said, a knowing look in his eyes. "The kind of leads that make careers—or break them. Well, my friend, you've always had a nose for the unusual. Just be careful out there. The desert is unforgiving, and some secrets are best left buried."

If only you knew.

"We'll be careful, Abdel," I promised. "But we need your help to get started. You said you could arrange transportation and some supplies?"

He nodded. "Yes, I've got a guy who can set you up with a decent vehicle and the basics. But listen, Gideon, whatever you're really after out there, whatever brought you all the way to Sudan... Is it worth the risk? The desert isn't the only challenge you may face. There is trouble brewing here in Sudan. Warlords are tormenting villages, and they've even begun probing the edges of the city to see how far they can push their strength."

I met his gaze steadily. "It's worth it."

Dr. Rahman sighed, removing his glasses to polish them on his shirt. "Very well. I'll help you as best I can. But promise me this: If things start to go sideways out there, if you find yourself in over your head... get out. No discovery is worth your life."

If only it were that simple. He had no idea what Vero and I had become. But I nodded anyway. "I promise, Abdel. We'll be careful."

"So, what are you looking for out there, other than something to do with Apedemak?"

I bit back the part about the medallion, and I wasn't sure he needed to see the necklace we'd discovered in Portugal. Instead, I focused on the riddle we'd uncovered.

"Centuries ago, there was a famous Portuguese explorer named

Diogo Cão who journeyed into Africa searching for what we believe is a lost temple of Apedemak. Cão died on his journey, but his first mate continued on. We uncovered the first mate's tomb a few days ago, along with a clue as to the whereabouts of the temple."

Abdel frowned. "You really have been watching too many movies."

"No," I insisted. "It's real."

"We found the first mate's tomb in the catacombs under Lisbon," Vero added.

Abdel looked at her then back to me. "Fine. Go on. What is this clue you found?"

"It says to journey to the land where the Blue and White Nile embrace, to the shadow of the sacred mountain, where ancient kings rest eternal. Apparently, there is a stone marked with the sigil of a lion head."

I left out the part about the hidden temple and the lion's seal that would grant us entry.

"We believe the mountain is Jebel Barkal."

Abdel listened then looked up at the ceiling, pondering our story.

"Well, this is the land where the two Niles converge to one," he said. "As for a sacred mountain, this is ancient land. Most local legends have a sacred mountain in them."

I felt a twinge of concern that maybe this would be much more difficult than I'd anticipated.

"But," he said, "Jebel Barkal is probably the place you're looking for. It was where Amun was worshipped in the ancient times of the Egyptians. And it was a major religious center during the height of the Kush Empire."

"Correct," I said. "And a UNESCO site."

Abdel shook his head. "Not anymore. It's been overrun by a warlord from the desert, an evil man set on causing chaos. His name is Kofi Adisa. He could make your journey even more treacherous. You'll have to be extremely careful. I would suggest making the drive at night. It's only a hundred kilometers, but it will take you at least five hours to get there. The nearest town to there is Dongola. Not much there, though."

"I understand."

"Well, if this is what you have to do, you might as well go in with as much information as possible."

For the next hour, we pored over maps and satellite images, marking potential sites and discussing the logistics of our expedition. Dr. Rahman's knowledge of the region was a huge help, and by the time we were finished, we had a solid plan, or at least as solid as we could manage given how much we were keeping from him.

"I've arranged for a vehicle and supplies," he said as we prepared to leave. "They'll be waiting for you at this address." He handed me a slip of paper. "The owner is a friend. He won't ask questions, but he also won't hesitate to report you if those other interested parties come asking with a good bribe. So be quick, and be discreet."

We stood to leave, and I thanked him for all the help. "If you ever need anything from me, don't hesitate to ask," I offered.

"I appreciate that."

Then he took my arm and pulled me close.

"Gideon," he said, his voice low and urgent, "there's one more thing you should know. The locals, especially the older ones... They speak of something out there in the deep desert. A guardian, they say, that appears to lost travelers. They call him Amari."

I frowned. "A guardian? Like a spirit?"

Dr. Rahman shrugged. "Who knows? It's probably just a story to keep people from wandering too far into dangerous territory. But if there's any truth to it... Well, be prepared for anything. The desert has a way of playing tricks on the mind."

"I'll be careful, old friend. I promise."

He gave a single nod then bowed slightly to Vero. "It was lovely meeting you. Take care of him, okay? He has a history of making bad decisions."

I laughed at the insinuation, but I also knew he wasn't wrong.

One decision, in particular. I felt like that was the one he had in mind too—my marriage.

It was weird. I didn't think about it much anymore. And it hadn't been that long ago. I suppose if the relationship hadn't been a sham, if she'd been a better person, and actually loved me, I would still feel a deep abyss in my soul.

But I didn't.

"I will," Vero said, snapping me out of my distant thoughts.

With those ominous words ringing in our ears, we said our good-byes, left the café and stepped back out into the sweltering heat of Khartoum. The sun was beginning to set, painting the sky in brilliant shades of orange and purple.

"He was nice," Vero said as we hailed another taxi.

I took a deep breath, feeling the weight of the medallion against my chest, the stirring of Xolotl's power within me.

A cab stopped at the curb, and we climbed in. Soon we were on our way to the address Dr. Rahman had provided.

I leaned back in the seat and tried to relax, but my nerves were a wreck. Even with superhuman powers, I was still human at my core, vulnerable to the same worries and emotions as everyone else.

Whatever lay ahead in the Nubian Desert—whether it was the Sector, this mysterious Amari, or the power we sought—I had a bad feeling something wicked was coming our way.

The taxi wound its way through the darkening streets of Khartoum, taking us farther from the city center and into an area of warehouses and industrial buildings. The address Dr. Rahman had given us turned out to be a large, nondescript garage with a faded sign that read Osman's Auto Repair in both Arabic and English.

I paid the cab driver, then we exited the beat-up old car and watched as the man drove off unceremoniously, on to his next fare.

I stared at the building for a few seconds, running over the details of the weather-worn façade, the metal roof, and the dirty gas pumps.

As we approached the entrance, a stocky man with grease-stained hands emerged from the shadows. He eyed us warily then spoke in heavily accented English. "You Gideon?"

I nodded, tensing slightly. Even though Dr. Rahman had vouched for this man, years of being hunted had made me cautious of everyone. I didn't see the red mist around him, and so far that little signal hadn't let me down.

The man—Osman, I presumed—grunted and jerked his thumb toward the interior of the garage. "Your ride's inside. Come with me."

We followed him into the dimly lit space, the smell of oil and rubber filling our nostrils. And there, in the center of the garage, stood our transportation: a rugged-looking Land Rover, its desert tan paint job chipped and faded, but its frame appeared to be solid.

"She's seen some miles," Osman said, patting the vehicle's hood, "but she'll get you where you need to go. Just don't ask where she came from, eh?"

I ran a hand over the Land Rover's pockmarked surface, feeling the history in every dent and scrape. This vehicle had stories to tell, no doubt. It had likely seen some things in the desert. I just hoped we wouldn't be adding any more bullet holes to its collection.

"The supplies are in the back," Osman continued. "Water, extra fuel, emergency rations—not that you'll need those. At least I hope you won't. GPS and sat phone too, but..." He tapped the side of his nose knowingly. "Maybe best not to use those unless you have to. Some people, they can track such things, you understand?"

I nodded, grateful for his discretion. "We understand. Thank you."

"Where are you going anyway?"

I considered not telling him. For all I knew, he could be a Sector snitch, but again, no mist, so I rolled with that.

"Heading north toward Dongola."

Osman whistled. "Drive fast. You'll have enough fuel to get you most of the way there. But you'll definitely need the two tanks on the back." He didn't say anything else, which I wasn't sure was better or worse.

As Vero and I loaded our personal gear into the Land Rover, I caught her looking at me with an odd expression—part excitement, part worry perhaps.

"What?" I asked.

She shook her head, a wry smile playing at her lips. "Just thinking about how crazy this all is. A few months ago, my life was so different. Now I'm about to drive into the Nubian Desert..." Her thoughts trailed off, and I sensed it was because we both knew Osman was either intentionally or unintentionally listening in.

I chuckled, but there was little humor in it. "Yeah. It's definitely not what I expected when I was talking to my high school guidance counselor about my future plans. But I suppose there's no turning back now."

"No," she agreed, her expression turning serious. "There isn't."

With a final check of our supplies and a handful of cash passed to Osman, we climbed into the Land Rover. The engine roared to life, a deep, reassuring rumble that seemed to vibrate through my bones.

I'd heard bad things about Land Rovers, mostly from friends who owned them. They were beautiful vehicles, with pretty interiors. But the engines were far from reliable, a fact that reverberated in the back of my mind as I thought about the five hours of driving through the desert at night. I seemed to recall the older models doing okay and being the vehicle of choice for expeditions across the sands, but maybe I was remembering wrong.

I waved to Osman as we pulled out of the garage and into the night. Within ten minutes, the lights of Khartoum were behind us.

The archaeologist in me felt a sense of excitement over what we might find. The same archaeologist felt dread settling in his stomach. We were committed now, heading into the unknown with nothing but our wits, our hidden powers, and each other to rely on.

The city gave way to dark hills and scattered villages and finally to the vast, empty expanse of the desert. The headlights cut through the gathering darkness, illuminating a lifeless, jagged landscape that seemed to stretch on forever.

We drove on through the night, the monotony of the desert broken only by the occasional cluster of rocks or the ghostly shapes of dunes in the distance. The conversation we began at the beginning of the drive—discussing trivial things to ease the tension—faded away after an hour.

After another ninety minutes, I was about suggest we find a place to stop and stretch, maybe top off the fuel tanks, when Vero suddenly sat up straight, her body tensing.

"Gideon," she said, her voice low and urgent. "Look."

I followed her gaze and felt my heart skip a beat. There, on the horizon, was a faint glow—not the first light of dawn, but something else. Something that pulsed and shifted in a way that no natural light should.

As we watched, the glow seemed to coalesce into a shape. It was massive, towering over the dunes, its form constantly shifting and reforming. For a moment, I thought I saw the outline of a lion's head, its eyes burning with an otherworldly fire.

"What is that?" Vero whispered, her hand unconsciously moving to grip the medallion around her neck.

Before I could answer, the apparition vanished, leaving nothing but the empty darkness of the desert night. But in its wake, I felt a surge of power unlike anything I'd experienced before. It was as if every cell in my body was vibrating, responding to some primal call.

Xolotl's voice spoke in my mind, which startled me because he hadn't said much since we left Khartoum.

"They have us surrounded."

CHAPTER 11

The sudden burst of light was blinding. One moment, we were driving through the quiet darkness of the desert night; the next, we were surrounded by a ring of harsh, white beams cutting through the gloom. I slammed on the brakes, the Land Rover skidding to a halt in the loose scree.

"Gideon," Vero's voice was tense, her fingers running over the medallion at her throat, "who is that?"

I squinted against the glare, trying to make out shapes beyond the wall of light. The quiet desert night was suddenly alive with dozens of headlights pointed at us, including several straight ahead that blocked the road.

"No choice," I growled, feeling the familiar surge of power from my own medallion. "If they don't want to talk, then I guess we fight our way out of it."

I took the risk of opening the door and stepping out into the glaring beams. I shielded my eyes with my hand as I peered ahead, wondering if I was going to simply be shot on sight or if there was going to be some kind of negotiation. Usually, from what I knew about these types, they were interested in getting something—

money, guns, supplies, or in some of the more disturbing cases, people.

As if on cue, a voice boomed out from beyond the lights, harsh and accented. "Step out of the vehicle with your hands up! Do it now, or we open fire!"

He spoke heavily accented English, but the guy was already proving to be a moron.

"Yeah, so, I'm already out of the vehicle. As you should plainly see with all those lights pointed at me. Would you mind cutting the high beams? It's rude to keep them on when there's another vehicle coming your way."

For a second, the voice didn't respond. Then I saw the silhouette of a man step in front of a vehicle directly ahead of ours.

I exchanged a quick glance with Vero. We both knew there was no talking our way out of this one. Whoever these people were—possibly Kofi Adisa's men—they hadn't come here to chat. But I doubted they knew anything about the medallions, or why we were here. They were bandits, land pirates, lowlife parasites living off others.

"I said put your hands up!" the man barked.

My heightened sense of hearing detected movement from the other vehicles, boots scuffing on the loose dirt and sand, the clinks and clanks of weapons jiggling as the men around us got into position to fire.

"What are you doing?" Xolotl asked. "Just kill them and be on your way. You see the mist, right? These guys are bad news. And there are more circling around behind—"

"I hear them," I said, cutting him off. "Do you detect anything out of the ordinary?"

"Other than a group of bandits getting ready to hit you with a thousand rounds of ammo?"

"I mean like Sector agents or specialized weapons?"

"Oh. No. Nothing like that. These guys aren't that advanced. And since I know you're worried about it, they don't have those acid rounds either."

"That's what I needed to know."

I slowly raised my hands over my head.

"Get down on your knees!" the leader barked. "And tell the other one to get out!"

Under normal circumstances, I would never have permitted a woman to get out of the car with these barbarians. That's what a coward would do. But our circumstances were anything but normal. I knew there was nothing these guys could do to either of us.

I looked into the SUV at Vero. She didn't seem scared. But she still hesitated, as if waiting for me to give the go-ahead.

I nodded.

She climbed out, raised her hands over her head, and walked slowly over to where I knelt.

She lowered herself down to her knees and glanced over at me with a grimace. "This could be more comfortable," she said.

"I know."

The ground was hard, and the loose rocks in the sand dug into our kneecaps.

The man who'd been shouting the orders stalked toward us, his silhouette growing as he drew near. I heard some of the other men encircling us start to move in as well, tightening the noose.

I saw the outline of a rifle hanging loosely in the man's right hand. It appeared to be an AK-47, a weapon of choice for many of his ilk in this part of the world. It was a reliable firearm, but the one time I'd used one on a friend's range, I felt like it rode up too much with sequential shots.

Once he was within thirty feet, the lights of the vehicles behind us illuminated his face. He was definitely local, with a thick black beard and a tan shirt with dark brown pants and black boots. The outfit looked like it hadn't been washed since it was made. His face was dirty, and a black turban covered his hair.

The guy looked like the poster child for terrorists.

When he was only twenty feet away, I spoke up.

"Good evening," I said in a cheerful voice. "Lovely night for a drive through the desert, isn't it?"

The man said nothing as he continued to approach us, a disapproving scowl on his face.

"Would you mind telling us where the nearest rest stop is? I had way too much water earlier, if you know what I mean."

"Silence!"

He stopped ten feet from us and leveled the rifle. He studied me for a few seconds, but his eyes were drawn to Vero, and lingered on her. He looked her up and down, his mind clearly going to vile places.

I knew what happened to women like her in areas like this. I'd heard stories on some of my expeditions, and also in the news I tried to avoid.

The lust in his eyes was primal, voracious. And my instincts told me to rip his head off and throw it back at the vehicle from whence he came, just to send a message to the rest of his men.

But I resisted.

"What are you waiting for?" Xolotl asked.

Just having some fun with him, I thought.

"You know, Gideon, I think I'm starting to like you."

Took you long enough.

"You should not have come here," the man said. He stepped over to Vero and looked down at her. He started to reach out his hand to brush his fingers across her face.

"Don't touch her," I said, my voice as hard as steel. "Unless you want to lose that hand one finger at a time."

He looked over at me with fury steaming in his eyes. For the moment, he forgot about her and moved closer to me.

"American, eh?" he said.

"Figured that out all by yourself? Let me guess, you're Canadian. Toronto? I don't hear the French accent from Quebec, so—"

He pointed the gun at my head. "My men are going to have fun with her while we tear your body apart."

"If you say so."

He frowned, then his expression changed. I could tell he was looking at the amulet hanging around my neck, visible between the unbuttoned part of my shirt.

"What is this?" he said, lowering his rifle until the muzzle touched the medallion.

"This?" I looked down at it then back to him. "Family heirloom."

Vero snorted.

He cast a scathing glance over at her but focused on me again.

Technically, I wasn't lying. Apparently, this thing had been in the family I didn't know I had since the dawn of humanity.

"Take it off."

"Sorry, chief. Can't do that."

"Take it off, or I will take off your head and remove it myself."

I sighed. "I mean, you already told me you were going to tear my body apart, so what's the difference?"

He raised the barrel and pointed it at my forehead. I saw his finger tense on the trigger.

"You're one of Kofi's men, aren't you?" I asked.

"You dare speak his name?" the gunman spat.

"We heard he's been causing trouble around here."

The mist spiraled around the gunman, as if begging me to end him.

It seemed like the guy was trying to think of something to say, a real zinger that would stump me just before he pulled the trigger to end my life.

"Kofi Adisa is the ruler of these lands. Soon, he will control the entire country."

"Yeah, I don't think so. Sounds like a bad person. Sort of like you. You strike me as a bad person. So I'm afraid I'm going to have to end you now."

For a second, the man looked confused. He quickly replaced that with an arrogant snarl as he tightened the trigger against his finger.

The rifle had to be close to discharging, and even though the bullet wouldn't kill me, it would still hurt. Even so, the temptation to make it look like it killed me, then pop up and scare the crap out of him, was strong.

I decided against it. The pain really wasn't worth the hilarious visual I would get of the guy freaking out at seeing a dead man stand up.

I summoned the power from the amulet, and in mere seconds my body transformed, morphing into the wolflike creature. The transformation was always a rush, a surge of primal power that never got old. I felt my body growing, muscles bulging and bones shifting.

For a moment, the man stared in disbelief at the change. Out of sheer instinct, he fired a round at my head even as the helmet tipped the muzzle upward.

The loud report echoed across the valley, but the round merely glanced off the top of my armored head.

I grabbed the end of the barrel as he fired another panicked shot. This one sailed out into the darkness behind me, or maybe toward one of his own men. Then I pulled it down and bent the thing in at an angle, rendering the weapon useless.

The whites of his eyes swelled in the headlight beams as he took a step back and clumsily reached for his sidearm.

To my right, Vero also changed, shifting into a terrifying armored bear.

The man finally drew his pistol and fired, switching between me and Vero. Sparks splashed off our armor, the bullets harmlessly pinging away and into the sand.

He emptied the contents of his magazine and kept squeezing the trigger even when the weapon clicked.

Finally, he stumbled backward, dropping the impotent firearm at his feet. He started to turn to run, but I stopped that right away.

I produced one of the spiral blades in my right hand and slung it at the man's ankles.

He only got four steps away before the sharp edge cut through his right shin. Before the pain and realization hit him, he took one more step, but this time landed on the bloody stump and fell over onto the ground.

Then the screaming began.

He grabbed for the bloody wound, howling something in Arabic. I understood a little of it but not enough to care.

I stalked over to him as he continued writhing and howling.

The only reason I could figure he didn't order his men to start shooting was that his feeble mind couldn't possibly grasp what was happening, or maybe he was afraid they might hit him.

Now, that fear evaporated, and he shouted with the last ounces of his strength for his men to open fire.

Muzzles flashed all around us, the warm desert air filling with the peppery sounds of reports. Some of the rounds hit our armor and ricocheted away. Others simply missed and flew into the night. It was dark, and the men were probably not the best-trained marksmen in the world.

I caught the blade and stood over him as his men tried to reload their weapons. A few random shots continued to fire, but none of them hit me where it would hurt.

The footless man was saying something in Arabic. It sounded like a prayer, and I definitely caught him saying the word "Allah."

I reached down and grabbed him by the neck, lifting him up off the ground so that his eyes met mine. His feet—oops, foot—dangled just below my knees, the wounded limb bleeding out onto the dry earth.

"God isn't on your side," I said to him.

I squeezed his neck, watching his eyes bulge. Then I lowered him down for a second just to get some momentum before I flung him eighty feet into the night sky.

ERNEST DEMPSEY

His body turned into a shadow away from the headlight beams of all the trucks around us.

He screamed on the way up, and on the way down.

The gunfire stopped for a moment, and I guessed his men were probably watching, unable to pry their gazes away from the horrific display of inexplicable superhuman strength.

The voice of the leader rapidly drew closer until, at the last second, his form reappeared in the light just before he hit the ground headfirst with a sickening crack and thud. The screams cut off instantly and were immediately followed by more gunfire.

I turned to Vero and shrugged. "Shall we?"

She nodded and let out a terrifying roar that shook the very air around us, a warning to our attackers.

The red fog swirled around every one of our assailants, marking all of the gunmen. These men had chosen their path, and now they would face the consequences.

"The mist judges them," I whispered.

"Indeed," Xolotl said in a somber tone.

I lunged forward, my powerful legs propelling me into the midst of our attackers to the front. They were everywhere, dozens of them, all armed to the teeth. But their weapons meant nothing against what we had become.

My claws tore through the first man like he was made of paper, the red mist swirling and thickening as it consumed his body, leaving behind only tattered clothes and a discarded rifle. I didn't even think about it, already moving on to the next target.

I produced both spiral blades and threw them to my right and left. The screams of the enemy told me the deadly weapons had hit several marks.

With a glance across the impromptu battlefield, I saw Vero in action. Her massive bear form was a whirlwind of destruction, swatting aside armed men like they were toys, each swipe of her paw a devastating blow.

The night air filled with screams of terror and the staccato of

98

useless gunfire. I felt bullets pinging off my armor, more an annoy-ance than a threat. These men had come expecting to ambush help-less travelers. Instead, they had walked into a nightmare.

Now, they were desperate. A few started to retreat back to their vehicles. But that wouldn't save them.

CHAPTER 12

The blades returned to me, and I was about to throw them again at the fleeing men, but one by one I saw them drop as Vero's arrows struck them down. I glanced over at her and saw her standing in shimmering golden Greek battle armor, no longer in bear form.

Another report popped to my left. The round thumped against my armor and fell to the ground. I turned and faced three more men with guns pointed at me, and charged.

They fired their weapons until the magazines ran dry. I was forty feet away when that happened. Then they tried to split up and run away.

I surged toward the one on the right first, catching up to him easily just as he reached an SUV's open door.

He jumped in, shifted the vehicle into drive, and stepped on the gas, spinning the SUV around while kicking up scree and dust.

I squinted my eyes and turned my head, but reached down in time to grab the back bumper with both hands—er, paws. Paw-hands.

First I pulled on the bumper, preventing the vehicle from

speeding away. Then I bent my knees and lifted the truck a few inches off the ground.

The engine roared as the wheels spun uselessly in the air.

I looked through the back window and through the windshield and spotted the other two guys running to another vehicle. The driver turned and looked over his shoulder at me, the whites of his eyes glowing against the beams from vehicles across the field.

I grinned then dropped the SUV back down to the ground as the RPMs neared the red line.

The truck hit the ground hard, jarring the driver. The wheels spun for a second before finding purchase. Then the SUV barreled forward. Before the driver could react, he plowed into his comrade opening the driver's side door of the other vehicle, pinning him violently between the two.

The sound of metal crunching and glass breaking accompanied the wreck. The collision was so hard, the second vehicle flipped over onto its side, crushing the third guy underneath.

Smoke and steam billowed out of the crumpled hood.

I trotted over to the wreckage, curious about what happened to the driver.

"Ugh, what a mess." The first victim had been sandwiched between the two trucks.

A hole surrounded by a spiderweb of cracks occupied the windshield. Then I knew what happened to the driver. I looked out beyond the two SUVs and saw him in a heap on the ground twenty feet away. The mist was already consuming his body, just like the other two.

The sounds of gunfire had dwindled to random pops in the night. I heard a man scream from across the battlefield and looked back to see another one fall to Vero's bow.

Another group of gunmen fired from behind open doors to their trucks positioned behind our SUV.

"More work to do, still," I half complained.

I charged forward, dipping between some of the vehicles en route to the gunmen. My jaws closed around the arm of a man trying to bring a heavier weapon to bear. His bones crunched as his scream cut short.

"Gideon!" Vero's voice caught my attention. "Rockets!"

I spun just in time to see a man hefting an RPG onto his shoulder, aiming at Vero. Without thinking, I leaped. My powerful legs carried me in a long arc through the air, and I crashed into the man just as he pulled the trigger.

The rocket went wide, exploding harmlessly in the desert beyond. I didn't give the man a chance to reload, my claws making short work of him. The red mist swirled, hungry, consuming.

For a split second, I surveyed the area, taking in the scene around us. The orderly ambush had devolved into chaos. A few men fled in different directions, abandoning vehicles and weapons in their desperation to escape. The desert sand was littered with empty clothes and discarded gear, macabre evidence of the fate that had befallen their owners.

A movement broke the darkness—a group of men making a stand near one of the larger vehicles. They had set up a heavy .50-cal. and were pouring fire in Vero's direction. Even with her armored hide, sustained fire like that could be dangerous, and those rounds packed enough punch to knock down just about anything.

I charged the gunner. The men were so focused on Vero that they didn't see me coming until it was too late. I crashed into their position like a freight train, scattering men and equipment like bowling pins. They were barely able to raise their weapons before death took them.

The machine gunner turned, trying to aim the big weapon at me. It may as well have been in slow motion. I grabbed the barrel of the gun, the metal shrieking as I twisted and tore it from its mount. The gunner fell back, terror plain on his face as the red mist swirled around him. I hefted it against my shoulder and fired a single shot.

I'm not trying to be grotesque or too descriptive, but there was very little left of his head and face. Just leave it at that.

I turned and opened fire on the others in the column stupid enough to stay and fight. The heavy rounds tore through their ranks with devastating effect. Some of the rounds pierced their vehicles, mangling the metal, glass, and tires along with the shredded bodies that had once driven them.

Vero was finishing off the last of them on the other side. She loomed over a single remaining enemy, who threw down his weapons and fell to his knees, putting his arms up over his head.

She held a notched arrow pointed at him, ready to feed the mist.

"Gideon?" she said. "What do you want me to do with this one?"

I walked over to her and stopped by her side.

The man was begging for mercy in Arabic, but he clearly didn't feel sorry for what he'd done. If so, the mist would have left him. It still danced around his form, waiting for his execution.

Normally, I would have told her to finish him off. In this case, however, I had another idea.

"You're going to use him as bait, aren't you?" Xolotl guessed.

Instead of answering him directly, I spoke to the guy.

"You work for Kofi Adisa, yes?"

He bobbed his head frantically.

"Good. Go to him. Tell him what happened here. Tell him that his reign of terror in this region is over. Tell him that if he wants to face us himself, we will be ready."

Fear drained the man's face.

"Do it," I reinforced. "Or she'll happily put that arrow through your face."

It had to be terrifying for the guy to be kneeling there, staring up at me in my monster form. It was no small miracle that he didn't pee his pants. Or throw up. Or both.

"Boo!" I barked.

He scampered backward then stood up and ran as fast as he could into the darkness.

Vero lowered her bow and watched as the man disappeared into the distance.

"You think he's going to bring Kofi to us?" she asked.

"Probably. Men like Kofi are so full of themselves. Massive egos. We eliminated a lot of his men tonight. This loss won't be insignificant to him. He'll be looking for payback."

"You sure that's what you want? I would rather us just go find the temple and be on to the next step of the quest."

I kept peering into the darkness. "Men like him do horrific things to innocent people. I've heard of his kind before. There was one in Uganda a few years back who used to go into villages and take kids from their homes in the middle of the night, then turn them into slave soldiers by brainwashing them. The atrocities he committed, and made those kids commit, were beyond terrible. Kofi is no different. I'm sure of that much."

"Do you think the Sector will try to use him? Give him intel about who we really are?"

"Maybe. Nothing is out of the realm of possibility with them."

Talking about them caused me to wonder why I hadn't seen the Division 3 agents recently. I knew they were primarily observers, but they'd been radio silent for too long.

I looked out over the scene that had returned to the original silence of the desert night.

As quickly as it began, the battle was over. We stood amid the wreckage of vehicles and the scattered remains of our attackers' possessions.

I shifted back to my human self and took a deep breath.

A sound caught my ear—movement from one of the overturned vehicles. In an instant, I was on alert again and shifted back to my wolflike form, stalking toward the source of the noise. As I rounded the hood of the truck, I saw him—another survivor, pinned under the vehicle's frame. The red mist swirled around him, but weakly, as if unsure.

The man looked up at me, his eyes wide with terror. He babbled something in Arabic that I didn't understand, holding up his hands in a gesture of surrender. For a moment, I stood over him, my jaws inches from his face, and considered ending him.

Instead, I stepped back, letting out a low growl of warning.

The man didn't need to be told twice. With strength born of desperation, he wriggled free of the wreckage and ran, stumbling and falling in his haste to get away. I watched him go, disappearing into the darkness of the desert night.

Vero stood beside me, a questioning rumble emanating from her throat.

I shook my massive head. "Let him go. Let him run back to Kofi Adisa with tales of monsters in the night. You never know. The desert might claim one or both of them before they can get back. But I want Kofi to know what happened."

As the adrenaline of battle faded, my body shifted and shrank, the armor receding, until I stood once more in my human form. Beside me, Vero's armor likewise disappeared.

We stood there in silence for a few moments, surveying the aftermath of the battle. The desert around us was a graveyard of vehicles and empty clothes, the only evidence of the men who had ambushed us.

"We should go. It's getting late."

She nodded.

We made our way back to our Land Rover, miraculously undamaged in the chaos of the battle. As I slid behind the wheel, my hands shook slightly. The power of the medallion thrummed through me, a constant reminder of what I had become—what we had both become.

"Gideon," Vero said softly as I started the engine, "are you okay?"

I took a deep breath, trying to center myself. "Yeah. I'm good. You?"

"Yeah. I would never have thought I would be after doing something like this, or any of the battles I've fought, the people I've wiped off the face of the earth. But it feels... right. Is that weird?"

"Yes. But no. It isn't. It's who we are now. It seems like the world is getting more dangerous, like evil is growing, tipping civilization to its breaking point on all fronts. I think that's why we have these now, and why we have to find the others before it's too late. Guardians like us are the only thing that stands between total destruction and humanity's survival."

I shifted the Land Rover into gear. "But it doesn't make it any easier to reconcile with the person I used to be. The archaeologist who dug up pottery shards and got excited about ancient inscriptions. That guy seems a million miles away now."

Vero reached out, placing her hand on my arm. "He's still in there, Gideon. We're still us. The medallions didn't change who we are, just... what we can do."

I nodded, grateful for her reassurance even if I wasn't entirely convinced. As we drove away from the battlefield, leaving the wreckage and the lingering wisps of red mist behind, I couldn't shake the feeling that we had crossed a line tonight. There was no going back to who we were before. All we could do now was move forward and hope that whatever power had chosen us knew what it was doing.

The desert night stretched out before us, vast and unknowable. Somewhere out there was the next medallion, the power of Apedemak waiting to be claimed. And beyond that... who knew? The Sector, Kofi Adisa, other forces we couldn't even imagine—they were all out there, moving pieces on a board we were only beginning to understand.

But for now, we drove on through the darkness, leaving the echoes of destruction behind us.

CHAPTER 13

J
ust past midnight, as the full moon hung high the eastern sky, I caught movement just over a hill to my left, just at the edge of perception. It seemed to pace alongside our vehicle. When I turned to look directly, there was nothing there but swirling sand. I suddenly felt like we were being watched.

"Did you see that?" My eyes scanned the desert around us.

She leaned forward, peering to her right. "See what?"

I shook my head, unsure how to describe it. "I don't know. Looked like a person. But moving really fast for a human."

Vero was quiet for a moment, her hand unconsciously moving to touch her medallion. "I don't see anything," she said finally. "But I feel it. Like we're being... watched."

"Or herded."

Were we being led by some unseen force? And if so, to what end?

I eased my foot off the gas, slowing the vehicle to a crawl. Maybe I should have done the opposite and gunned it.

"There," Vero blurted, pointing straight ahead.

I'd been gazing off through the window and not seen the silhouette appear on the road ahead of us.

Against the backdrop of the bright, full moon, the dark figure seemed almost like an apparition, absorbing all the light from my headlights. I couldn't make out a face, or any other details.

I slowed down until the SUV came to a stop and then shifted it into park.

The figure stood perfectly still. The only motion came from strands of his cloak fabric fluttering in the breeze.

"What should we do?" Vero asked.

I wasn't sure, but I knew we couldn't just sit there. I briefly considered going around it, cutting off the road and throwing the SUV into four-wheel drive. But the terrain on both sides looked treacherous. I'd gone off-roading most of my life as a youth, heading out on Saturdays and Sundays with friends and family, sometimes in an SUV, sometimes on motorcycles.

I knew what I was doing with that kind of driving. But nighttime was different. I only needed to go a little out of the way to get around this... person, but I had a feeling that wouldn't change anything.

Whoever or whatever this was would simply reappear in our way again.

"He is not an enemy," Xolotl said. "Turn off the engine and get out of the car."

"What?" Both Vero and I said it at the same time.

We glanced at each other.

"He is here to help," the voice in my head added.

I sighed, turned off the engine, and killed the headlights, even though the doubt inside me kept saying that was a bad idea.

Vero didn't ask what I was doing. I had a feeling she was getting the same instructions from Artemis.

I removed the keys from the ignition, and we opened our doors at the same time, leaving them open as we walked around to the front of the vehicle.

"There's no mist around him," I noted.

"Yeah, I know," Xolotl said. "I told you. He's not here to hurt you."

So it's a he. Okay.

"Hello," I said, walking toward the figure. I waved in a friendly gesture, still unsure if that might spook the stranger.

He said nothing.

"Do you need a ride or something?" I continued. "Where you headed?"

The wind shifted. It had been blowing gently sideways, but now it came from behind us, as if this person drew in all the air from the desert. Sand blew around us, swirling in clouds that dispersed into the dark sky.

I glanced over at Vero as we continued forward. She reached her hand up to the medallion around her neck, as if preparing to call on the power again.

"You needn't do that," the figure said, his voice booming across the sands like a roaring freight train. The wind blew back toward us, bringing the dust and sand with it.

We shielded our eyes with our forearms, narrowing our eyelids to slits.

When the wind died down, I lowered my arm and found the man standing a mere ten feet away from us, as though he'd teleported from his previous position.

Now I could see his face, along with his tattered robe.

He was Sudanese, with dark skin and a shaved head. His eyes looked nearly black, and despite my superhuman powers, I felt a little afraid to look into them. The man stood about my height, just a shade over six feet. His light brown robes hung loosely off his shoulders and brushed against the ground at his bare feet.

A tattoo of the Eye of Horus was inked onto his forehead a few inches above the nose. Several dots were also tattooed under his eyes in a line that ran across his cheek bone, then down to his jaw.

He wasn't young, but something about him didn't exactly seem old either. Based on his appearance, it would have been a reasonable guess to think he was probably in his late seventies, maybe early eighties, which seemed contradictory, but I had this weird suspicion that he was much older than that.

"Who are you?" I asked, finally able to find my voice.

He twisted his head toward me in an almost robotic fashion. It was an even, mechanical movement that sent a chill down my spine.

"I am Amari. Servant of Amun, the one you call God, or the Creator."

That was unexpected.

I noticed additional tattoos peeking out from under the V neck in his robes but couldn't see what they were.

"Nice ink," I said, pointing to his chest.

The man grinned. Surprisingly, his teeth looked like they were fairly well maintained. I'd expected them to be yellow and dirty, or missing.

He pulled the robes apart so we could see the rest of the artwork.

The head of a male lion stared back at me. The tattoo's attention to detail was spectacular to the point where it almost looked alive.

"I also serve Apedemak," he said.

Vero and I shared a knowing yet pleasantly surprised glance.

I reached into my pocket and produced the necklace we'd found in Portugal.

"We are looking for Apedemak," I said, holding out the necklace to the man.

He eyed the object for a moment then looked back up at us. "I know you are, Guardians. You are Gideon Wolf, servant of Xolotl."

"Heh," the voice in my head laughed. "You hear that, servant?"

"I wouldn't say servant," I corrected.

"I would."

I ignored him.

The man looked at Vero. "And you, I see Artemis is with you."

"She is," Vero answered.

"It is unusual for two guardians to travel together without the others. According to guardian history, each walks the earth alone, protecting their realm until..."

He faded off, seeming to choose his next words carefully.

"Until what?" I pressed.

"We can discuss that later."

I didn't like the way that sounded. If it was something dangerous, or like bad news, I'd rather get it out of the way now and move forward.

That said, I pushed away my curiosity for the moment. "You're a shaman, aren't you?" I asked. "A medicine man?"

"I am called many things, but yes. I serve that purpose to the people of the desert."

"Great. So, you know why we're here. Can you show us how to get to the hidden temple and find the Apedemak Medallion?"

The shaman inclined his head, as if assessing us both.

"I can show you the path to Apedemak. But are you strong enough to walk it?"

My instincts were to say yes. I'd done things I could never have imagined before—in my old life. Vero and I were superhuman, gods walking among mortals. But I hesitated. I had a feeling the question itself was the first of a series of tests we were about to face.

"There is no way I can know that without doing it. But I am ready to take the first step."

"Very good," Xolotl whispered in a creepy tone.

The shaman grinned. "Good. Follow me. We will spend the night in my village."

"We can give you a ride," Vero said. "You don't have to go on foot."

"And it will save time," I added.

The man's grin only adjusted slightly, taking on a mischievous air. "I will go on foot. Try to keep up."

I glanced over at Vero, who reflected my questioning expression. The man turned and started trudging away into the darkness.

"I guess we follow him," I said.

We returned to the SUV, climbed in, and buckled our seat belts, though at the time I wasn't sure why.

"This is going to take forever," I complained, turning the key to start the ignition.

"It's his show," Vero said. "Maybe it's not far from here. Like just beyond those rocks or something."

I started to say maybe but then realized the guy was gone.

"Crap. Where'd he go?" I asked.

Vero peered through the windshield and out the window on her side.

I looked around too but couldn't spot him.

Without thinking, I shifted the SUV into drive and accelerated ahead, spinning the rear wheels on the scree beneath.

"I hope we didn't lose him," Vero said, still scanning the dark horizon for any sign of the shaman.

"There," I said, pointing straight ahead.

The headlight beams raked across the man's figure nearly a hundred yards ahead.

"How?" Vero wondered.

"Maybe we just go ahead and assume everything we're going to encounter from now on in our lives is super weird."

"Deal."

We narrowed the gap between us and the shaman. He was practically flying, even though I saw his feet touching the ground as he ran along the road. It was like every step he took was ten for a normal person.

I kept my foot on the gas pedal as we neared sixty miles per hour.

"He's running almost the same speed as a cheetah," I noticed. "That isn't possible for a normal human. The fastest man can go just over twenty-seven miles per hour. But not sixty. And not at that age. And not for this distance!"

We'd already covered a half mile in our chase to catch up to the man.

The SUV bumped and jostled on the uneven road. A couple of times we caught a few inches of air and crashed back down to earth. The sport suspension on the vehicle helped me keep control of the wheel, but the ride was still like something in a rally race, or one of those desert races I'd only seen highlights of on obscure sports channels.

Once I'd reeled the guy in to around the fifty-yard range, I eased off on the throttle and matched his speed.

At one point, I thought I saw him glance back over his shoulder, still grinning as if he was amused by the chase.

Then suddenly, he raised his right arm and pointed off the road and into the desert.

I frowned at the gesture then watched him veer to the right. He leaped over a rut next to the right side of the road and kept running, momentarily disappearing from view.

"What's he doing now?" Vero wondered.

"I have no idea. But this whole thing just keeps getting weirder. Hold on."

She grabbed the handle over the window. Pretty much everyone I knew had a name for it. Because this is a family story, I'll not mention what my friends and I call it.

I let my foot off the throttle, feathered the brakes, then cut the wheel hard to the right as I resumed acceleration.

The truck fishtailed to the left, but I easily corrected it, and the vehicle surged off the road, jumping the shallow ditch. We landed on the other side, and the shaman's figure came into view again.

We were going uphill, and on a much rougher patch of terrain than the road ever offered.

I gripped the steering wheel as hard as Vero clutched the handle above the window. We rocked back and forth with every bump and hole and mound we hit. I knew the truck had been through some rough spots in her day, but she was old, and I wasn't sure how much longer the bolts and rivets would hold up under these conditions.

A terrible vision of us blowing a tire or busting an axle came to my mind. I knew the latter was unlikely, but at this point I'd thrown logic out the window and into the dark Sudanese desert.

Keeping up with the shaman proved more difficult off-road as we climbed a long slope.

I kept wondering where he was taking us. True to form, Xolotl remained mum on the subject.

Just as temptations to stop the vehicle and look at a map bubbled into my mind, I noticed a subtle glow on the horizon beyond the top of the hill.

Sunrise wasn't for several more hours, so I knew this had to be a town, village, or settlement.

The shaman abruptly stopped at the summit and turned to face us as we barreled toward him.

When we were twenty yards away, I pumped the brakes, praying the lines hadn't been severed on the rocks or against the jagged, hard ground.

The SUV rolled to a stop next to the man, and then I saw where he was taking us.

Down in the basin on the other side of the hill sat a sprawling village of huts and cinder-block buildings.

Amari turned to me and pointed a bony finger down into the settlement. The guy was breathing normally, as if he'd just woken up from a long sleep. He'd been running nearly sixty miles per hour, and the last stretch was uphill. I couldn't fathom how he wasn't gasping for air.

"This is Nbahu. You will stay here for the night."

I could feel Vero's questions drilling into the side of my head. Was this really a safe place to stay for the night? The place was Third World with a serious rat infestation of terrorists lurking possibly anywhere in the darkness surrounding the village.

The last thing I wanted was for us to wake up with our heads on the ground next to us in a hut.

Sure, we had these powers, but we had to sleep at some point. And when we did, it was just like normal humans. We were completely vulnerable.

Then again, it would have been rude to turn down the hospitality. "Hey, thanks for the offer, but your hood looks super sketchy, so maybe we'll just come back tomorrow after we spend the night in a more reputable place."

That would have gone over like a turd in a punchbowl.

And it wasn't like there were a bunch of five-star joints around here. Or even two stars.

"Thanks," I mustered. "I know we're both tired after the travel, and the ambush."

"Of course. I'll make sure you are comfortable. Follow me."

"Are you going to do the running and jumping thing again?"

His coy grin didn't give me an answer either way.

"No. I will go slower this time. It would be reckless to go so fast through the village."

CHAPTER 14

A mari led us down the other side of the hill and onto the beaten path that passed for a road. As promised, he moved much slower than before.

I wasn't sure why he couldn't simply hop in the back seat and tell us where to go, but he, like the others I'd met, seemed highly eccentric.

We reached the bottom of the hill and continued toward the village. Bonfires visible from the top of the ridge burned brighter down here, and they were spaced out evenly around the settlement's perimeter.

"Where do they get the wood for those?" Vero muttered, befuddled.

I'd been wondering the same thing.

"Yeah. There aren't many trees out here."

"You mean any trees. I haven't seen one since we left the city, and those were few and far between. Just a few palms out here, and I don't know how many of those are around."

"He provides the fuel," Xolotl answered.

I wondered what he meant but got no further response.

My mind wandered to both logical and far-out possibilities, but I decided to rein that in for now and simply pay attention to our guide as he led us beyond a two-foot-high wall of rocks that encircled the village.

"Not going to stop anyone with that wall," I remarked. "It must not be there for defensive measures."

"Judge things by their size, do you?" the voice asked.

No, not always, I thought. *Just for practicality. Do you always rip off lines from one of my favorite movies?*

"I've never seen a movie."

So, you just plagiarize by nature.

He didn't say anything else, probably perturbed at my responses.

Amari turned to the right and walked ahead in the gap between the wall and the first houses around the internal perimeter. After a few minutes, he stopped, and crossed his arms as if to say *this is where you park your truck.*

I switched off the engine and climbed out, with Vero exiting on the other side.

"Collect your things," Amari said. "My home isn't far from here."

I partly wondered why we hadn't just driven all the way to his house, but maybe rolling an SUV through a village distinctly devoid of automobiles might have drawn more attention than desired.

We certainly had a knack for doing that all on our own.

Vero and I opened the back and retrieved our gear.

As I slipped my rucksack on, I peered out beyond the burning pyres toward the darkness and the hill we'd just come from.

"Awfully quiet here," I noticed.

She finished strapping on her bag and followed my gaze. "Too quiet?"

"Could be." I turned and faced the nearest buildings. "Why don't we hear the sounds of dogs or cats, or babies screaming?"

"Maybe they do a sort of lights-out thing after dark to keep everyone inside their homes."

"Yeah," I half agreed. "I guess."

Even so, I thought it odd that we hadn't heard anything. And come to think of it, I hadn't seen another soul either. It was as if the entire village had been abandoned.

Part of me started to wonder if Amari was indeed who he claimed to be.

I started to say something about staying on our toes but refrained. The guy could probably hear us, and on top of that, I felt the nagging draw of fatigue pulling on me.

My body was heavy, and I needed sleep.

We were just going to have to roll the dice and trust this guy.

I closed up the SUV, and the two of us walked around to the front, where Amari stood waiting.

The cool evening air was dusted with a hint of frankincense and vanilla. Perhaps a touch of cinnamon.

"Follow me," Amari said unceremoniously.

He turned and started walking into the village between two huts made of earth and stone.

As we passed through the narrow opening, I noticed candlelight flickering in the windows but still detected no signs of life other than us.

I held my questions for the end of the show, figuring our guide would eventually tell us what was going on.

Walking through the settlement, I realized how immense the place was. It had looked decently large from the hilltop earlier. Or had it? Was my mind playing tricks on me?

I shrugged it off as the desert causing my mind to wander to strange theories, questioning my senses.

We snaked our way through more huts until we arrived at what I guessed was the center of the village. A single hut stood in the center, surrounded by a circle of stones. A fire burned in a pit about thirty feet in front of the home.

The structure reminded me of the first one I'd seen. I couldn't believe it had been nearly two years since the events in Mexico, teed off by the execution of my wife in a hotel room at the hands of the cartel.

That first encounter with one of these medicine men was a haunting experience that had defied logic and the senses. There was no reason for me to suspect this would be any different.

We followed Amari to the rickety wooden front door, where he paused, looked back over his shoulder at us, then pulled on an iron latch and pushed the door open.

The odor of incense wafted out, tickling my nostrils. Inside, the hut was completely dark—pitch black, as if the light from the fire outside couldn't reach beyond the threshold.

Amari motioned for us to enter, but I felt a sense of apprehension sweep over me.

I saw the same concern on Vero's face.

I sighed. We'd come all this way. And there really weren't any other alternatives nearby. On top of that, I didn't feel like running into more of Adisa's men. So I stuffed away the worries and stepped into the hut.

The instant my foot touched the floor on the other side of the threshold, candles flickered to life all around the room. I felt a gust of wind rush over me and ripple through the hut.

Except it wasn't just a hut. Not like the one I'd been in back in Mexico.

On the outside, the building appeared to be made of earth and whatever rocks Amari could find. And it looked like it was only maybe five hundred square feet.

But on the inside, everything was like a mirage.

The square room expanded thirty feet into every direction. Instead of an earthen floor, as I anticipated, my foot touched down on polished wooden boards.

A rustic kitchen to the left occupied the corner. There were comfortable chairs surrounding a fireplace to the right, each cushion covered with colorful quilts.

Two open doors revealed bedrooms, one to the left and one

beyond the back wall. From what I could see, the rooms were clean, and the beds were made. Beds. Actual beds. Not like a pile of straw with sheets over it. The frames were made from polished wood to look like miniature logs. Or maybe that's what they were.

I'd seen the same kind of design in cabins I'd stayed in before when visiting Pigeon Forge and Gatlinburg. In fact, the entire layout looked similar to those places.

"You have your own private bathroom as well. You'll be staying in that one," Amari pointed to the room in the back.

I stared at the man, astonished by the revelation.

"What?" he said. "You didn't think I had indoor plumbing?"

For a second, I couldn't find the words. I was too dumbfounded, and from the look on Vero's face, I could tell she was facing the same struggle.

"To be honest," I confessed, "no. No I did not. I thought this was going to be—"

"A mud hut with no amenities?"

"Well, yeah." I looked around at the place just to make sure I hadn't imagined it. "Are all the other huts... I mean homes here like this one?"

Amari inclined his head. "Perception is reality. And reality is perception. I perceived this place in my mind. And all the other homes in our village."

"But on the outside—"

"I would think you of all people would understand that what we see on the outside isn't always a reflection of the inside. We keep the exterior of the homes here looking small, humble, unattractive, in order to avoid more attention from Adisa and his men than we can handle."

"Doesn't he still come here to steal people to serve in his army?" Vero asked.

"He tries, yes. So far, he hasn't made it into any of the homes. But last week, some of his men made it through the perimeter and took a few of our children. I was unable to hold them off entirely."

I frowned. "Perimeter? Hold them off? That wall you have out there wouldn't keep out a bicycle, much less a band of heavily armed raiders."

"Again, perception is reality," he corrected. "Look at this home. On the outside, you would believe there is no possible way it could contain so much space."

I recalled thinking it had to only be five hundred square feet on the inside. But standing here now, It was easily a thousand, or more.

"That wall," Amari continued, "creates a division between the realities. It is a veil to keep the eyes of the wicked from easily discovering this place. They have been here before, but that doesn't matter when you look for something your eyes can't detect."

"So, you're using some kind of—"

"Magic?" He shrugged. "Some might call it that. I thought my friend in Mexico explained this to you. But we are all able to shift reality, to move between the dimensions. Some of us are better at it than others. Tell me, Gideon, when you first met the shaman in Mexico, did you see his hut?"

"Yes. When I came out of the jungle."

"And when you left it, was it still there?"

I thought for a second even though I knew the answer. I was starting to question my memory. "No. At least, I didn't see it."

"And the temple in the jungle?"

"I didn't see that either, although I fell in a hole."

"It is the same. These sacred places sit on what some would call holy ground, places that are stronger than others, where the veils between reality are thinner and can be more easily manipulated."

I'm just an archaeologist. So, all of this metaphysical mumbo jumbo was starting to break my brain a little. I wondered what Vero thought of it. She was a bartender, a small business owner. On the outside, someone might not think much of that. But I knew her to be highly intelligent. One of the signs pointing to that I picked up early on—she doesn't speak much. Instead, she listens. That's a trait, I learned, that the smartest people in the world have.

"Fascinating," she said. "What causes Adisa's men to be able to spot this place sometimes?"

"The veils shimmer now and then when there is a disturbance in the timelines. If his men happen to be within view, they can see beyond the veil for a moment, or even several minutes. That is what happened last week."

His expression turned sad. His eyes drooped, and his jaw slackened.

"You mentioned finding the Medallion of Apedemak. Unbeknownst to Adisa and his men, the key to finding the lion god's secret temple is hidden in the ruins where he maintains a base of operations."

Okay, so this medicine man, who lives in a quaint, magical cabin in the desert, was talking in plain, albeit accented English, and was discussing an enemy's base of operations as though he were some kind of military tactician. This night just kept getting weirder.

"Why do I feel like there was an ulterior motive in bringing us here to your village?"

The shaman maintained a somber, stoic gaze. He peered into my eyes, boring into them.

"You already know why I brought you here. As with all things in the universe, there are always two. Two sides, good and evil. Light and dark. Positive and negative. Physical and spiritual. And there are always two reasons you are here: to find the Medallion of Apedemak."

"Let me guess the second one. You want us to get back the children Adisa took and wipe him and his men off the face of the earth."

Amari didn't move, didn't even flinch. "To get the children back, yes. Taking out Adisa and his men would be, how do you say, icing on the cake? Once you have discovered the amulet, Apedemak can return to protect the people of Africa from the forces of evil."

"Sounds like a big job for one person," Vero said. "The whole continent?"

I was thinking the same thing. Then again, there were only seven guardians for the entire planet. To say we were outnumbered would be the biggest understatement of all time. Thinking about it in those terms really hit me hard. Before, I was just up against bad people doing bad things. But they ran organizations. Taking out a group was one thing, but a whole world of evil...

"You will not be tested above which you are able," Amari said.

I knew that quote. I'd heard it numerous times when I was a kid. Actually, it had been pounded into my brain by my religious parents. But it had always stuck with me, especially in dark times where I thought about giving up, when it seemed the entire world was against me.

"First Corinthians 10:13," I said quietly.

"Yes. A wise text to remember, especially when you seem overwhelmed by circumstances."

I nodded. "Yeah. I guess it is."

"Do you want us to sleep in shifts?" Vero asked, changing the subject after a yawn. "We can keep watch over the village."

"That won't be necessary tonight. It is late, even for Adisa and his men. And he is preoccupied at the moment."

"Preoccupied?" I asked. "How? And how do you know that?"

"You permitted a few of his men to escape. I expect by now at least one of them made it back and is relaying the news of what happened during their ambush on the two of you. Of course, Adisa will not believe it. Not at first, but he is aware of the legend of Apedemak. To him, at least for now, it is only that—a legend. I suspect now, though, he may become a believer having lost so many of his men. He will plan a hunting party for the morning. When he and his men leave the ruins, they will not take the children with them and will only leave a few guards behind to make sure they do not escape."

"This guy really knows his stuff," Xolotl said. "You should listen to him."

I am listening to him.

"Just saying. He makes a lot of sense."

I ignored the statement. I already thought the same thing, and my unseen companion knew that. He was only trying to be irritating. And he was succeeding.

"You will be safe here for the night," Amari added. "Tomorrow evening will be the best time to attack, when they are more susceptible, and when you can use the cover of darkness."

"Thank you," Vero said. Her soft tone reflected her obvious appreciation.

"You're quite welcome, Guardian."

Something still nagged at me. The same thing that had struck me when we entered the village.

"Where are all the people?" I blurted. "Walking through this place, I didn't see or hear any signs of life."

"They are in their homes. I have instructed them not to leave their houses after dark. Their movement or sounds could disturb the veil around the village. So they remain hidden and quiet. It is inconvenient in some ways, but there isn't much reason for them to be out after dark. The desert is both dangerous and boring at night. Once Adisa and his army are defeated, we will be able to do as we please at any time of day."

The answer made sense. Although I did feel bad for the people not being able to go out and enjoy the stars. Here in the middle of nowhere, without any light pollution save for the pyres burning outside, the view of the sky was simply amazing.

"That makes sense," I said. "And thank you for giving us a place to crash for the night. I appreciate it."

"It is an honor to host you, Guardians." He turned and walked over to the door on the left, paused to look back and give us a nod, then disappeared inside and closed the door.

I looked at Vero, who was already staring at me. "I guess we should get some shut-eye. Sounds like we have a big day ahead of us tomorrow."

She nodded. "Yes. I just hope his plan works."

CHAPTER 15

I woke up to my heart racing. I looked around the bedroom but didn't see any sign of Vero anywhere. Through the shuttered window, I could see it was still night outside.

I pulled off the sheets and slipped out of bed, pulled on my pants that I'd left on the floor, and stood. I was sweating, even though the room was surprisingly cool, almost like it would be in a cave.

The bathroom door was open, but it was dark inside. And empty. *Maybe Vero went out for a drink of water.*

I walked cautiously over to the door, and pried it open just a crack. I peeked through the opening then opened it wide until I saw a figure sitting on the floor in front of the hearth on the opposite side of the room. It was Amari, staring into the flames as they danced, casting eerie, flickering shadows across the walls of the room.

Cautiously, I stepped out of the bedroom, leaving the door open.

I moved across the floor and stopped behind one of the chairs surrounding the fireplace.

"Amari," I whispered. "Where is Vero?" I could see now that she wasn't in the house, unless—however unlikely—she was in Amari's room.

The medicine man turned his head around almost like an owl and stared at me with vapid, lifeless eyes.

"Amari? You okay?"

The man said nothing. Instead, he merely continued staring as if I wasn't there. Then he turned his head around and resumed whatever he was doing before.

Shivers went up and down my spine and raised the hairs on my arms and neck.

The only thing I could guess was that Vero must have woken up and gone outside to make sure everything was okay.

I'd been surprised at how easily I'd fallen asleep, and how well I'd slept up until the moment I roused. Even against the drag of exhaustion, my nerves tugged hard on my senses to keep me awake.

Within minutes, that anxiety had surrendered the fight.

I walked over to the door and paused with my hand on the latch. I glanced back over at Amari, who still sat there with his legs crossed, peering into the fire.

"Weird," I breathed.

Then I raised my voice. "I'm going to check outside. Okay?"

No response. This time, he didn't even turn his head to face me.

"All right. Fine. He's clearly meditating or something."

I pulled on the iron handle and tugged the door open. A gust of air rushed past me, just as it did when I'd entered the house.

For a second, I hesitated to leave the safety of the hut, but I pushed on anyway and stepped out into the chilly desert night.

The door abruptly slammed shut behind me, nearly causing me to jump out of my pants. I looked at it as if the thing were possessed, then continued forward.

The bonfire still roared in the pit in front of the hut. The flames twisted and climbed, licking the air before disappearing. I walked over to it and stood several feet away from the edge of the pit. The fire's warmth radiated all over my skin.

Then I saw something in the darkness beyond the flames. A

dense fog lingered fifty yards away from where I stood, between the huts in their rows surrounding the path to the shaman's home.

I puzzled over the mist for a moment, wondering how it could be here in such a dry, desolate place. Then again, I'd seen plenty of things that didn't make logical sense. Heck, I was one of those things.

Suddenly, two red orbs emerged in the fog. They glowed bright red and seemed to be coming toward me. I took a step back, realizing that what I saw were two eyes. Whatever they were attached to was coming my way.

I tried to summon the power, to shift into the monster, but nothing happened. I felt no surge rush through me, no energy pulsing in my veins. I reached my right hand up to my neck to feel the medallion.

Only then did I realize it wasn't there. I rubbed my hand around my upper chest, but the amulet was gone. I looked down, then around on the ground, but there was no sign of it.

Had it come off in my sleep? Had I dropped it in the hut? Or... had Amari stolen it?

"That's not possible," I muttered.

Still, the eyes continued toward me. I took a step back just as the full figure appeared from the folds of the mist.

"No," I said, shaking my head in disbelief. "That can't be."

There, a mere fifteen yards outside the ring of stones surrounding Amari's hut, stood the Chupacabra.

The battle armor that had protected me in combat, glimmered in the flames.

I took another step back.

"Where are you going, Gideon?" the creature asked. His voice was deep and cold and raspy.

"This isn't real," I said, suddenly hoping this entire scenario was just a dream.

The monster took a giant step toward me. "What is reality, Gideon?"

He kept coming, and when he reached the circle of stones, stopped short.

I stood still, thinking there must be some kind of magical barrier he couldn't get through.

"Give me the medallion," I ordered. "It belongs to me."

"It belongs to whoever bears it," the creature answered. "I see no medallion around your neck."

"What do you want? If you came for it and you stole it, what else do you want from me?"

The monster grinned, bearing its fangs.

Now I understood the horror enemies felt when they stared at me when I was in that form.

"I want you, Gideon. But you don't have the medallion to protect you now. Xolotl can't help you. You are just a weak, pathetic human, incapable of anything. You couldn't even protect your wife from a few thugs. How will you defend yourself, and Vero, from me?"

I swallowed back the fear and clenched my jaw.

There was no way I could beat him, whoever he was. I'd been on the other side of that armor. I'd taken hundreds of bullets. Explosions didn't kill me. There was only one thing that could, and that was to take the creature's head.

Out of the corner of my eye, something gleamed in the firelight. I looked that way, and saw a sword lying in the dirt. Its curved blade extended from the black handle in a similar design to a katana.

"Yes," the monster said. "Pick it up, boy. We may as well make the fight interesting."

I started to move toward the weapon, but the beast lunged forward as if to cut me off. I dove toward the blade, rolled to a stop, and picked it up as the creature charged.

He growled and leaped over the stone wall, closing the gap between us in a terrifyingly short amount of time.

"I guess there was no magical barrier after all," I muttered, standing and taking a defensive position.

The creature brandished its sharp claws, the very claws I'd

used to rip apart enemies. I braced myself, waiting for the first attack, deep down knowing that I wouldn't last more than a few seconds.

He lunged at me, swiping his right paw at my neck to clean off my head and end the conflict in one stroke.

I ducked under it, feeling the wind swoosh through my hair. Then I countered, slashing the blade at the creature's midsection. The edge glanced harmlessly off the armor, and sparks crackled at the impact point.

For a moment, I couldn't believe I'd actually landed a blow— without any of my special powers. It had all been me.

But before I could enjoy another second of that minuscule victory, the beast spun and struck me in the back with the bridge of his paw.

I didn't measure the feet I flew from the impact, but it had to be close to thirty.

When I landed on the hard ground near the edge of the stone ring, I rolled a few times before coming to a stop. The sword clattered out of my hand five feet away. Then the pain hit me.

The delayed reaction of the creature's powerful strike sent a terrible ache through my back, as if he'd crushed internal organs.

I lay there, grimacing as the beast stared at me, the eyes glowing bright red as if the anticipation of the kill made them burn somehow.

"Weak," the creature muttered and took a heavy step forward that shook the ground beneath me.

I coughed hard. Blood splattered on the dry earth. *That can't be good.*

The monster kept coming, slow, deliberate, as if taunting me with his approach.

"Get up," he said.

Yep. Definitely taunting at this point.

I clawed at the ground, desperately trying to drag myself toward the sword. It was only feet away, but it seemed like a mile. Not that it would matter. I'd gotten lucky with the shot I took. And look where that got me.

But something pushed me to keep going. My only options were to lie there on the ground and let him have an easy execution-style kill, or I could go down swinging.

"Yes," the beast snarled. "Get your pathetic weapon. As I said, it will make things more interesting."

I scratched at the earth, pushing with my toes against the hard, rough scree.

He kept coming. I didn't think I would reach the sword in time. He was nearly on me as I stretched out my fingers. The second they wrapped around the handle, I felt a surge of energy pulse though me. Maybe it was just adrenaline fueled by the faintest sliver of hope. Whatever it was, I felt strong enough to roll to the right just as the monster scraped his claw across the ground where I'd been only a moment before.

I sprang to my feet and backed up, holding the sword in front of me as I stood at an angle, giving him as little a target as possible.

Dust and sand spewed up from the ground in the wake of the creature's attack. He growled in frustration then looked at me, rage burning in his eyes.

"Good," he said. "Make it fun for me."

"Why are you doing this?" I asked, retreating another step.

"Because you are not a guardian. The shaman in Mexico lied to you. All of them have been lying to you. You think you're part of some ancient lineage of heroes who stand against the forces of evil? Without the medallion, you're nothing, Gideon. You're a pathetic, weak human."

He took a deliberate step toward me, then another. I matched him with two steps back for every one of his.

"Look at you now," he went on. "You're afraid. Because you know I'm right. You believe an archaeologist who spent his life in books and ditches could somehow be some kind of chosen one, a warrior sent to defend humanity? There are no heroes, Gideon. Not you. Not your little girlfriend."

Every insult dug into me, worming its way into my soul—the part of me that deep down knew he was correct.

I'd never done anything truly amazing in my life. I certainly hadn't been a fighter. I couldn't even recall the last time I'd been in a fistfight other than the one that happened in sixth grade. I had something of a temper but was able to regulate it enough that I never got myself into trouble.

Now, though, every taunt he threw filled the cup of iniquity inside me until the last one caused it to overflow.

I breathed hard but not from exhaustion. Furious anger flamed through me. My muscles tensed. I dug my feet into the ground, ignoring the jagged bits of debris in the dirt and sand.

"You're wrong about me. About us. And you're lying."

For half a second, the beast paused. It analyzed me in that brief moment, as if trying to surmise if I actually believed what I said or if I was bluffing.

It shook its head.

"It doesn't matter to me either way, whether you believe what I'm saying or not."

"I think it does," I snapped, nearly cutting him off. "Why else would you bother coming after me? Why this?" I rolled my head around to indicate our surroundings. "Why, now, are you trying to convince me to give up even as you say you want me to fight? I don't believe you are what you seem to be."

The creature's right eye twitched. It was an unusual movement, not just born of anger but almost as if he was trying to keep something inside. What it could be, I had no idea. But whatever it was, it definitely wanted me out of the picture.

"You don't know what you've gotten yourself into, Gideon Wolf. There are things behind the veil that would make you beg for death."

"I've seen behind the veil. Fallen angels. Good ones too. There isn't much you can throw my way that would shock me."

The creature laughed. "You think you're the only monsters in this world? You and your little girlfriend?" He took another step forward. "The things that you and the rest of humanity have written off as myth or legend are more real than you could have ever imagined."

I frowned. "Yeah, no, I got that. Now, are you going to bite, little doggy? Or are you going to keep barking?"

I could tell the jab hit him. He turned his head slowly. "Time to die then, Guardian."

He roared and surged forward, charging at my position with reckless fury.

I waited, every second feeling like it would be my last.

Then, a moment before he reached me, I spun around, scooping dust and dirt up with the flat of my blade. I slung it into the air in one swift movement, spraying the creature's face with debris.

He'd raised his right arm, ready to cut me down in a single, devastating strike, but when the grit hit his eyes, he lost his vision. I stepped aside and let him pass, his hulking mass shaking the ground under my feet.

He wiped at his eyes as he continued moving forward, not able to see the short wall in front of him. His left foot found it first and sent him toppling over onto his face.

I jumped toward him even before he hit the ground. I knew I'd only get one good shot at this, and I had to make it count.

I leaped over the wall and raised the sword as the creature rolled over, still wiping at his eyes, growling in anger.

He must have gotten enough of the debris cleared because he pulled his paws away from his eyes in time to see me standing over him as I brought the blade down toward his neck.

He shot up his paws to block the attack, but the blade cut right through them and sank deep into his neck and didn't stop until it struck the ground below.

The creature's body began to tremble. I rolled to the side and crouched a few feet away as a bright light spewed from the neck. I held out the sword, ready for another attack even though I'd completely separated the monster's head from its body.

The ground shook beneath me. And the light grew brighter until I thought it would either wake up the entire village, send a beacon to Adisa and his men, or both.

Then a wave of light exploded across the desert, blasting through the houses and into the hills around us.

I shielded my eyes for a second, then once the light was gone, I lowered my arm and looked at the body. A huge viper wiggled out of the creature's neck and slithered away, stopping briefly to look back at me with what I can only describe as disdain in its eyes. I'd never thought reptiles showed any emotion. But it was clear to me that whatever this thing was, it was not happy with me.

Then it turned and danced its way along the path out of the village until it disappeared.

I finally started breathing again, taking in the air in huge gasps. I lowered the sword to my side, feeling a twinge of relief drip into my chest.

The body of the monster started evaporating before my eyes.

"What the—?"

I left it at that as I watched the creature disappear, leaving nothing but the desert floor where it had lain.

I stepped over to the spot, stabbing my blade around the area, but it really was gone.

What was all this?

I wasn't sure I'd get an answer anytime soon. Maybe it was a dream. Or maybe it was some kind of test Amari was running on me. Before I could ponder further, I saw something move beyond the fire-light. It was faint, barely detectable at first, but as the thing moved again, I saw the distinct outline of its silhouette against the backdrop of the starry horizon.

It was a lion.

"Apedemak?" I breathed.

The lion seemed to stare at me for a moment, though I couldn't see its eyes from that far away. Then it turned and started walking away.

"Apedemak? Wait! I'm here to find you! We need your help! I'm trying to find the..."

Without realizing it, I had trotted twenty yards as if I might chase down the animal. But it was gone now, as if the night had swallowed him.

I slowed to a stop, knowing I would never catch the creature.

Suddenly, the scene began to melt around me. The village, Amari's hut, even the fire appeared to liquefy and slowly collapse on itself.

"Amari?" I shouted. "Hello? Anyone?"

The sword in my hand also turned to a viscous goo, dripping to the ground. Then I realized the ground was also melting, and I was sinking into it.

"What is this?" I yelled. "Someone help me!"

CHAPTER 16

I shot up out of the bed and looked around the room. Vero wasn't in the bed. Through the window, I could see the dim sky of morning outside.

"Vero?" I said, scanning the room as if she might suddenly appear from some unseen hiding place.

My eyes darted around, checking the floor, the bed, my hands.

"Was it all just a dream?"

Then my brain snapped back to Vero.

"Vero?" I said louder, pulling on my pants as I stumbled toward the door.

Just as I finished zipping them up, I yanked open the door and looked out into the living room and kitchen.

Vero stood by the counter, pouring a cup of hot coffee. Odd the aroma didn't hit me first. That always preceded visual confirmation.

She smiled over at me. "Good morning, sleepyhead," she said.

I glanced to the left, expecting to see Amari by the fire. He wasn't. The leftover embers from the night before smoldered in the hearth.

"Where did he go?" I asked, knowing I sounded both desperate and a little crazy.

"Amari?" she answered.

I noted his bedroom door was open, but no one was inside.

"Yes."

"He went to see someone in the village. I believe he is bringing us someone who can help us find the clue in the ruins."

My breathing slowed a little. I felt the doorframe, running my fingers along it as I inspected it to make sure it was real.

"Are... you okay, babe?" Vero asked.

My head snapped toward her. Then I sighed. "Yes." Again, I looked around at my feet, then at the room spreading out away from me as though at any second it might revert back to the terrible vision from my dream. "Yeah. I'm okay."

"You look... like you've seen a ghost."

I shook my head and shuffled away from the bedroom. *Coffee. I need coffee.*

"I'll say," Xolotl chirped. Despite being handcuffed with the voice for roughly two years, it caught me by complete surprise in that instant.

"Ah!" I barked with a start, glancing around the room for who might have spoken to me.

"Relax, big guy," it said. "It's only me."

"Right. Only you."

Vero arched an eyebrow. "You sure you're okay? What's he saying?"

"Nothing," I lied, shaking it off. "Just startled me. It takes a while to get used to hearing that voice in your head when you wake up from a good sleep."

That much was true. Coming out of any dreamy rest to the voice of some unseen deity that lived in your head would have shaken even the most hardened souls.

"Nice recovery," Xolotl teased. "Real smooth."

Shut up. I have questions for you later.

"Fine. Whatever."

"I know what you mean," Vero agreed. "I still haven't gotten used to it. But Artemis doesn't pry; she's not as intrusive as your guy sounds."

"Count that as a blessing."

"You know what?" he said.

I ignored him.

"Thanks for making coffee," I said to her.

"No problem. It's actually pretty good. I had low expectations."

"That's a surprise. I moved closer to her and pecked a kiss on her cheek. It was still strange that she was in my life now. I'd been with my ex-wife for a long time. I hadn't even been in the right mindset to start seeing new people again. But this had happened so quickly, so naturally, that I hadn't been able to fight it.

"Then again," I added, "everything in this village seems to be a surprise."

"No kidding."

I slipped behind her and found a beige mug sitting next to a French press. I poured the dark brown liquid until the cup was nearly full then returned the press to its place.

I held the mug to my lips, inhaling the warm, nutty, chocolatey aroma. It seemed to penetrate my foggy, bewildered mind. I tilted the mug to my lips then tipped it up to take a sip.

"Did you sleep okay last night?"

I coughed a few times, spilling a little coffee, then set the mug down and looked for a paper towel. I didn't find one of those, but I managed to discover a dark green rag in a drawer.

"Not really," I said in a prickly tone.

Vero raised a suspicious eyebrow.

"Sorry," I said, wiping up the mess. "Just a little edgy this morning."

She watched me closely for nearly a minute before she spoke again, her arms crossed and her right hip pushed out. I knew what that body language meant before she said a word.

"Are you going to tell me what's really going on? Or are you just going to act crazy all day?"

Just then, the door opened, and Amari stepped into the room.

"Good morning," I said, narrowly escaping the subject. "Where did you go?"

Amari looked suspicious but said nothing as he stepped aside to allow another person to enter the room.

A young Sudanese man, probably in his early twenties, stepped through the doorway into the hut. His tall, lean frame was accentuated by his long limbs and easy movements. His skin, a deep, rich brown, contrasted sharply with his dark gray attire. He wore loose-fitting clothes that flowed around him with every step—a long-sleeve tunic that reached down to his thighs and matching pants that gathered slightly at the ankles. The fabric was simple, yet durable, designed to endure the harsh desert environment. His face was sharp and defined, with high cheekbones and a strong jawline. His eyes, dark and reflective, held a quiet intensity, revealing a possible depth of thought beyond his years. His short, curly hair was neatly trimmed, framing his face. As he entered, he paused for a moment, his gaze sweeping the interior, taking in the familiar surroundings with a mix of weariness and determination.

There was something about him that struck me amid all this. It was the look on his face, or maybe in his eyes. I could sense that he was brave but cautious, perhaps a result of growing up in such a dangerous place.

"This is Asim," Amari said. "He will be helping you locate the ruins and navigate through Adisa's men."

I stuck out my hand toward the younger man. He looked down at it for a moment, as if uncertain what to do. Then he reluctantly gripped it and shook it as if surprised I would honor him with such a greeting.

"I'm Gideon," I said, letting go. "And this is Vero."

He grinned and bowed his head to her.

"It is good to meet you both," Asim said.

Amari shut the door and nodded toward the French press. "Would you be so kind to pour me and my friend a cup of coffee?"

"Oh yeah. I'm so sorry. I'll brew another batch." Vero turned to the French press expecting it to be empty. Instead, the container was full again, nearly to the brim.

"What the—"

"I've just come to accept he's a wizard," I said.

She looked back over at our host as if also wondering the same thing.

"I think you'll find Asim extremely useful on your quest to find the clue in the ruins. He's lived in this area his entire life, so navigating the desert and all its dangers is second nature to him."

"You are kind, great teacher," Asim said. "But I have much to learn."

Amari grinned. "He's humble too."

The shaman moved into the kitchen as Vero stepped out of the way. "Don't worry about it, my dear," the old man said. "I'll pour it."

"Sorry. I was just—"

"I know. Seeing such wonders isn't part of a usual day for you. It's all right."

Amari found a couple of mugs in a pantry above the French press and set them down before filling them with fresh coffee.

He passed one to Asim, who accepted it with a gracious bow of the head. Then Amari leaned back against the counter and held the mug to his lips.

"I can show you how to get to the ruins. Getting there should be easy. But getting in; that is a different story."

"Yeah, I kind of expected that," I said, taking the first sip of coffee since I spit out the first one. "Doesn't help we probably really ticked off Adisa by killing a bunch of his men last night."

A grin slipped past Asim's defenses. "Yes," he said, quickly returning his lips to their previously neutral state. "Amari said they ambushed you on the road. That was their night patrol."

"*Was* being the key word there," Xolotl chimed in for the first time in a blissful ten minutes.

"He will, no doubt, be very angry," Asim continued. "He will have to replace those men with new ones, which will put a strain on his resources."

"Well, that's good to hear," I said, diving into the mug again.

"Not necessarily," Amari countered. "When Adisa needs something, he sends out his men to take it from nearby villages, including —as you know—this one."

"You think he may come here?" Vero asked.

"It is certainly possible. The veil is strong now. I do not believe he will find us."

"Strong? Now?" I asked.

"Yes, it changes with the cycles of the moon. When the moon is gone, our village is much more visible to enemies."

I wasn't going to even try to explain that one scientifically.

"Okay, so just to be safe, we'll try to move quickly." I turned to Asim. "How long will it take to get there?"

"Thirty minutes. We will need to go the last bit of distance on foot so we don't alert Adisa's men to our presence."

"Yeah, rolling in there kicking up a cloud of dust behind your truck would probably not be the best approach," Xolotl said.

"When do you think we should go?" Vero asked.

"Tomorrow night," Amari answered. "That will give you time to prepare. After dark more of Adisa's men will be drunk, celebrating the spoils they've collected. That will give you an advantage."

I kept thinking we were being a bit silly about this whole strategy thing, and I certainly didn't like the idea of letting the captives spend an entire day and night in a warlord's camp. Vero and I could just shape-shift into the monsters and tear the entire base apart. Boom. Done. Dust off the hands and be on our way.

Amari was holding something back. I could feel it. Or maybe it was just paranoia.

"We will approach from the east before the moon rises," Asim said, sounding more like a military general than a shepherd, or whatever he was. "The hills on that side will also help give us cover. Many large rocks to hide behind."

"Okay," I said. "Sounds good. You got any guns on you?"

"No. Only a sword that has been in my family for generations."

That won't be much help in what is sure to be a gunfight.

But the mention of the bladed weapon piqued my interest. He didn't have it on him. There was no sheath or scabbard visible, so I assumed he'd left the sword at home. Still, I couldn't help but wonder if there was a correlation between that and my terrifying experience the night before.

"So it is settled," Amari said. "We will have breakfast after our coffee. Then I can show you around the village."

He took a long sip of his coffee then lowered the mug and said, "So, Gideon. Tell me about the dream you had last night."

CHAPTER 17

After spitting out another slurp of coffee, I wiped my chin and found the rag again to clean off the counter and the front of the cabinets below it.

"Sorry," I said, setting the mug down near the French press.

"It's fine," Amari said, smiling.

"What's he talking about?" Vero asked. "What dream?"

I shook my head as I finished wiping things down for the second time. "Nothing. It's nothing."

"Is that why you were acting so weird this morning when you woke up?"

"I don't know. I mean, yeah. Okay, the dream was pretty messed up. And it all felt so real."

"How do you know it wasn't?" Amari offered.

I thought about it for a moment while I folded the rag on the countertop to buy me a few extra seconds, but that didn't help. "What do you mean?"

"The question is straightforward. How do you know what is real and what is imagined? Or is there really a difference between the two?"

I inhaled deeply and sighed, picking up the mug again—this time hoping I'd gotten all of the spit takes out of the way.

"I don't know. I guess what your senses detect is real."

"But in the dream," Amari countered, "your senses feel and see and smell and hear everything, just as they would in this reality."

"What are you saying? That we live in a simulation? Or that everything is a dream?"

I'd heard those theories before from various scientists and theorists. One of my favorite fiction authors even discussed it on something called the *Wordslinger Podcast*, which I found interesting because neither of the guys on that show had any sort of credentials to discuss the notion. Then again, maybe fiction writers were way ahead of the rest of world. Their wildest imaginings of science often, eventually, became reality.

"We live in a universe of perception by senses," Amari explained. "Of course, there are the things unseen that lurk behind the veil."

"Like angels and demons?"

"Yes, but not only those. Beyond the five basic senses are the infinite timelines, which is how prophets of so many cultures were able to see into the future. Of course, they only viewed a few, sometimes only one of those timelines based on the current events of their day. But the possibilities are unlimited."

I sensed Vero wanted to ask a question, meanwhile Asim merely stood there listening respectfully.

"This is interesting stuff. Really," I said. "But what does it have to do with the dream? I thought I was going to die."

"When we dream, the veil between worlds is stripped away. Sometimes we experience fantastical things that defy logic and reason. Other times, our dreams feel ordinary, like a walk on a sunny day or sitting down for a meal with friends."

"I always thought that certain dreams were foreshadowing events to come," Vero interjected.

Amari turned to her, the apparently humble smile still stretching across his face. "That is a common belief. And it isn't incorrect. As I said, all of the timelines exist in every moment. So, if you are able to travel to one of them in your dreams, you may be able to see future events for the one you return to."

My head was spinning at this point. And all I wanted to know was why I'd had the dream in the first place.

Our host must have sensed my lack of patience and understanding because he looked to me again. "Tell me about your dream."

Sometimes, after waking up from a dream, no matter how vivid, it was forgotten within seconds. This one, however, had stuck deeply in my mind.

I told him about what happened, how I woke up in bed and couldn't find Vero. I explained that he was there, sitting by the fireplace. I told him how he looked at me in the dream, how his eyes were vacant, almost lifeless, as if he were in some kind of trance. Then I told him about the battle outside, the sword, how I defeated the Chupacabra, and about the figure of the lion I saw in the distance before the world started melting around me.

Amari listened quietly, allowing me to finish. When I was done, he stood there looking serious for a minute. The smile had disappeared from his face, replaced by a concerned expression. I wondered if he was trying to think of an explanation or if he already knew the meaning of it all and was figuring out how to give me bad news without freaking me out.

"This serpent you mentioned," he said, finally breaking his silence. "What did it look like?"

I shrugged and shook my head. "I don't know. A snake. I mean, it looked venomous. Like a viper. Not a rattlesnake, but maybe a cousin. I don't know much about snakes, honestly. The farther they stay away from me, the better."

Amari turned away and paced over to the hearth. He stared down into the fireplace, crossing his arms in the folds of his robe.

"What does that mean?" I pressed. "The snake. Do you know something that you're not telling me?"

There was no getting around it. The part about the serpent had visibly changed his demeanor.

"He's close now," Amari mumbled.

"Who's close now?" Vero asked.

Asim continued to remain silent, listening and absorbing the conversation like a sponge with legs.

The shaman didn't answer. Instead, he kept staring into the fireplace, lost in his thoughts. "I thought we had more time," he muttered.

"More time?" I stepped closer to our host. "Amari, what's going on?"

He took a deep breath through his nostrils then slowly turned to face me.

"You have a mission you need to complete," he said. "Get to the ruins. Find the clue. It will show you the way to the hidden temple of Apedemak."

I reached out and touched his shoulder, as if that would somehow shake him out of his trance.

"Amari. What's going on? Why did the mention of the serpent shake you?"

He looked down at my hand on his shoulder and then back into my eyes. "You must go, Gideon. The sooner you find the medallion of the lion god, the better. You mustn't linger here any longer."

"Fine. We'll go. But you have to tell me what's gotten you so worried. What is it about that snake that rattled you?"

The man blinked several times, as if that would buy him a moment or two.

"It's him," Asim said. "Isn't it?"

I spun around and looked at the younger man. Vero directed her gaze at him as well.

"It's who? Will one of you tell us what's going on?"

"Yes," Amari said. "It is him."

"Seriously, man," I cut in.

"The serpent you saw is a powerful being. It is normally

forbidden for beings beyond the veil to enter a human's dreams. For him to do that must have taken an enormous amount of power."

"Who?" I pressed. "Who was it?"

Amari leveled his gaze with mine. Black clouds seemed to swirl in the darkness of his eyes. "He is known by many names to different people," he began. "He is a trickster, a god of enormous power."

Okay, I didn't expect that. I was thinking maybe one of the Sector agents—fallen angels—had somehow snaked their way into my head.

"This god has the power to change shapes. He was, or is, known as the Lord of the Desert, Master of Storms. He brings chaos, disorder, and war. The vast, treacherous sands, the dunes, the sandstorms —all mirror his violent, desolate nature."

The shaman's eyes grew distant again, and it was as if he was peering through me.

"Who is he?" I asked, desperate to get some clarification.

"He was the brother of Osiris and the uncle of Horus in the Egyptian pantheon."

The answer hit me harder than the monster had in my dream.

"Wait a minute. You don't mean..." I started to say that wasn't possible, but I knew better. None of this new life of mine was possible according to my old understanding.

"Yes," Amari confirmed. "Set has returned."

CHAPTER 18

I shook my head. Partially to clear the skepticism from my old self and partly to deny that the ancient Egyptian god was actually here, in the present day, and apparently my enemy. "How?"

"The veil is all that keeps the shadow world at bay and separate from our world. There are many scriptures, of many different faith traditions, that tell us we humans are actually gods who are walking in darkness, oblivious to our power. And most never find it because they are consumed by materialism, a tool of the dark one. Some, however, were created above us, while others attained a status higher than ours through their understanding of the universe.

"Set was one of the first. He and his family were here in the most ancient of times, beyond the time of the Ice Age and the great cataclysm."

"You mean the flood? Or the Younger Dryas?"

"Yes, sort of. But long before then. As the story goes, Set murdered his brother Osiris, the father of Horus. Bent on revenge or justice or both, Horus fought his uncle and defeated him, returning the world to balance and light."

I knew the story but let him keep going.

"Horus' victory over Set was a symbol of triumph of light over dark, day over night, and good over evil. But it wasn't only symbolic. It was very real. Horus lost an eye in the battle with his uncle, and ever since, the Eye of Horus has been one of the most important symbols in Egypt and around the world."

"So if the story of Set is real, that means Horus is real too?"

"You sound surprised, Gideon, which I find interesting. Horus was one of the original seven guardians of Earth. Like with the one who resides in you, the power of Horus is contained in a medallion, awaiting the next to wear it."

I couldn't say anything. I was too stunned, even though I probably shouldn't have been. The wildly insane had become my normal.

"So that is the next medallion we have to find," Vero realized.

"You must focus your attention on locating Apedemak," Amari cautioned. "Never look into the future. Now is all that is real."

"But Set," I contested. "What did last night mean? I was fighting against my own power. What would have happened if I lost?"

"You would have died," Amari said as if it didn't concern him.

Fortunately, this time I didn't have coffee in my mouth. "What? Are you serious?"

"The body cannot live if the mind is dead. And if the mind believes it is dying, truly believes it, then yes, you would have died."

"How is that fair? I was facing an... an ancient god? And not just like one of the minor ones. Set was... is one of the big dogs. It's a miracle I beat him."

"Is it?"

I started to reply then hesitated.

"Yes, the medallion allows you to harness the power of Xolotl. It makes you nearly invincible. But that isn't your only source of power. You defeated Set without it. You stood alone against one of the most powerful deities from the ancient world, and you defeated him."

"Why do I get the feeling I'm really lucky to be standing here right now?"

"Maybe you are. But I doubt that's the case. You outwitted Set, and beat him in battle. He is, no doubt, skulking over it at this very moment, but it isn't the last we've seen of him, unfortunately. The trickster gods are sneaky. While not all are purely evil, he certainly is."

Well, that didn't sound good.

"Do you mean he may come back into my dreams again?"

"I doubt it. He doesn't return to a place where he was defeated. His ego consumes him. It was part of the reason he killed his brother. He couldn't stand having someone equal to him or more powerful."

"Sounds like a sore loser," Vero commented.

"Yes. But he is still extremely dangerous. You must be vigilant on your quest to find Apedemak. It is obvious now that Set and the forces of evil are taking greater risks to prevent you from succeeding. They know that once the guardians have returned, their play to plunge civilization into darkness will be at grave risk."

I didn't even want to think about what that would look like. The entire world controlled by sinister, powerful forces? What would happen to the people? What would become of cities, towns, villages like this one? Would they all be enslaved? And to what end?

"I sense the question you're considering," Amari said.

"You do? As in, you're reading my mind?"

"No. No one is capable of doing that. But it seems you're looking to the future, to what could be if Set and his allies succeed."

"Sounds like he was reading your mind to me," Xolotl chirped.

"What would it look like?" I asked. "What is the end game for the dark one and all his minions?"

"That, young Guardian, is the question to end all."

For a second, it seemed like he wasn't going to answer it. He left his words hanging, looking at me awkwardly.

Then he waved his hands, creating an invisible sphere in front of him. He closed his eyes as he continued manipulating the space. He was whispering something, but no one had any idea what he was saying. It was in a language we didn't understand.

Suddenly, I saw something appear in front of him, as if the invisible globe he'd been forming with his hands magically came into view. I peered into it, trying to see what was inside the ball. It looked dark, though, with black clouds speeding by in a gray sky. There was land, but it was stark, jagged, lifeless.

I felt my hair bristle from a breeze, but the door and windows were all closed. I pulled my eyes from the sphere and looked around the room. Except we were no longer in Amari's hut.

We stood in the middle of a vast wasteland that looked eerily similar to the one inside the ball. I looked back to it and saw the room where we'd been standing a moment before it disappeared, and the shaman lowered his hands to his side.

"What in the world?" I breathed.

Vero walked over to my side, quickly grabbing my hand.

"This is the future of Earth if the forces of darkness emerge victorious."

Amari's words hung as thick as the air surrounding us. It reeked of pollution and a million terrible odors, as if the planet itself was in a state of decay. The cold winds whipped around us, adding to the feeling of utter desolation.

We stood on what had previously been a city street in a densely populated area. Crumbling buildings stood around us, overrun by rotting vegetation that seemed to get either not enough light, not enough water, or both, to continue growing.

This was the fall of man, the result of humanity's folly. Unending wars, disregard for the balance of nature, and eventually infection of moral decay had produced this.

I could feel it all around me.

"Where are all the people?" Vero asked. "Are there any left?"

"Yes," the shaman answered. "There are some. The population was reduced by ninety percent in this reality, shortly after your time."

"So, this can still be avoided?" I said.

"Of course. Human choices change the outcomes. Some changes

are bigger than others. The fact that you are now on a mission to find the other medallions has delayed this possible future."

"Delayed?"

"It could still come to be should you fail. It will just happen later."

"No pressure," I joked.

"But where are the people?" Vero asked again.

"There are none in this city. Or what's left of it," Amari clarified. "Less than a billion survived the end. Nearly all of them are now slaves to the ones in charge. The dark one continued to push human- ity, polarizing them to extremes until they destroyed each other. Civil conflicts happen in every developed nation. The Second World countries didn't suffer as much, not at first. They were mostly spared from the initial destruction. When the dust settled, only a few remained—those loyal to the ones who'd been pulling the strings for hundreds of years."

That sounded familiar. But I kept the thought to myself.

"Why?" Vero wondered. "Why do this to the planet? Even those loyal to the dark prince need food, clean water, shelter."

"Indeed. And there are a few of them left, allowed to survive to maintain the herds. What few realize is that everyone is expendable to the forces of evil. They would sacrifice living things if that's what they believed was necessary."

"So, what's the point? Why would the dark prince keep some humans alive? Why not just have them all kill each other?"

"The question you must ask yourselves is, what is the point of all this? The entire war that goes on behind the veil, the spiritual conflict in heaven so many scriptures highlight from long ago, and battles that still continue to this day—what is it all for?"

That was a good question, and I wasn't sure I knew the answer. I thought for a minute, scanning the bleak cityscape, the drab sky, the ruins of what was once a proud, lively city.

"The answer lies in the dark one's motivation," Asim said, speaking for the first time since we arrived here.

"Yes," Amari confirmed.

"His motivation?" Vero said. "He has always been called the consumer of souls from what we learned."

"They called him Ha-Satan, but you already know that. You know the names by which he is known. But what possible reason could he have for doing all this to the planet?"

Then it hit me. The epiphany was stark, disturbing at its core. But it was the only explanation that made sense. "We're in a revenge story."

The shaman nodded but said nothing.

"The ones that were cast down, the ones who have always sought to cause misery and chaos on earth—their motivation the entire time was to break the Creator's heart, and by doing so drive the entire universe into darkness."

"Yes," Amari whispered. "Wiping humanity out entirely would be too easy. Almost merciful. But enslaving us, pushing us to the point where no one dares utter the name of the Creator, leaving us in utter despair without hope for anything else... That is the ultimate cut to the one the dark prince believed wronged him."

"That's messed up."

"Of course, he will do everything in his power to change the outcome."

"Go down swinging."

"Yes."

Standing there in that wasteland, seeing what would become of the planet and its people if I failed, shook me to the depths of my soul. I couldn't let that happen. Failure was not an option.

The world around us suddenly vanished, and we found ourselves back inside Amari's hut. It took a second to orient myself again.

I looked over at Asim, who stood there silently, as if awaiting instructions. "Can you put together a layout of Adisa's compound?"

He nodded. "Yes. I have seen it many times. I can draw it out for you."

"Good. We need to plan a point of entry. Sweep in, annihilate everyone."

Amari shook his head. "No. It cannot be done that way."

"Why not? Seems to have worked out so far. Do they have some kind of special weapon we don't know about?"

"No. But they have hostages. And at the first sign of trouble, Adisa and his men will use them as human shields. Or worse, they'll start killing them until you surrender. This mission will require a more discreet approach."

"I don't like the sound of that," the voice in my head complained.

I didn't like it either, but it didn't sound like we had much of a choice.

"Not to worry," Asim said. "I will guide you through the compound. I know all their patrols, their schedules, and locations."

"I'd rather not put you in danger," I said. "Hang back once we're there. We can handle it."

Asim shook his head. "No. I am going with you."

I glanced over at the shaman with a questioning expression. "He always this stubborn?"

"Not usually," Amari admitted. "But in this case, he has good reason to be."

"Why's that?" Vero asked.

"His younger sister is one of the hostages."

CHAPTER 19

Amari sent his young apprentice to get some food from a marketplace I hadn't seen when we came into the village. I figured it, like all the people, must have been hidden after dark.

Our host set about making preparations for the meal, pulling plates out of one of the cabinets, utensils from a drawer near the sink, and glasses he filled with clean water.

I couldn't believe they even had indoor plumbing out here, much less pure water to drink and cook with, but I assumed it had something to do with the shaman and the strange powers he wielded. There were no power lines anywhere to bring electricity here, so none of it made logical sense.

"What happened to his sister?" Vero asked while Amari continued making preparations.

Amari set a bowl down on the counter. "Kofi Adisa returned a few weeks ago, when the veil was thin. He and his men raided the village. They took some of the children, a few women too. Three of our men were killed trying to resist. The others knew better than to try to fight them with no weapons."

"Sounds like a bunch of weak beta males if you asked me," Xolotl said in my mind.

I shook my head. "Do you think they're still alive?"

"Yes," Amari said. "They usually put them to work. Although the women often face a fate worse than death."

He didn't have to elaborate. I'd heard terrible things like that before coming out of lawless places such as this. It wasn't surprising, but the barbaric, horrific nature of it still shocked.

"How old is his sister?" Vero asked.

"She is eleven."

"Jeez," I blurted. "That's awful."

I felt overwhelmed by a sudden sense of righteous anger, the kind that made me want to wipe Adisa and all his men off the face of the earth. My blood boiled, and I sensed the power of the amulet pulsing through me.

"Yes," Amari agreed. "So you see why Asim is set on going with you. He must find his sister. To him, there is no other way."

I could understand that. I didn't have any siblings, but if I did, I would feel the same way, the same sense of responsibility. There was, no doubt, a festering sense of guilt inside Asim's heart and mind.

The door opened, ending our conversation abruptly.

Asim stepped inside and closed the door. He held a basket full of fruit, bread, and vegetables.

Okay, there is no way that stuff is locally grown.

Then again, maybe I was wrong. I'd seen videos online featuring farmers who turned the deserts in the American Southwest green with special farming techniques that required little rainfall. I still didn't fully understand how it was possible, but I'd seen the results and they were astounding.

"Thank you, Asim," Amari said, shuffling over to the young man. He took the basket and returned to the counter where he'd laid out a knife.

"Of course," Asim replied with a nod.

"The food should be ready shortly. If you would like to sit at the table, I will bring it over."

"Are you sure you don't need some help?" Vero asked. "I know my way around a kitchen."

"Same here," I volunteered. "Happy to help."

"That won't be necessary. Besides, you're my guests. And you three have plans to make."

Asim stuffed his right hand into the folds of his tunic and retrieved three sheets of paper. The material was worn and gave the appearance of something much older. There was no keeping things from the elements out here. Or maybe that was the best he could get in the middle of nowhere.

Detailed drawings etched across the sheets, displaying a comprehensive, overhead view of Adisa's compound.

"Did you draw all this?" There was no hiding my astonishment.

"Yes," Asim said, glancing over at me. "Why?"

"It's just so detailed. Did you use a drone to get a better look at this place?"

"No."

"Asim has a high level of spatial intelligence," Amari interjected from the kitchen.

"He must," Vero added, poring over the layout.

Asim pointed at an area labeled Main Gate.

"This is where most of Adisa's shipments come through. And it is where they send out their forces to conduct patrols or to raid a village."

"What did we run into on the road?" I asked.

"That was a patrol. They sweep the roads thirty kilometers to the north and south, capturing anyone unfortunate enough to cross their path. Sometimes people slip through if they are changing shifts."

"That seemed like a really big shift," Vero noted.

"Yes," Asim agreed. "It is. Kofi Adisa likes to show off. He believes that fear will keep all the villages in line and obedient—cowering to his might."

"What percentage of his men did we run into on the road?" I wondered.

"Usually, he keeps two-thirds of his forces at this compound." He tapped the map again. "And the front gate will be the most heavily guarded."

Asim circled his finger around to the back, where an area was drawn to illustrate a hill or small mountain that abutted the fortress.

"There is no way in through the rocks here," he said. "The temple entrance is here." He pointed to the base of the hill situated in the rear of the compound. "There are two more entrances here and here," he said, running his finger to a location to the north and south. "He has built fences with razor wire on the top and bottom. Going through those could be risky. And there are towers every fifty meters surrounding the perimeter, each equipped with high-powered lights that constantly scan the surrounding desert for threats at night."

"Okay, so how do we get in? One of the side entrances?"

"No." Asim moved his finger to the northwestern part of the hill. "There is a narrow path that winds up to the top of this rock." He then tapped on the corner nearest one of the watchtowers. "The guards never bother to look at this mountain because they don't believe anyone would try to come that way. And since it's so narrow, any invaders would have to go in a single line, which would make them easy targets."

"But for a team of two—" I said.

"Three," Asim corrected. "You'll need me to make the plan work once you're inside."

I didn't like the idea. This guy didn't look like much of a fighter. While Vero and I had a little supernatural help, he would be on his own. I had no clue if he even had any kinds of weapons, apart from the family sword he mentioned earlier.

Still, this was one of those scenarios where I could argue with him until I was purple and the guy would still insist. The truth was I had to trust him, and if he said we'd need him once we were beyond the perimeter, I believed it.

Of course, if he got killed that would mean we were without a guide. I'm sure we could eventually find what we were looking for, but it would be messier, and potentially more dangerous.

"Fine," I surrendered. "So we get close to this guard tower. Then what? Take out the guards?"

"Yes," Asim confirmed. "With your abilities, you should easily be able to make the jump from the rock cliff to the tower."

I wasn't sure what he meant by "should."

"How far is this jump?" Vero asked, echoing my thoughts.

"Only twenty meters."

I arched my eyebrows at the response. "That's not an easy jump."

"It will be for you two."

"How do you know?"

"I told him," Amari answered amid the sounds of pans rattling and vegetables sizzling.

"Okay, yeah," I said. "Twenty is doable. But that doesn't mean it's easy. And how many guards are we talking about?"

"There will only be two stationed on each tower. Once you take out the first two, I will climb down the cliff and then up the tower to maintain the spotlight. If the light stops moving, the other tower guards will notice and immediately suspect something is wrong. It will be dark enough for you to make the jump without being seen by the other towers, so that part isn't a problem."

"Unless we accidentally knock over one of the lights."

"Well, yes. So try to be careful when you make your landing."

He made it sound like it was easy.

"How are you going to climb down? Is that cliff steep?"

"Yes. It is straight down. I will have a rope anchored at the top. It won't be a problem so long as I'm not spotted by anyone on the ground. This area, however, is usually unoccupied."

"Okay," I said. "So once you're in the tower, Vero and I hit the ground. Then where do we go?"

"There is a cave here amid the ruins," Asim said, pointing at a position at the base of the rock formation. "It will be guarded, and there is no real way to sneak by them."

"How heavily guarded?" Vero wondered.

"Usually four men are there. Unfortunately, you'll have to be more direct with your attack. Unless you can climb walls."

"We've done weirder things than that," I said. "What's in the cave? Adisa's personal living space?"

"No. That is over here, in a heavily fortified section of the ruins. They've rebuilt sections of an ancient palace that was here to provide him living quarters while the rest of his men live in tents or shanties."

"Sounds fair." I shook my head at the thought of being one of his servant soldiers.

Asim continued. "If Adisa is there during our attack, he will most likely be in that palace. At night he likes to retire there and..." He faltered. Whatever he had been about to say must have bothered him because his lips started quivering, and tears formed in his eyes.

Amari must have sensed the man's pain because he paused what he was doing in the kitchen and turned around.

"Your sister is fine," he said, his voice sincere and calm. "Nothing has happened to her. And soon, she will be with you again."

How the old man could possibly know that remained to be seen, but Asim didn't question the man. He accepted it, and his expression of worry and sadness stiffened to one of resolve.

I diverted the subject back to the mission. "You said if Adisa is there. Where else would he be?"

"Sometimes he rides out with his night patrols. There is no pattern to this decision, and I have watched their compound for a long time."

"This guy needs a hobby," Xolotl said.

The voice startled me because he'd been silent for so long.

Well, it's not like there's much to do out here.

"No kidding," he answered.

"Inside the cave," Asim continued, "is where you'll find the clue to the location of the hidden temple."

"Will there be more men in there?" Vero asked.

"Possibly. They store munitions in there as well as other supplies. But most of the time, I think the only men there are the ones guarding the entrance."

"He thinks? That isn't comforting," Xolotl said.

Give the kid a break. He's doing the best he can.

"What is it we're looking for?"

The blank look in Asim's eyes told me the guy didn't have a clue. Before I could complain, Amari cut in.

"In the back of the cave, you will find an ancient chamber, built in the times of the old kings and queens of this land. They went there to worship the Maker and pay tribute to Apedemak. In this chamber, you will find the clue you seek."

"Okay," I said. "So we infiltrate Adisa's compound. Get into the cave. Find the clue. And get out."

"And the hostages," Amari added.

Right. I'd forgotten about that little piece of the puzzle. This wouldn't be a simple smash-and-grab job. This would also be an evacuation, likely under heavy gunfire.

I didn't even bother asking how many hostages we were talking about even though Amari said it was just a handful. It would be a tricky thing to get them out of the compound without any of them being harmed.

"Sounds like we'll need a diversion," Vero said. "Anything in mind?"

Asim shook his head. Then he stopped as if an idea had popped into his brain. "There is a large fuel tank near the back of the compound on the other side of the cliff. They use it to fuel all their vehicles."

"I like the way this kid thinks," Xolotl said, anticipating the plan.

"You're thinking of blowing it up."

"Do you think you could?" Asim asked.

"Definitely. That won't be a problem. But making sure none of the innocents get hurt . . . That's another matter."

"They won't be back there. They're usually kept in this building here. That's where all the prisoners are." He tapped on a large structure situated just outside the palace. "It's a building they constructed just for the purpose of housing those they capture. The walls are thin, made of weak metal, same as the roof. But those inside are under constant watch."

"Okay," I said with a nod. "We can work with this."

The plan seemed pretty straightforward. Except for the fact that we didn't know what the clue was. And that we had to somehow herd a bunch of people to safety. I figured we'd probably steal some of Adisa's vehicles to transport them. But I still wanted to know what the clue was.

"What is this thing we're looking for in the cave?" I asked.

Amari plated some of the vegetables and slid the dish to the left on the counter. "I don't know what it is. I've never been in there."

I frowned. "Wait a minute. If you've never been in there, how do you know the clue is still there?"

"I don't," he confessed. "But you'll find out once you're inside."

I tried to keep my jaw from hitting the floor. This mission was going to be difficult enough, but now knowing that the thing we were looking for might not even be there wasn't exactly encouraging.

This wasn't going to be as straightforward as it seemed.

CHAPTER 20

"Kill the lights."

The order was assertive and blunt and seemingly out of character for the reserved, humble Asim.

"Keep going straight toward the rock."

I did as he instructed, switching off the headlights to the SUV. The desert in front of us vanished into the black of night, only offering outlines of rocks here and there that were tall enough to block the pale light of the sky behind them.

Straight ahead, the silhouette of the mountain was an ominous sight to behold. It climbed high above the desert plains, cast against the backdrop of a half-moon and billions of stars in the cloudless sky.

I slowed down a little, wary that we may end up plowing into an unseen rock or a deep ditch.

"Just stay on this path, and you will be okay," Asim reassured.

I didn't know what "path" he was talking about. It was basically open desert that had maybe been used by vehicles before. But there were no traces of tire tracks or even the ruts caused by the occasional vehicle.

I clenched my jaw, gritting my teeth while gripping the steering wheel with white knuckles. Seriously, I felt like any second the road was going to drop out in front of us and send us headfirst into a big ditch, effectively ending our little operation before it began.

Minutes dragged on with agonizing slowness as we approached the enormous rock.

"You're sure they won't have anyone positioned on the top of that thing?" Vero asked, peering up at the rock from the back seat, her head between us.

"I have never seen men stationed there."

"So tonight could be the night," I said. "Would be just our luck."

"There is no threat there," Xolotl said. "Asim knows what he's doing."

Every now and then, the voice in my head redeemed himself from his usual annoying comments and provided real assistance. How he was able to see in so many directions, and at such distances, I had no idea. I could only guess that it had to do with some kind of extrasensory, perhaps interdimensional perception. But if that was it, was he doing that through me as an avatar? Or on his own?

I knew he wasn't going to give me the answer, so there was really no point in even asking. That was one of those things I felt like he enjoyed keeping from me, like a secret a child holds from other kids —or their parents. It was an important reminder that the spiritual— even spirits themselves—could be as petty as anyone else.

"Careful here," Asim said, cutting off my train of thought. "The path bends to the left. It will lead us to the trail leading up the back of the rock."

Again with the path. The only thing remotely making it a path were the rocks and mounds on either side of where we were driving. And I could barely see any of them. We were driving purely on what the moon illuminated, which wasn't so bad after my eyes got used to it, but still, I would have preferred at least the glow of the parking lights to guide our way.

I steered the SUV through the bend then straightened out

again, keeping our speed comfortable in case I had to suddenly slam on the brakes, which I kept thinking was going to happen any second.

Drawing nearer to the mountain, the giant rock towered high above us. It looked as though it was only four or five hundred feet high at its peak, but out here on the flats of the desert, it was an imposing sight.

"Over there," Asim said, pointing to an area bathed in the mountain's shadow.

It was darker there, and difficult to see, but I trusted the man. I had to. I didn't have any clue about this place other than what we'd discussed beforehand.

I took my foot off the pedal and allowed the truck to roll to a halt at the base of the rock, then used the hand brake to keep it there while I killed the engine. That was an old trick I'd used back in high school if I was being followed by another car. I'd shut off the lights and only use the hand brake for slowing down since, at least in my vehicle, it didn't cause the brake lights to illuminate.

I glanced back in the mirror to find the same was true with this SUV.

"The path is just over there," Asim said, nodding toward a section of the rock that was hidden in the darkness. The moonlight only cast a residual glow on this side, which could make the going a bit trickier.

I scanned the upper areas of the rock for any traces of the red mist, which would signal bad guys stationed there, but I detected nothing, and I suspected Xolotl would have said something if there was a threat to be found.

"You catch on quick," he whispered with a sharp, sarcastic tone.

Ignoring him, I opened the car door and stepped out into the chilly, dry desert air.

The temperature had dropped significantly since we left Asim's village, which I knew would happen just as it had the night before.

Asim collected a gear bag from the back of the truck while Vero and I stood by the grill and waited. We wouldn't be using any equipment. Just the powers bestowed upon us by the medallions.

Even though I should have been brimming with confidence, worry needled my mind, pummeling it with doubts.

"Follow me," Asim ordered as he passed us, heading toward the rock.

At the base of the mountain, I finally noticed the path when we were twenty feet away from it. And Asim was right when he'd called it narrow. The trail was no more than two feet wide, and as we ascended, working our way up the switchbacks, there were several spots where it tightened to only a foot in width.

On more than one occasion, I caught myself looking down with trepidation. Sure that if I fell, I could summon the monster and probably land on my feet at the bottom. Probably. But then I would have to change back to my human self to make the climb again because my alter ego was too bulky to navigate the trail effectively.

Just past the halfway point, Asim paused and looked back at us. "Are you two all right?"

I was breathing heavily, and my legs burned. I figured Vero was feeling the same way. But our guide seemed unaffected by the climb up the steep path.

"Yeah," I said, panting. "All good." I knew if I shifted into the Chupacabra, I'd be able to bound up the slope with no problem. But I might also slip.

Asim also appeared to be unfazed by the distance between where we stood and the desert floor. How many times had he done this? He spun around and continued upward.

Beyond the peak of the rock, a dim glow radiated from the other side, casting a corona of light just above its inky outline.

Lights from the compound.

We picked our way along the rocky path until we arrived at a plateau, then continued halfway across until most of the enemy's camp was in view.

I couldn't see the buildings closest to the rock, or the cave entrance that I figured was somewhere below us, probably to the right. Asim's drawings of the compound and of the size and scope of Adisa's base of operations were surprisingly accurate.

The ancient ruins that made this such an important historic site had been completely overrun by Adisa and his barbarians. I doubted UNESCO knew anything about all this. Not that they could do much about it. A bunch of suits rolling up out here to tell Adisa to get lost wouldn't go over well. Likely not even the UN white-helmet peace-keepers would dissuade him.

Still, it disgusted me to see it. The preservation of history had been my life's work. And this... this was just crapping all over a site that contained so much shared human heritage, and it still had so much to reveal.

We stayed close to the shadows of an outcropping in case one of the men on the towers happened to look our way. But most of where we were perched was untouched by the light from below.

The first watchtower—the one we would jump to—was exactly where Asim said, and the same distance from the rock's edge to the three-foot wall that protected the guards inside. The structure, while old, appeared sturdy, made from steel that had weathered over time in the desert. The roof on top was made of corrugated tin to provide shade to the men who occupied it during the day.

"I would not want to be one of the guys there at high noon," I commented.

"No," Vero said. "That would be way too hot. And I don't imagine they stay well hydrated out here. Where do they get their water?"

"There is a spring inside the cave," Asim said. "They've connected pipes to it so water can be collected and dispersed throughout the encampment."

Seems like Kofi Adisa has thought of everything.

"Over there is where you will jump," Asim said, pointing to a ledge that jutted out from the plateau.

We weren't quite halfway to the top of the mountain, and based on the height of the tower, I guessed we were probably eighty feet off the ground. That realization caused me to wonder why the climb up had been so difficult. It wasn't as though we'd done eighty feet of stairs. Maybe I wasn't in as good a shape as I thought.

"At least I'm strong," Xolotl chimed.

"True," I breathed.

Asim set his bag down on the ground and pulled out a long black rope. Then he moved forward to a boulder that had broken free of the mountain. The bulky stone looked like it weighed at least a ton, and I imagined what it might sound like if it rolled off and hit the ground below.

Of course, the thing wasn't going anywhere. No one would be able to push that, except maybe me or Vero in our creature forms.

I watched Asim loop his rope around the thing and tie it off, knowing that it would be more than sufficient to support his weight as he rappelled down. He pulled a harness out of his bag and slipped it on, buckling a carabiner through two loops on the front, then an additional tool I'd never seen before.

"What is that?" I asked, keeping my voice low.

"Brake. I'll need to go fast so I'm not spotted by any of the other guards."

"Wow." How many times had he done this before? "Is rappelling something you do often?"

Asim shrugged. "Now and then. I used to take my sister out climbing on the rocks near our village."

His answer was muted with a tone of regret.

I didn't press the issue any further and waited until he was locked in and ready to go. He clipped a flashlight to his belt then turned to us. "Ready when you are."

Vero and I nodded.

It seemed sudden, but there was no point in dallying about. Might as well get down to business.

"You know," Vero said. "I could just take those two guards in the watchtower with a couple of arrows."

"Right. We should have thought of that."

"What arrows?" Asim asked, looking at us like he was missing something that should have been obvious.

Vero held out her hand, and a bow appeared. She raised it and took aim, pulling back on the string.

Out of thin air, a shimmering arrow notched above the grip.

Asim's eyes opened up like window shutters. He didn't say anything—didn't ask how that was possible—he merely gazed in awe at the sight.

"You should probably change," Vero said. "Not sure you can make that jump as a human."

I obeyed and summoned the power of Xolotl, shifting into the Chupacabra in seconds.

Again, Asim looked awestruck by the visual. His jaw even hung open a little.

I prowled over to the edge of the cliff. If the guards had looked my way, they may have seen me in the residual light from below, but they were too busy peering out into the desert, twisting the spotlight back and forth in a monotonous pattern.

I reached the precipice and looked back over my shoulder. I nodded, and Vero returned the gesture.

She loosed the first arrow, and it sailed just past my right shoulder. I heard the wind bristle across it as it flew toward the target.

The missile struck the first guard in the left ear. He didn't react; didn't reach up to feel what had happened. He simply wobbled then collapsed, dead before he hit the floor.

The other guard spun to see his partner dead on the ground, but before he could even look up to see where the attack had come from, Vero loosed a second arrow. The projectile struck the man in the bottom of his throat. He staggered back, hitting the side wall before he fell to the floor with the other body.

I took a few steps back to get a running start then leaped. I soared across the expanse at incredible speed, sticking my arms out like Superman. The landing was tricky, and I had to fly between the roof and the wall to not draw attention. The sound of a monster my size hitting the sidewall would definitely raise a few eyebrows, and for the moment, we were trying to do this the quiet way.

I flew just under the roof then tucked and dove onto the floor, landing just to the side of the two bodies. I rolled until I hit the side-wall with a thud, then stood and took the spotlight in my hands and continued the steady rhythm the guards had been using.

While I did, I glanced over the edge of the railing to my right. Adisa's goons were spread across the compound. Some were walking around with rifles hanging loosely from their shoulders, definitely not the way trained military personnel would do it. They appeared lackadaisical, and not ready to fight if something were to suddenly happen.

Though, to be fair, there was nothing that could have prepared them for us.

After morphing back into my human body, I turned to the side and watched as Vero shifted into her bear form. She took two huge steps and leaped over the gap the same way I had done. As her body sailed through the opening between the sidewall and the roof, she shifted back to her human self, hit the floor, and rolled to a stop just sort of the opposite wall.

I frowned down at her. "Yeah, now that I see you do it, I probably should have done it that way."

She stood up, dusted herself off, and shrugged. "What can I say? You're not a woman."

I grinned sardonically and shook my head. "Very funny."

"I wasn't being funny."

"Oh, I know."

She moved over to the back edge of the platform and looked out over the wall. "So many of them," she muttered.

"Yeah. It's a sizable force, no question."

"And Asim's sister is down there somewhere, frightened and uncertain what is going to happen next."

I heard the sadness in her voice, her own fear that sounded almost motherly for the young girl.

"Take the light," I said, stepping aside so Vero could continue the sweeping motion. She grabbed it by the handle and began the steady motion while I moved to the sidewall facing the cliff.

I made out Asim's shadowy figure on the rocky perch. His dark brown clothes helped make him less visible to the casual observer.

I watched as he leaned out over the precipice face-first and slowly began his descent, walking his way toward the ground below.

He's got some cojones to do it Aussie-style like that.

I kept my eyes on him as he reached a quarter of the way down. Then something caught my attention to the left. A guard was heading straight toward Asim's landing spot. The gunman walked with a drunken gait, as if he'd been pounding shots of booze for the last three hours.

He ambled sluggishly over to where the fence met the rock mountain and paused.

"What is he doing?" I asked myself in a hushed voice.

Red mist swirled around him, as it did all the men I'd seen in this place so far. There was no reason to expect otherwise. I would have been more surprised if there was a single guy in this place who didn't have that death mark wrapping around them.

"Oh, you have to be kidding," Xolotl said, a sound of disbelief clear in his tone.

I felt the same blend of concern and disgust as I watched the man stop almost directly under Asim and unzip his pants to relieve himself.

CHAPTER 21

To his credit, Asim had spotted the guard and stopped his progress down the rock face, but now the lights of the compound illuminated his figure. The only thing keeping him remotely unseen was the color and shade of his clothes. They blended almost perfectly with the rock, which told me Asim had picked them out for just such a reason.

I wondered how long he could hold out in that spot with the guard standing beneath him. A bead of sweat rolling off his skin, a bit of debris breaking loose from the rock face, anything could give Asim away.

I stood there, paralyzed, trying to figure out how to handle it before our friend's strength gave out and he was forced to do something drastic.

"Hey, V?" I said, stepping back toward Vero. "We have a problem down below. You mind taking him out?"

"Sure," she said, handing the spotlight back over to me.

"By the way," I added, "he's taking a leak. So try not to be too disgusted."

"Ew. Why didn't you use your blade thingies?"

"Felt more like an arrow job to me."

She rolled her eyes and moved over to the sidewall, notching an arrow in her bow. "Seriously. That's gross. You guys just go anywhere you want, don't you?"

"Pretty much," I admitted.

She shook her head, then took aim and loosed the arrow.

I leaned over the wall in time to see it sink through the center of the man's spine. There was no way to know for sure, but I figured it probably severed his spinal cord on its way to, and through, some vital organs.

He twisted around, grasping at the protruding arrow, then fell to his knees and over onto his side.

Asim glanced over at us as if to say thanks and then ran down the cliff face until he reached the bottom.

Vero looked back behind us to make sure no one had seen what happened. I checked the nearest guard tower, but those two guys were preoccupied with their mundane task, and engaging in what must have been pointless, or at the very least, uncivil conversation.

"Nice," I said to Vero.

"Thanks." She sidestepped to the wall to her left and looked down. Most of the compound was swarming with activity. But this little area was left unattended, probably because Adisa's men felt the guards on the tower could handle anything or anyone that tried to get in.

Once on the ground, Asim unclipped the rope from his harness and sprinted to the tower base. I lost sight of him when he disappeared behind the wall and floor.

"He okay?" I asked.

Vero took another look down.

"Yes. He's coming up now."

I kept sweeping the light back and forth, matching the speed of the men in the other tower as best I could.

Vero opened a door cut into the sidewall, and Asim appeared, climbing into the nest. He breathed heavily from the ascent and sat there on his backside for a minute to catch his breath.

"Okay," I said. "Time for phase two of the plan. Where is this cave again?"

Asim nodded slowly and stood. He pointed back to the rear of the compound where the mountain rose from the earth.

"You'll go around those tents in the back. You will know it when you find it. Just try to be quiet. Any sounds of trouble might spook Adisa, and when a man like him gets scared…"

We knew what he insinuated. Evil men like Adisa would do almost anything in the name of self-preservation when backed into a corner. They'd give up their own family members if it meant they could keep breathing for another thirty seconds.

If the alarm were raised, we'd have to ramp up the timeline for our search.

Vero nodded, pulling the scarf around her neck up over her face and the matching hood over her head. She knew women weren't always treated with respect in this part of the world. Violent crimes against women were astronomical here, while the conviction rate of such acts remained abysmally low.

"Good luck," Asim said.

"We'll get your sister back," I said, almost as much to ease his anxiety as my own. The fact was we didn't know for sure if his sister was even still alive, and if so, where she was being kept. All we had to go on was what Asim told us. For now, that would have to be good enough.

The only part of this plan I had doubts about was the order in which we were to do things. Seemed logical that we should go after her and all the other prisoners first then find the clue. To me, the immediate threat to human life was more important. But Asim had insisted it must be done this way.

I chose to trust him.

He'd gotten us this far. Unless this far was some kind of elaborate trap. That would mean Amari was in on it too.

The doubts started circling in my mind. Our entry had been too easy. We faced minimal threats. I didn't know if I was just being paranoid or more alert to threats around us.

"It's not an ambush, kid," Xolotl said. "None of these guys know you're here."

"You're sure?" I whispered.

"Am I sure? When have I steered you wrong?"

"It seems like always, but I guess you haven't. You did miss the sniper, though."

"Funny. Now get moving."

I nodded, looked over at Vero, then vaulted over the wall toward the center of the giant rock. I hit the ground running, barreling toward the first tent on the left. I cast a quick glance to my left down a path that led around the outermost buildings and tents. No guards. Yet.

I hurried to the nearest structure—a small shanty with metal sides and roofing—and ducked into the shadows behind it.

Then I watched as Vero took the same tack. She gracefully made the jump down to the ground, rolling as her feet touched the rugged surface, then back up into a sprint until she joined me behind the building.

We waited, our backs against the corrugated wall, watching for any sign of trouble. Up on the tower, Asim continued sweeping the desert beyond the perimeter with the spotlight. So far, no one had seemed to notice.

I leaned around the corner and looked down the path. I spotted two gunmen just as they turned to walk down one of the alleys. I felt a little lucky they hadn't seen me. Or maybe they were the lucky ones.

"Okay, all clear," I said, stepping out into the open once more.

I skirted along the buildings and tents, passing narrow thoroughfares until I reached the one where the guards I'd spotted had turned. I looked down that way and saw them still meandering away from the rock mountain toward the center of the compound.

I heard the sounds of laughing from several of the buildings. Evidently, Adisa's men were having a good time. Hopefully not too good a time.

My mind drifted to Asim's sister. *At least I don't hear screaming or crying.*

I knew that didn't mean everything was okay, but it would have to do for now.

I peeked around the corner again and spotted the cave entrance thirty yards away. Just as Asim predicted, there were four guards, two on either side of the opening to the mountain.

Each of the men was holding a rifle slung over one shoulder. Two were smoking cigarettes while they talked. Their casual demeanor was hardly fitting of their station, and I wondered how Adisa would react if he saw them taking their job so lightly.

Maybe he already knew, and like the guards, assumed no one would get that far into the encampment without being detected.

Not that it mattered. They could have been holding those rifles in a ready position, fingers on triggers, and the result would be the same. The only difference was that, due to their lack of concern, they would fail to get off a single shot, thus leaving the rest of the compound unaware to our presence.

I plucked one of the spiral blades from my right hip and held it out away from my body.

"Think I can get all four with one throw?" I asked Vero in a hushed tone.

"If they were all in a single line, yes, but they're not."

She was right. The men weren't in any kind of formation.

"Good point. I'll get the two in front. You get the two in back."

She answered by producing the bow and pulling back the string to notch an arrow.

"Ready?" I asked.

"Ready."

I stepped out from the shadows and side-armed the disc at the first of my two targets. A half second later, Vero loosed the first arrow at the nearest man standing next to the rock façade.

The blade easily cut through my target's neck, then sliced through the second's throat, severing their heads from their bodies.

Vero's arrow struck her first target in the base of the skull and protruded out through the man's mouth. Before he fell against the wall, the second arrow zipped past him, sinking deep into the last guard's right eye.

The four men fell to the ground. The heads of the men I'd taken out popped free and rolled a few feet away from the bodies.

I know. Violent. And the truth was, I wanted to vomit. Seeing a couple of heads just rolling on the dirt wasn't something I'd ever accept as normal. But hey, it came with this supernatural territory.

Jeez, if my professors could see me now, well, they'd probably be terrified. "Hey, Gideon, what you been up to lately? You were always one of my favorite students."

"Oh, nothing, Dr. Bortles. You know, ruthlessly killing lots of evil people with the power of an ancient amulet I discovered in the Yucatan that shape-shifts me into a mythical monster."

Honestly, they'd probably laugh thinking I was joking. And I'd have to let them believe it.

I rushed toward the cave entrance with my right hand extended. The spiral blade returned to my grasp, and I clipped it to my hip in midstride.

When I reached the cave entrance, I looked to the left down the main "street" of the encampment.

There were dozens of armed men standing around; talking, laughing. Many huddled by a large fire in the center of the encampment.

I slowed down as I passed the guards' bodies, watching carefully to make sure no one saw us. It seemed none of Adisa's men were paying any attention to the cave. Part of me wondered why they would. It was guarded by four guys. And any intruders would have to get through all of them first before they even got close to the cave entrance.

The other part of me kept thinking this was all too easy, which only heightened my senses.

"You're right to think that way," Xolotl said. "Many a warrior has fallen to a false sense of security."

I didn't respond, but I knew he was right.

We had to stay alert.

I quickly ducked into the shadows of the cave and watched the men fifty yards away as Vero passed by and took a position on the other side of the tunnel.

We shared a questioning expression as if we both wondered if we'd been spotted, but neither of us answered. We were on radio silence now.

I turned and looked deeper into the passage.

The first twenty feet of the cave looked like a natural formation, crafted by the hands of time and weather. But beyond that, the corridor appeared to have been honed by human hands with ancient tools that had long since rusted away. The tunnel's well-defined shape could not have been replicated by nature. The lines, the smooth sections, the flat floor beneath—all pointed to the work of skilled craftsmen long ago.

The initial forty feet were dark, with the only light coming from the camp outside. Farther in, single light bulbs were fixed to the tunnel's ceiling. Wires ran from one to another, and along the wall to the floor, then outside to what I guessed was probably a generator.

There were no power lines out here, and I hadn't seen any solar panels, though those would probably work well in a place that almost never got rain.

I shook the random thoughts from my mind and pressed ahead, leaving the shadows behind.

We kept moving, with me in front and Vero close behind keeping watch of the rear. The passage veered to the left for thirty feet then cut back to the right. At the corner, I stopped and took a peek around.

At the end of the tunnel, roughly sixty feet away, a brightly lit room opened up. I didn't see any gunmen, but I did notice a few wooden crates stacked against the far wall.

I motioned for Vero to follow me and moved ahead, creeping quietly on the tips of my toes. The shoes on my feet scuffed against the hard floor more than once, and I cursed myself for being so clumsy.

When we reached the opening, I held up my hand and stopped at the threshold. There were no voices. No sounds of machinery. The chamber was completely silent, muted to the noises of the encampment just outside.

The room was probably eight hundred square feet, as best as I could guess. This ancient place was a hodgepodge of wonder and total disregard of historical integrity. Dozens of crates, like the first ones I'd seen, lined the walls almost all the way to the ceiling, hiding an entire wall of hieroglyphs in the shadows of their stacks. One to my right had been pried open. I looked inside, lifting the lid to get a better view, and saw several rifles packed within.

The wall straight ahead hadn't been covered up, and I moved closer to study the intricate imagery portraying a story from long ago.

"Can you read it?" Vero asked.

"It's not like most Egyptian hieroglyphs I've studied." On top of that, Egyptology wasn't my primary career focus, so that didn't help. But I'd seen enough to know my way around it. The designs of these images, however, were slightly different. I figured they might be close enough for me to decipher. If I could get past the crates of weapons.

"Who's arming these guys?" I wondered.

Vero tapped me on the arm and pointed at the floor to the left.

"What is that?" she asked.

I followed her gaze to the floor and immediately realized that was what we'd come here to find. And I had no idea what it was.

CHAPTER 22

"It looks like a giant dial," Vero said.

I couldn't disagree. But I couldn't confirm it either.

While the rest of the floor looked the same—carved from the rock of the mountain—the portion that caught our attention was made from another kind of stone that didn't appear to be native to this place, at least not this mountain.

"Granite," I said, bending down to run my fingers over the smooth surface.

The dial looked almost like a table set into the ground, with three separate inner rings fixed within it. Each ring featured images of animals and other shapes carved into the stone, with the outer ring displaying seven, the second innermost ring with five, and the smallest one with three. A single carved line from the center of the circle pointed out toward the rings and the symbols.

Sand and grit filled the gaps between the rings and the center.

"This must be it," I realized. "This is the clue we're looking for."

"Yeah, but how does it work? It doesn't look like we can turn the hand in another direction. I'm guessing we have to line up the right symbols."

I grinned at her intuition. "You'd make a pretty good archaeologist. Well, for a bear," I joked.

She huffed a laugh. "Funny."

"I guess we have to rotate the symbols and get them in the correct order."

I studied the engravings again. The huge stone rings looked heavy, and moving them would take an immense amount of strength. That might have been the only reason Adisa's men hadn't attempted to move them. Or maybe they tried and didn't get anywhere with it. I wasn't about to give a scumbag like Adisa any kind of credit. He probably thought it was just a cool flooring design.

"What's the order these things are supposed to be in?" Vero asked, looking over at me.

"Not sure," I confessed, shaking my head as I scratched the side of my furry head.

I knew that some piece of this must point to an image of a lion. The problem was, each ring contained one of those, and it was the same one. On top of that, those images matched the one on the necklace we'd discovered in the catacombs.

"That's the same image from the necklace," I commented, my mind starting to work through the puzzle. "But it must have to be done in a certain order. So, you see my dilemma."

"Yes," she agreed. "All three have the same one."

I turned and looked to the back wall again, and at the hieroglyphs that sprayed out across the surface. Traces of the colorful paints used thousands of years before to adorn the images still lingered in the dust.

Suddenly aware that we were wasting time, I pointed at the crates to the left. "We need to get all this out of the way so I can see the entire wall."

Vero nodded and immediately pulled on the bottom crate of the first stack. Her superhuman strength was more than capable of getting the objects out of the way without my help, so I set to the other side and began doing the same, all the while listening closely with my enhanced hearing to detect if anyone was approaching.

It was only a matter of time. Sooner or later, someone would come by to relieve the four guards at the cave entrance, or simply walk by and find four sets of empty clothing where they'd met their demise. That part might throw a guard for a loop for a few seconds, thinking the men were playing some kind of trick on him.

I could see it playing out in my head, and it was kind of funny except that the scenario would likely lead to the entire compound's firepower raining down on us.

Vero was already sliding the second stack out of the way while I finished my first. "That's good," I said. "Those last few are far enough away I can see behind them. Would you check the tunnel to make sure no one is coming?"

She nodded and retreated back into the corridor.

I maneuvered two more stacks of the heavy crates out of the way so I could see all the images on the wall. As I finished pulling the last of the wooden boxes, I happened to glance at the end of the one on top. It was stamped with a logo, a white image of what looked like an eagle with three stars behind it.

I frowned and looked around, realizing that all of the crates featured the same logos.

"That looks like an American thing," I muttered.

"Yeah. It sure does," Xolotl agreed. "What do you think it means?"

"I don't know. But it can't be good. And I definitely don't like where my first instinct is taking it."

"You mean—"

"All clear for the moment," Vero interrupted, returning into the chamber's light. "But I wouldn't count on that for long."

"Okay." I nodded. "Keep watch while I try to figure this thing out."

I stood back, inspecting the wall's spectacularly preserved images.

On the far right, in the bottom corner, was an image larger than the others, one that seemed to preside over the right half of the layout. This picture looked like a man with the head of a jackal, or some other doglike creature.

A chill shot through me, and my skin crawled.

"Set," I said. The lights almost seemed to dim a little at the mention of the name.

Maybe it was just my imagination. But after my little run-in with that deity in my dreams, I wasn't throwing out any possibilities. For all I knew, he could have led us here to trap us.

I looked over at the dial and saw the same image of the jackal-headed man on the two larger rings.

Then I checked above the one on the wall and started to work. I knew these hieroglyphs, most certainly rooted in the Egyptian style, needed to be read from top to bottom, but could also be read right to left or left to right.

These weren't standard, though, and as I analyzed the images in the columns, I started doubting whether or not I was doing it correctly.

I took another step back, deciding to get a bigger perspective of the entire story. From what I could tell, this was an accounting of both history and a foretelling of the future. At the end stood Set, wreaking havoc on the people of the world. On the other end was the sun disc representing Amun, and the beginning of time here in this realm.

All of the hieroglyphs seemed to converge on the image in the very center of the wall, the lion man, Apedemak.

I moved closer again and traced the nearest lines to the figure of Apedemak. "I think this says that he stands on the line between chaos and prosperity."

"Okay," Vero answered. "Does that give you a good idea of what to do?"

"I think so."

I turned to the huge dial and noted the corresponding images I believed to be the correct order.

Starting with the innermost ring first, I found two gouges where it appeared hands could fit to pull or push the stone around.

I could barely squeeze my thick fingertips into them. "I gotta switch back," I said. "Can't get my fingers in here."

"Okay. No sign of trouble yet."

"All right." I shifted back into myself and easily gripped the two slots. Crouching and leaning back, I pulled the wheel. The sound of stone grinding on stone rumbled through the chamber. There was no way an ordinary human could have done this on their own. If I didn't have the medallion... Well, then again, I wouldn't have been in this spot anyway.

I kept shimmying backward until the sun disc was aligned with the arm in the center. When I stopped, a loud thud boomed from underneath us, shaking the entire room.

"What was that?" Vero asked, turning away from the passage.

I looked around, uncertain. "I don't know. Either I just started an ancient booby trap that's going to crush us, or something unlocked."

"Which is it?"

"I'm fifty-fifty on that."

Before she could respond, Xolotl interrupted. "Someone's coming."

Vero must have been alerted too and quickly took a defensive stance. "What should I do?"

Part of me hated putting her in danger. After all, on the inside she was the sweet bartender I'd fallen for back in Mexico when my entire life was one dark night of the soul. But I had to remind myself—often—that she was a guardian, just like me, and she could handle herself.

"Buy me some time."

She responded with a curt nod and stepped quietly into the darkness. Whoever was coming into the cave was about to come face to face with a nightmare.

184

I looked back at the rings in the floor, at the likeness of Apede-mak. As before, two slots cut into the stone allowed for a sort of over-lapping grip. I slid my hands into them and started to pull.

The middle wheel started to move as I dragged it around. I'd nearly centered the lion man over the arm when gunfire erupted in the passage.

I looked up, momentarily distracted. The screams of the men meeting a brutal end at Vero's claws reached my ears.

Unfortunately, I should have stayed focused on my job. Instead, my hands slipped out of the slots, and I felt the wheel slip into a notch—with the wrong symbol matching.

It was a cat. But not the lion god, Apedemak. It was a Persian, if I'm not mistaken. But it was not the correct symbol.

The walls on either end exploded in a rain of rubble and dust. Fragments showered me, and I ducked down, covering my head and eyes against the projectiles.

I didn't hear the sounds of the men out in the tunnel. Vero must have finished them. That confirmation came when I heard her shout my name.

"Gideon?"

All I could see were clouds of dust and chunks of rock all around me.

My ears weren't ringing. That was a good thing. And it also led me to believe what just happened wasn't an explosion.

"Gideon? You okay?"

I made out her human silhouette rushing toward me, stirring the dust around behind in her wake.

Then I heard the deep, ominous sound of what could only be extremely heavy stones sliding toward us.

Through the settling dust I saw the walls closing in on either side of us, and where they had been smooth-cut before, now sharp spikes carved from the rock itself converged toward us.

They weren't moving quickly, so that was the good news. And we could still get out of here. The exit was a mere twenty feet away.

Sure, there would be hordes of enemies we'd have to fight through, but it wasn't anything we couldn't handle. I hoped. There were the hostages to consider, and Asim was still—hopefully—up on the watchtower pretending to be one of Adisa's lookouts.

But we were so close. And I got the feeling that if we just bolted for the door and let this ancient iron maiden—minus the iron— cover the dial, that might just be it for tracking down the hidden temple. From there, finding the Apedemak Medallion would prove much more difficult.

Screw it, I thought. *We're here. Might as well get it done. Or get crushed trying.*

Then I wondered if, because the only way we could lose our lives was by losing our heads, we would just be pinned and skewered by all those spikes for all eternity.

"Yes," Xolotl said. "That is exactly what will happen."

"That's a fate way worse than death," I spat.

"Not what I was thinking you'd say," Vero said, looking down at me.

Her arm shifted into a human one, and she held it out to help me up.

I stood and looked quickly over at the dial.

"I have to reset that middle one," I said.

The walls continued closing in.

"I'll see if I can slow them down," Vero said.

I fitted my hands back into the slots while she rushed to the wall on the left. She found a large enough gap between the spikes to lean into the moving death trap.

Meanwhile, I pulled the wheel again, this time fitting the mark of Apedemak over the dial's hand.

I stood up, thinking maybe I could dust my hands off and take a second now that I'd corrected the earlier error. But life wasn't always like that. And neither was this elaborate trap.

The walls kept coming.

Vero dug her boots into the hard floor and pushed.

The grinding slowed but didn't stop.

"I can't hold it," she gasped. "I can only slow it a little. Hurry and move the last piece."

Vero didn't have to tell me twice. I was already crouching over the largest wheel before she finished the sentence.

"You know," Xolotl said over the rumbling stone, "there's a good chance that if you get this wrong, those two spiked walls could actually speed up and crush you. Right?"

"Not helping," I said.

"No? Well, would it help to know there are more men coming this way?"

"Oh come on."

"Yeah. Seems like about ten or so. No, check that. Twenty."

I glanced over at Vero, who must have just received the same intel. She looked at me for directions.

"Just hold the wall a few more seconds."

I pulled on the slots of the third wheel. It was the heaviest of all, but I still managed to move it, albeit with more effort than the other two. I shuffled my feet backward as I dragged it around, desperately hoping I didn't slip or lose my balance and drop the thing back onto another wrong icon.

The sudden sound of gunfire interrupted my concerns, and I nearly lost my grip. Fortunately, my left hand stayed in place while the other slipped a little, and I kept the wheel moving.

Vero was already facing the oncoming enemies while she leaned against the wall. Bullets snapped through the air, smashing segments of the priceless hieroglyphs to chunks of unrecognizable debris.

I kept pulling, faster than before. "Why does the jackal have to be the last one on this old combination lock?" I complained against the amplified sounds of gunfire in the confined, rocky space.

A bullet struck me in the back, and I winced. It exited through my upper right chest. Then another ripped through my leg.

Without stopping, I willed my armor to appear around me, and as I thought it, my head, torso, and legs shifted into that of the beast, surrounded with the metallic protection I needed.

Now the rounds pinged off me. But I still had my human hands and arms to pull the wheel.

"Two more spots," I urged, coaching myself like I was in a gym trying to do two more reps of some impossible exercise.

The walls drew dangerously close. The sharp spikes were mere feet away from me. Had I not moved so quickly, I wouldn't have been able to complete the full turn. Vero had been pushed near as well. She'd shifted too, for protection. But now she was wedged between the thick-based spikes like a fish caught in a net.

Then, as if we needed one more challenge, I saw a grenade roll past the two of us and stop a mere two yards away.

I dropped the wheel into place and reached my hand out to Vero.

She grabbed hold, and I pulled just as a loud clack echoed from beneath us.

One second, we were there in the chamber, nearly skewered by the spiked walls. The next, I felt the floor under us drop away. My weight pulled Vero free of the wall, tugging her down into the darkness a split second before the grenade exploded.

The short, fiery burst briefly illuminated the walls around us for half a second. I felt and heard the shrapnel hit my armor, and a few places it didn't cover. That didn't concern me.

What did was I had no idea how far down this drop was going to go.

CHAPTER 23

At first, I thought we were going to fall hundreds of feet until we hit the ground in a painful, awkward way that would have killed any normal mortal.

But I hoped instead we'd land fine, and I'd be able to pull off some kind of hero landing.

You know. Those cool ones they do in the movies where they jump from some high place and land with one knee bent and hit the ground with their fist?

Yeah, that didn't happen here. We fell for less than three seconds, crashing to the ground in a pit as dark as the heart of evil itself.

I landed on my right side and immediately rolled to my feet, peering into the blackness. I heard Vero moving nearby.

"You okay?"

She grunted. "Yeah. I'm good. Where are we?"

I saw her eyes glowing in the darkness from behind the sockets in her helmet.

Of course, I didn't have a flashlight. Or a glow stick.

I felt around the air in front of me until I touched against her armor. "There you are," I said.

I sensed her change back into her human form too, though I couldn't see the transformation.

"What is this place?"

"I don't know." I looked up toward the chamber where we'd been just a moment before. "I guess those walls sealed it shut."

"There's something on the ground here," Vero noticed.

I kicked out my foot and felt it brush against something heavy. I reached down and ran my fingers over it, then against something next to it. "It's their weapons. Their entire cache just got wrecked by that deathtrap."

"At least something good came out of it. Any ideas?"

Suddenly, flames burst around us. They burned from torches we couldn't see on walls we had no clue surrounded us.

"Or that could happen," she added.

I spun around, scanning the room. It wasn't entirely dissimilar to the vibe I got from the hidden temple I initially fell into, the one that started this whole mess.

The chamber was cut like a giant rectangular box, and the stone down here wasn't the same rock we'd seen above, with a lighter color looking more like sandstone. Hieroglyphs adorned the surfaces all around us, and unlike those in the above room, these had retained all their vibrant colors throughout the ages.

"This is incredible," Vero said. She spun around slowly, taking in the surroundings.

"Yeah," I said with a nod.

Both walls on either side of us were divided by a thick line that ran horizontally toward the doorway at the other end. The line on the right was a beautiful turquoise color, while the one on the left wall was bright white.

"The two Niles," I realized, stepping forward toward the doorway.

Vero walked by my side, and I felt our fingertips brush against each other. I grabbed her hand, sensing she might be nervous, and held it as we walked carefully across the room.

"When I was in Mexico," I said, "in the hidden temple there, it was sort of like this. Torches flickered to life on their own. And I heard a voice speaking to me."

"Do you hear it now?" she asked, more curious than afraid.

"No."

"I'm still here if you want me to talk," Xolotl said.

I simply shook my head.

"There is something different here, though," I continued. "Obviously, the Egyptian-style hieroglyphs on the walls weren't there."

"You don't think this is actually where the amulet might be, do you?" Vero asked.

"Could be, but if so, wouldn't Amari have told us? And the clue in Jack's book about this place... It seemed pretty clear this was only the next step."

"Definitely feels too easy for it to be here."

"Right," I agreed.

I remembered Asim was still—hopefully—up in the watchtower doing his thing. After the explosion and all the noise coming from the cave, I guessed most of Adisa's men were rushing that direction to take care of the problem, but all they would find was a blocked-off entrance to their weapons storage room, and probably what was left of the men's clothes that belonged to the guys Vero took out.

As we passed under the stone archway into the other room, the blue and white lines continued with us and out to the other side. More torches flamed to life in the next chamber, and once inside, we could see the two lines run down to the floor and into the center of the space, where an eerily familiar golden box sat atop a three-step platform.

"What is that?" Vero asked as we approached with caution.

I pored over it with every step until we reached the bottom of the platform. The ancient ark was rectangular in shape, made from pure gold. Its surface was smooth and polished, and in the light of the flames it shimmered and danced, casting eerie shadows around the room on the blank walls.

The sides of the ark were covered in hieroglyphs and pictures showing battles and religious scenes. These decorations were carved into the gold and filled with blue lapis lazuli.

At each end of the lid stood a foot-high figure of Apedemak, the lion-headed god. These figures were also made of solid gold. They had detailed manes and small rubies for eyes. The figures faced outward, as if guarding the precious container.

Between the two Apedemak figures, the lid had a raised picture carved into it, a classic example of an ancient bas-relief. This picture showed Apedemak winning battles against mythical beings, monsters from a time long forgotten. It was painted with bright colors that were still visible after thousands of years.

In the center of the lid, amid the battle scenes, was a raised circle designed to look like the sun. *Great, another dial.*

"It's an ark," I said, finally answering Vero's question. "Similar to the one from the Bible. Ark technology and design were things the Egyptians developed, though they didn't fully understand the power of what they'd created. These things were more than holy relics. They could draw static electric power from the arid deserts and geostatic pools in the region to be used in religious ceremonies. Priests would unleash the power in a fantastic display, causing the people to think it was one of their deities speaking to them. Later on, Moses studied in those Egyptian schools. He knew all about arks, and probably made some in his shop class."

I glanced over at her with a mischievous smirk.

She replied with an arched eyebrow. "Shop class, huh?"

"Something like that. Anyway, when Moses was told to create a new ark for the most holy relics of Israel, he understood the full power of what it could do. It wasn't just for electrical shows. It was the first super weapon of the age, hearkening to a more ancient time when such things like this may have been more commonplace, and more devastating."

"That sounds... dark."

I shrugged. "The world was wiped out by a cataclysm just over twelve thousand years ago. Much of that stuff was lost to the flooding after the Younger Dryas."

"So what are we supposed to do with this one? If it's got all that... power you described, isn't it dangerous?"

"I think so, probably. Even if it hasn't been charged by being moved, carried on wooden rails like the one in the Bible, this could be a geostatic hotspot."

"Jeez, are you always this neurotic?" Xolotl asked. "I'm kidding. I know you are. And in case you're wondering, I don't detect any kind of potential power surge from this thing. It appears to be dormant."

"That's a relief," I muttered.

"What?" Vero asked. Then she realized I was talking to my invisible friend.

"It looks like we have to turn that dial to unlock it."

"Or to unleash some kind of terrible curse that kills us both."

"Yeah. Or that."

"What?" She looked at me surprised. "You're not supposed to agree with that."

"Hey, it could be. But I doubt it. We wouldn't have been led here just to be wiped out by some kind of ancient, magical booby trap." At least, I hoped we weren't.

Our hands slipped apart as I ascended onto the second step. I stood there, staring down at the dial. In its center, a circle had been carved into the gold, and within that circle was a mirror image of the necklace we'd discovered in Portugal.

I reached into my pocket and removed the disc, letting the chain dangle through my fingers.

As I held it out closer to the dial, the flames around us flickered as if brushed by a breeze.

"You know what you're doing, right?" Vero asked.

"Not really," I confessed. "But we didn't come all this way to do nothing."

I unclasped the chain and let it fall at my feet, then gently placed the disc into the center of the dial.

Nothing happened, but I didn't expect anything. Not until I turned the knob.

"Here goes," I said with a look back at Vero.

I wrapped my fingers around the dial and twisted it to the left, thinking that's how all things were loosened.

At a quarter of a turn, something clicked inside the ark. Out of caution, I stepped back down to the floor next to Vero and watched.

A loud, sudden burst of air hissed out of the lid like it was shot from an air compressor.

Then a blue mist began to seep out. It spilled through the narrow opening between the lid and the main body of the ark, slowly at first, but with greater volume and speed with every passing second.

Vero and I instinctively took a step back, retreating from the substance. I started thinking maybe she'd been right about there being some kind of curse inside the ark. I also wondered if Xolotl had been wrong.

The flames around us began to wane, as if smothering themselves.

I glanced back over my shoulder toward the doorway, but it was gone. The opening we'd come through moments before was a solid wall.

"Um, Gideon?" Vero said. "Any idea what this is? Artemis isn't sure either."

"You two are so impatient," Xolotl answered in my mind. "Relax. You're about to see something unlike anything you've witnessed before."

I had to trust him, even if I didn't like his attitude.

The lid started to rise above the ark's body. The eyes of the two Apedemak statues glowed bright red, mingling with the eerie blue light from within the container to create a sort of purple haze above the fog.

The bright light from the figures' eyes grew stronger, illuminating the walls and the ceiling thirty feet overhead.

The blue mist continued spilling out of the ark. It was up to our knees, and filling the room fast—like a pool.

Vero reached out and took my hand again, and we moved closer together.

"I don't like this," she said. "Should we transform?"

"I don't think it matters," I answered.

The mist reached our hips then our torsos. Then our necks.

"I hope this isn't some kind of poisonous gas," she blurted.

Then, within seconds, we were completely covered in the fog.

CHAPTER 24

I looked around in panic. I still felt Vero's hand in mine, but I couldn't see her. I couldn't see anything except the swirling purple clouds enveloping us.

"Gideon?" Vero said, her voice unsteady.

"It's okay. It's weird. But it's okay."

The mist didn't seem to have an odor or taste, and breathing it in had no effect on me. In fact, it was almost as if it wasn't actually there.

Without warning, the light vanished from the room for a terrifying second. Then, just as suddenly as the room had darkened, a new light appeared above us—projected into the air from the dial on the ark.

"Whoa," I breathed.

"That's... incredible."

The fog was gone, and over our heads hung what looked much like an augmented reality map of Africa. The outline glowed orange, with our current location marked with a circle, as if the gods were saying, "You are here!"

Then, an arch appeared on the map where we were and stretched east across the Sudan until it finally stopped. A blue line wiggled through the area past a dot, where the arch ended.

The word *Naga* etched itself into the air next to the location.

"Naga," I said out loud.

"Do you know it?" Vero wondered.

"No. I don't know what it is. But I guess we'll have to find out."

I continued to stare up at the incredible display. It was like something out of the near future but without the need for special goggles or glasses.

"So, that is where we'll find the next medallion," I said.

"That's great, but how are we going to get out of here? There's a wall where the door was."

A new light appeared straight ahead of us. It was the same orange color as the map outline overhead, but this one outlined a doorway.

Vero and I looked over at each other then started toward the exit, or what we believed to be the exit. It could have been an opening to a bottomless pit on the other side.

Luckily, that wasn't the case. We both stopped at the threshold, then I remembered the disc from the necklace.

"Hold on," I said and hurried back over to the ark. I stopped, looked around for another second, then picked up the disc and hurried back to where Vero waited.

"I have a feeling we may need this again." I held up the talisman then stuffed it into my front right pocket.

I walked through the doorway first, still wary that it could be some kind of trap or even a portal into another dimension.

Instead, it opened into another passage, this one narrower than the way we'd come in. The walls were bare, though cut to a smooth finish. Luckily, the orange line of light continued to stream overhead to illuminate our path.

"Where do you think this comes out?" Vero asked, keeping her voice low.

"I have no idea. But be ready in case we burst out of some door into a mob of Adisa's guys."

The tunnel made a sharp ninety-degree turn before the path started to slope upward. The corridor only looked about fifty yards to the top, where the opening gave way to a dark blanket studded with stars that sparkled like diamonds.

I quickened my pace, knowing Vero would have no trouble keeping up. We only slowed down when we drew near the opening. Mobs of angry voices overpowered the droll sounds of Adisa's encampment. It sounded like pandemonium had broken out in the compound, and I immediately realized we could use that to our advantage.

We stopped short of the opening, and I faced Vero. "We have to get to the building where they're keeping the hostages. Do you remember where that is in case we get separated?"

"Yeah," she nodded.

"Good. I have a feeling this is about to get really messy."

"Fine by me. Anyone who does the kinds of things these guys have done deserves what we can give them."

The right side of my lips curled into a grin. I loved her conviction, though it was a bit dark.

I took the last few steps to the top of the passage, then stood in the shadows of the doorway.

Men were running by, all heading to my left. We must have circumnavigated to the other side of the encampment, which meant we were opposite of Asim. I looked up to a watchtower on my right and noticed the spotlight beam sitting still.

"They've pulled all hands on deck," I muttered. "Adisa must be scared. And if they're all going to the cave entrance, we might be able to slip past undetected."

"We better move fast then."

I nodded in agreement as I watched another squad of ten guys rush past our position and down the path along the rock. I didn't see any others coming our way and figured that was the last of them.

"Okay," I said. "All clear. Keep moving."

I transformed into the Chupacabra and burst from the tunnel, sprinting across the wide path to a narrow opening between tents and sheds. One of several ancient pyramids loomed straight ahead. As I picked my way through the nomadic dwellings, I passed ancient stone structures left by the Kush people who lived in this region thousands of years ago.

Still, the sounds of the men shouting—now from behind us—echoed through the air. I could only guess what they were doing. Maybe they thought they could break through the new barrier that had nearly crushed me and Vero.

I slowed down as I neared the center of the compound. The walls to Adisa's personal dwelling towered overhead, though they were uneven and crumbling in several places.

I'd seen this structure from the mountain, but down on the ground and up close it seemed much more imposing.

Slowing down, I crept alongside a beige tent until I reached the corner. There, I paused and looked back over my shoulder to make sure Vero had kept up. She was right on my heels and waiting for my next move.

I leaned around the corner and looked to the right, then left, before retreating back to cover.

"The entrance is at the other end of this path."

"Any guards?"

"No, but there will be at the front. No way Adisa left this place unguarded."

"So, we storm the front? Or try to slip in some other way?"

At first, I hadn't even really considered the second option. I just figured we'd sneak around until we got to the front door then go berserk.

Her question got me thinking. I looked up at the walls, guessing they were maybe thirty feet at their highest point. Definitely doable for us. I'd jumped that high several times in this wolflike form.

The only problem was from this vantage point, I couldn't tell if there were guards up on the parapets or the narrow walkways atop the wall. It was best to assume there were, but that didn't tell us where they were positioned.

"Screw it," I said. "We go up over the wall and take out the ones with the high ground first."

"Good plan. I'll be right behind you."

I passed her a curt nod then turned, stepped out into the open, and leaped.

I flew up and over the edge of the wall, clearing the block railing by five feet before dropping down onto the landing.

Two seconds before I landed, I'd seen two guards walking to the left toward the back of Adisa's building. Now, crouching low, I produced the twin blades—one in each hand—then flung them at the two targets.

Vero landed just behind me in time to see the spinning blades cut through the men's necks. Both victims wavered for a moment then fell at the same time—their heads toppling off on the way down.

I extended my hands to catch the spiral blades then held them at the ready for the next target.

We both turned the other direction and peered down the wall walk. Vero obviously preferred using her projectile weapons in human form, and shifted quickly before she produced her bow and drew the string back, aiming at the first of two men marching the other direction. She loosed the first arrow then the second immediately after.

The two missiles pierced through the center of both men's backs, felling them like small, dead trees.

We stayed low and shuffled over to the inner wall and peered over the edge.

"That's a lot of wall guards," I said, noting at least twenty more men, each assigned to patrol the area in pairs.

"You can never be too careful," Vero responded. "Never know what kind of monsters might be out there."

I glanced over at her and chuffed a laugh. "You're pretty funny for a bear."

"And you're pretty charming for a wolf... or dog thing."

"Thanks." I swept my gaze across the layout again. "You think we should split up and meet on the other side?"

"Sounds like a good plan."

"Okay. I'll go left. See you over there."

She nodded and took off, nearly racing while keeping low enough to avoid detection from the other guards.

I maneuvered toward the other end of the wall. I'd seen two guards coming toward this corner a moment before, and knew they'd be here within seconds.

I crouched, hidden behind the stones, until the men came into view.

The one nearest me did a double take, looking down at the monster crouching in the shadows. The crimson smoke swirled around them both.

I made quick work of both, tackling them to the ground, then with my wolflike hands, grabbed their faces and smashed the back of their skulls into the stone. The crack would have turned most people's stomachs.

It was an acquired thing, I guess.

The men instantly stopped moving, and I rushed forward down the line, ducking into a little lookout balcony to remain out of view of the next two.

I looked out toward the opposite wall, the front of the structure where I knew Vero was laying waste to the wicked men who worked for Adisa. I couldn't see her over the wall, but I knew she was there, meting out brutal, violent justice.

After waiting ten seconds, I poked my head around the corner and peered down the wall walk.

The next two had stopped to look down toward the rock where all the commotion had drawn the attention of nearly the entire compound.

I grinned at their inattention and stalked out of my hiding place, on the hunt again.

CHAPTER 25

By the time I reached the northern wall, I'd left a trail of carnage along the walk that painted those walls the color of the kidnappers' blood. Soon the bodies would be gone, so it wouldn't be that bad for long.

I looked down the way and saw Vero taking out two more with her bow. She'd really taken to the weapon, which made sense considering who was riding with her in her mind.

I didn't know as much about Artemis as I would have liked, but her skills with a bow had been legendary. Skills that had, apparently, been passed on to Vero.

Vero finished off the last two guards before hurrying to meet me at the halfway point on the walkway.

She looked me over as a mother would a child after a day at school. "You good?"

"Yeah. You?"

"Of course. Easy."

I nodded. "Too easy, perhaps."

Inching closer to the inner wall, I stood up and peered down into the courtyard. To the left, the front entrance was blocked by a grated metal gate. Looking through the opening, I noted two guards on each side.

They were facing out, so I didn't count them as problematic. Not yet.

There were, however, still eight more guards in the courtyard, stationed in various positions. If we vaulted over the wall and down onto the ground, every one of them would open fire, thus sounding the alarm.

We didn't have that kind of time. If the main group of Adisa's forces returned here at once, getting the hostages out safely would become much more difficult. On top of that, we still had to get eyes on the prisoners. Asim had told us where he believed they were being held, but what if he was wrong?

"Based on what Asim said, the hostages will be kept back there in that area." I pointed to the back left of the ruins.

Beyond the wide courtyard, a set of steps led up to the entrance to the dwelling of ancient Kush kings. Past that, a series of rooms lay covered in military camouflage netting and beige tarps. The roofs of the ancient buildings had long since deteriorated, so Adisa and his men had used whatever they could find to create shelter over their leader's quarters.

"Seems like a lot of work to cover all that," I noted. "Would have been simpler to just put up individual tents in each room."

"Right?"

"This guy has an ego. He'll call it his palace even though the roof might be duct-taped together."

"What should we do about getting in?"

"I don't know," I admitted. "If we take out one or two at the same time, the others will see it, and our little surprise party will be over."

I noticed Vero staring at a bonfire that roared in the center of the courtyard. She seemed mesmerized by the flames that licked the air ten feet above the ground.

"Would be nice if we could use that fire for a diversion," she said.

I hummed my agreement. Then an idea bubbled to life.

"Hold on," I said, producing the spiral blade from my right hip. Cocking my head to the right, I lined up one of the larger logs in the middle of the fire and reared my arm back.

"When they rush to see what's going on, we take off the other direction and drop down on that landing over there." I pointed to the top of the steps.

"Already going," she said and turned to hurry down the wall walk.

I took one last look at the fiery target then spun the blade at it. I wanted to get a head start and make for the corner behind Vero, but I needed to know if the idea worked.

The spiraled weapon zipped through the air, striking the intended log and splitting through it with precision and power.

Sparks exploded up into the air. The top of the pyre teetered then began tumbling down into itself, spilling charred and burning logs out of the shallow pit and onto the ground.

The guards responded immediately. They couldn't afford for any sparks or embers to blow free and set fire to the meager roofing that covered Adisa's quarters.

I ducked down and sprinted after Vero.

She reached the corner five seconds before me and vaulted over the interior wall down to the landing.

I followed after, without bothering to check if the area was clear.

Fortunately, every guard in the courtyard had rushed to the bonfire like moths to the... okay, I try not to use clichés. So, let's say, like moths to the fiery beacon of death. Yes, that's better.

I extended my hand as the spiral blade returned and caught it easily, which now that I thought about it, would be really dangerous if it weren't enchanted or whatever Jesse had said.

"Come on," Vero said, pulling on my arm as she made for the entrance.

We passed through into the inner palace. Stone walls lined the hallway on either side. The tarps and netting overhead rippled in the breeze.

The first two doors we passed opened into what appeared to be storage rooms full of supplies such as food, water, and ammunition. Then we passed two more of the same.

"This guy is something of a prepper," the voice in my head whispered.

He was right about that. Adisa, it seemed, was either really prepared for the worst, or he was simply greedy and this was his way of amassing material goods.

We reached an intersection where the hall split in four directions and almost walked headlong into two guards.

The mens' first reaction was to look at us with surprise. The second after that, they realized we were intruders. They leveled their guns at us, but that wouldn't save them. Vero shifted into the bear. We each took a gunman to slash apart before they could fire a shot.

While the mist consumed them, we changed back to human and looked down the corridor straight ahead that led to the rear of the palace building.

"I think it's this way."

Vero said nothing, and the two of us continued forward.

The corridor from the intersection to the rear was maybe fifty yards, give or take. Light bulbs hung from the walls, strewn together with long wires that ran to some unseen generator or battery bank.

With every step, knots of anxiety tightened in my gut. The men running this camp were savages, led by a ruthless, cruel warlord. I'd heard of the type before, heard stories of what they'd done to people. Adisa was no different, and even though this unlikely journey had toughened me in ways I could have never imagined, there were still some things I never wanted to see with my own eyes.

I prayed silently that none of the prisoners were being tortured, or something else, by Adisa's men.

The sound of a man's gruff laughter filled the corridor. It echoed past us until it faded down the hall.

Vero and I paused, waiting to see if someone would appear, but no one did.

Every room we passed had been empty of people but packed with cots and personal belongings I figured belonged to more of Adisa's men. Luckily, none of them were here at the moment. But that could change any second.

More laughter spilled out into the passage. It was the kind that curdled your blood, haughty and arrogant, bent on the enjoyment of something horrible.

I moved faster, my eyes focused on the last door in the back corner. Based on what I remembered, that had to be the way into where they kept prisoners.

Part of me questioned my memory and the directions we'd studied with Asim.

"No turning back now," Xolotl said. "But there are four men in there. Just so you know."

Vero and I shared a glance, both understanding we'd just heard the same bit of intel.

I stopped just before we reached the doorway and listened.

The men inside continued talking and laughing. I didn't understand much of what they were saying, but that wouldn't matter. Soon, they'd all be dead.

I shifted into the monster again and stepped into the doorway so the men inside could see me.

The room was huge and had perhaps served as private quarters for a queen long ago when this place was in its prime. Fabric tarps stretched from wall to wall, providing shelter from the elements above.

The four men sat on the floor around a short square table. Several coins and bills were piled in the center. The men held cards in their hands, though I didn't recognize what game they were playing. They weren't poker cards. Maybe it was a regional game.

The instant I appeared in the doorway, their collective jovial demeanor dampened. Their faces darkened to expressions of fear and worry. They'd foolishly left their weapons leaning against the wall to the left. Not that those would have done them any good.

For ten seconds, none of them said a word. They couldn't even let out a gasp.

They were probably trying to figure out if they were hallucinating or not. Based on the hookah near the table, I figured they'd either been smoking tobacco or opium or both. And if it had been opium, I must have looked like the devil incarnate.

My plan had been to step inside, rip them apart, and free the prisoners. But there was a problem with that.

Beyond the four men and their little card game—at the other end of the cavernous room—stood a massive jail cell that ran from the wall on the right to the one on the left. I'd expected to find the prison here, watched by four inept guards. But what I hadn't anticipated was that it would be empty.

CHAPTER 26

Vero stepped into the room next to me and peered straight ahead at the empty, makeshift jail.

"Where are they?" she asked, concern lacing her voice.

The four men's eyes widened even more at the sight of the bear —a talking bear. They remained frozen, paralyzed by fear and wonder, though one started subtly scooting away from the table toward the rifles leaning against the wall.

"I don't know," I said. "They should be here."

"This complicates things."

I stalked over to the guy who was trying to slide his way over to the guns, reached down, and picked him up with one hand. I held him high enough that our eyes were level. His feet dangled and kicked over the floor, unable to find purchase.

"Where are they?" I snarled.

The man's bloodshot eyes searched me for clarity. He shook his head vehemently, speaking in a dialect of Arabic I didn't understand at all. His brain was clearly unable to find any sort of psychological purchase that made sense.

I looked back down at the other three, who were too scared to move.

"Any of you speak English?"

The red fog swirled around them, pulsing and glowing as if it had its own heartbeat.

The guy on the other side of the table, one with matted black hair and a dirty face, slowly raised his hand.

"You do?" I confirmed.

"Yes. I... speak a little."

"Good." I turned back to the guy I was holding in the air. His nose was crooked and ruddy. Half his stained teeth were missing. And he smelled like a herd of camels and goats after a rainstorm.

I twisted his body then threw him into the wall. His head hit first with a satisfying crunch. Maybe the violent head trauma killed him. Or maybe it was the broken neck. Possibly both. Either way, he dropped to the floor like a sack of beans and never got up.

One of the men shouted in fear at what I'd done.

I peered down at him, letting the guy stare into my glowing red eyes while I spoke to the one who understood English. "Tell him to be quiet."

The translator did as I said, and the man resigned to trembling quietly.

"Now," I said. "Where are the prisoners?"

The man looked puzzled for a moment, as if he were trying to process the words and make sense of them in his mind.

"The people that were in there," Vero said, pointing to the prison cell at the other end of the room.

The guy looked up at her, then over to the bars, then back to me. "They... aren't here."

I closed my eyes and breathed slowly, taking in a long breath of air to quell my frustration. We didn't have time for this. Either he was stalling, or he knew less English than advertised.

I reached down and picked up the man to my right and lifted him over the floor. He yelped, shaking his head as he clawed at my wrist in a feeble attempt to free himself.

"Where. Are. The prisoners?" I said, emphasizing each word. "Where were they taken?"

The second question seemed to clarify things in the translator's mind, evidenced by the epiphany suddenly mirrored in his eyes.

"Dongola."

Finally, we were getting somewhere.

"Why were they taken to Dongola?" Vero asked.

He looked over at her then back to me. "To... be sold. They left camp... about two hours ago, I think."

I didn't like that answer. And I showed him how much by tossing the man I held into the air then punched his face so hard it sent him over the table and across the room, where he hit the floor and rolled to a stop against the wall.

"Who is selling them?" I demanded.

The man shook his head.

A new sound filtered into the room. It came from down the corridor just outside. Shoes scuffing on stone, the jangle of metallic equipment or weapons, the angry shouts of men, all signaled that we were running out of time.

Whether Adisa's men had figured out there was a problem here in the palace or were simply sweeping the area for signs of the intruders, they would be here within the minute.

I picked up the third guy, holding him by the neck. "Tell me. Is it Kofi Adisa? Is he selling them?"

The man's lips quivered, and I thought he might soil himself as he stared at me, contemplating which would be the more dangerous thing for him to do—answer or not.

I brandished my claws, extending them from my paw-like hand. The sharp points penetrated the man's throat. Dark crimson flowed from the wounds in his neck as he gurgled, kicking his feet, desperately trying to make noises my grip wouldn't allow.

I looked down at the translator.

"Last chance. You're the only one left." I tossed the dying man to the side and moved closer to him. "Is Adisa with the caravan?"

The man swallowed, finally ready to give up the goods. "Yes. He... is the one who makes... the business."

The English was awkward, but I got the picture. Adisa was the one who made the deals. There was, however, one more piece I felt like I should know.

"Who's the buyer?"

The man shook his head. From the look in his eyes, it seemed like maybe he genuinely didn't know that one. But if that was the case, he'd worn out his usefulness.

I leaned down and grabbed him by the tunic, lifting him high above the gaming table.

I let him look at the other three, their bodies been consumed by the red mist. Of course, to him, it merely looked as though the corpses were disappearing into the thin air.

"What... are you?" he asked.

I bared my teeth in a malicious grin.

"I am the darkness shadows fear," I answered.

The noises from the hall drew closer.

"They sound pissed," Xolotl said.

Vero turned and stepped toward the door. The first men through would be walking into a buzz saw. And we would let them.

"How many?" I asked my unseen companion.

"What?" the man in my grip asked.

"Not you," I clarified.

"More than ten. Less than five hundred."

"Not helpful."

"Isn't it, though?"

I grunted my frustration and redirected my focus on the man I held aloft. "This is your last chance. Who is the buyer?"

He shook his head. "I swear... I don't know. They're from China. That's all I heard."

"China?"

The sounds outside the room rose to a cacophony.

The man nodded vehemently. "Yes. I heard Kofi say something about the men from China. But that is all. I sw—"

I'd heard enough. I spun around like a discus thrower and whipped the guy at the doorway.

He screamed for exactly one second as he flew horizontally at the exit. Then the scream cut off instantly when the back of his head hit the left of the doorframe, crushing the back of his skull and warping his neck at an awkward angle. His momentum carried him through the opening and out into the passage.

I'll be honest. That had been my intention, you know, to give a good scare to the approaching mob. Imagine you were one of them, charging through the halls of this ruined palace, ready to take down some intruder, then suddenly, one of your comrades flies through the doorway with the back of his head caved in.

He hit the wall outside and dropped to the floor, which would have also given pause to virtually anyone approaching.

The sounds lessened for a few seconds.

I imagined the men were trying to figure out what happened to the dead guy in front of them.

"Hey," I said to Vero, quietly enough that only she could hear.

She looked back at me.

My eyes shot up to the fabric ceiling overhead. "You want to take the rear? Meet me in the middle?"

She nodded, understanding my idea like I'd passed it to her telepathically.

Vero bent down and jumped hard into the air, ripping through the ceiling with her claws as she disappeared into the night.

I heard her land on the wall that separated me and the angry mob. From there, she'd move down the line and get behind them. Then we could meet in the middle.

It was a better plan than the two of us trying to go headlong into the enemy. They'd get more shots at us, and while those wouldn't kill us, as always, they would hurt like... well, you know.

On top of that, we were both so huge in our monster forms that fighting alongside one another in that corridor would prove clumsy and difficult, and would slow us down.

I strode over to the doorway, hearing the sounds of the oncoming men approaching—albeit this time with a tad more caution.

I paused on the threshold, waiting. Shadows danced across the floor and the far wall, cast by the sloppily hung light bulbs strung together on the stones.

The first guy to appear looked like he was in his late twenties. His dark face was clean shaven, but that was the only thing clean about him. None of these guys cared much for hygiene, or maybe they just didn't have access.

The guy held his rifle with the stock against his shoulder, but instead of aiming up at my head, the barrel lowered slightly.

"You look surprised," I said. "Not what you expected?"

He started to take a step back. He also tried to shout, but I slashed his throat with a sharp claw and kicked him against the wall, where he fell by the clothes of the other guy I'd thrown through the doorway.

Then I stepped out and met the seething mob.

They packed the corridor from one side to the other, dozens of lines deep from what I could see. The men pointed their weapons at me, aiming down the sights with eyes full of fear and wonder. The red mist here was so compacted that it seemed to flood the room.

I let out a loud roar that shook the floor under their feet. It was so powerful, the guys on the front line shuffled back a step.

Then one gave the order to fire, and the passage exploded with the thunderous booms of AK-47 reports.

Before the first round could touch me, I dove back through the opening into the prison room. Bullets snapped through the air where I'd been a moment before, no doubt smashing into the stone wall at the end of the hallway or ricocheting dangerously back toward the shooters.

I waited for a few seconds. The gunfire died. A man shouted an order. I guessed he was telling the front line to move forward.

But any progress they made was interrupted by a loud thud from somewhere down the passage. Then screams of terror filled the air, cut off by more gunfire.

I jumped back out into the corridor, unsure if the men would still be facing my direction or the other.

It was the latter. They'd all turned to meet the threat from the rear, undoubtedly thinking that I'd quickly gone around behind their ranks.

Vero towered above them all by at least a foot. I saw the bear's head dipping forward and then rising again as she tore through the lines, sending men flying up into the ceiling or against the walls.

Bullets sparked off her armor as she waded through the enemies, claws slashing through the men desperately trying to defend themselves.

Those nearest me began to back up, desperate to retreat from the creature. But they backed right into me.

The second the guy in front realized he'd run out of real estate, he turned and looked up into my eyes. He shouted, but his voice cut off as I stabbed my claws into his chest.

Half of the men in the corridor pointed their weapons at me. But only the ones in front could fire. If those in back had done so, they'd have picked off their own.

I grabbed the rifle closest to me and ripped it out of the gunman's hands and swung it at him, breaking the thing over his skull. His head caved from the brunt force of the blow. I didn't watch him fall. I was already onto my next victim.

I grabbed at the spiral blades on my hips and clutched them as I charged forward into the ranks of terrorists. With my arms extended, I began to spin—like the Tasmanian Devil I'd seen in cartoons as a kid. Except in this case I was cutting through bad guys like the smell of raw sewage through an indoor wedding.

The power of the medallion coursed through me, mixing with the rage I felt for what Adisa had done to so many innocent people. His men paid the price, falling all around me as I neared the center of their lines.

I barely saw Vero coming my way. What had been an extraction mission had turned to bloodlust for these evil men. Tonight, we would give the mist all it could consume.

I felt a bullet sting a piece of flesh on my right side just below the ribs and immediately looked to the man holding the rifle as I paused my onslaught.

The expression in his eyes almost looked apologetic, as if he knew he'd made a huge mistake.

He fired again, but I ducked under the shot, swept the blades beneath his belt, and carved through both legs in a single, devastating strike.

His upper body wobbled before he fell onto the ground, face-first. He wriggled around, trying to crawl through the vanishing bodies of his comrades, as if he thought he could escape. I knew he'd bleed out before he made it out of the building and left him to his demise as I pressed ahead through the last gunmen desperately trying to defend themselves.

I made quick work of the wicked and finally emerged to meet Vero in the middle of the fallen.

I looked around, my chest rising and falling deeply as I caught my breath. Even with the supernatural power, that kind of fighting required an intense amount of effort.

"There'll be more of them."

She nodded in agreement. "We should get back to Asim. He could be in trouble."

"Yeah."

We took off, sprinting down the corridor. We left the palace structure and emerged on the landing on the edge of the courtyard.

None of the guards were out there. They'd all come flooding into the building to assist with the attack. The gate was open too, and the four men who'd been standing just beyond it were also missing— probably being consumed by the red mist back in the palace.

Once through the gate, we turned left and continued down the path until we reached the corner of the ruins. I only slowed enough to glance down the alley to the left before picking up speed and pressing ahead. I didn't care if we were spotted now. In fact, that would probably be a good thing as far as Asim was concerned. I'd rather have all eyes and guns on us than him. We could take it.

More sounds of angry men filled the air. Voices shouted. Guns fired. It seemed as if they were firing them into the air like I'd seen some terrorist groups do on television footage, usually shouting threats at the United States.

We reached the outer perimeter of more makeshift dwellings and stopped at the foot of the easternmost watchtower.

One of the men in the nest started shouting.

"Well," I said, "we've been spotted."

A battle cry rose into the night as reinforcements were alerted to our location.

"I'll take out the guys in the tower," Vero said. "I can give you cover from there."

It was a good plan. I grinned at her. "All right. Let's do it."

She shifted into her human self to scale the ladder on the side of the tower.

I stepped out into plain view again so the men above could get a good, terrifying look.

I smiled and waved to him like I was some kind of sadistic were-wolf. I was going for the scary clown look, but maybe that didn't make sense to African terrorists raiding villages in the middle of nowhere.

Maybe I could have just stood there. The guy was already freaking out. But I figured why not have a little fun while making sure he or his partner didn't look behind them at the woman quickly scaling the ladder.

"Hey!" I shouted. "You two! Idiots! Yes, you!"

I doubted either of the guys knew what I was saying. It wasn't like there was a good school around here to teach English. At least not in this encampment.

They both bought my little ruse and aimed rifles down at me. The sounds of another mob drew closer, their angry voices echoing between the shanties and tents. The men above opened fire, their weapon reports peppering the noise of the approaching crowd.

I dove out of the way to the left then sprinted into the nearest alley.

The last I'd seen Vero, she was only eight feet from the top of the tower. I figured she was there by now, and the abrupt cutting off of rifle fire confirmed that hypothesis. I poked my head back out and saw her standing behind the wall in the tower. The men were out of sight, their bodies hidden behind the barrier. But I saw the grim, red light pulsing as the mist began its macabre work.

Vero produced her bow and notched an arrow, aiming at one of the guards in the next watchtower.

Those men must have seen me, or their comrades shooting my way, because they opened fire on my position, sending rounds through the thin, metal wall of the shanty I leaned against. Dirt and rocks splashed around me from the barrage of bullets.

One gun stopped firing. Then the next.

I looked up at Vero, who glanced down at me, pointing down the perimeter pathway.

I peeked around the corner in time to see the first ranks of the mob rushing around a corner near the second watchtower.

Vero notched another arrow and let fly.

The missile struck an oncoming guy in the chest, felling him instantly. The men around him and behind him kept coming, as if nothing had happened. Vero fired again, and again, loosing arrows at blurring speed.

More charging terrorists fell. Some tripped over the dead, causing more chaos. But still they came, firing their weapons wildly at Vero's position.

The deafening sound filled my ears. I winced and looked up at Vero. She ducked behind the wall to avoid the hail of bullets.

"My turn," I whispered.

"Yeah. I was wondering when you were going to step in, or if you were just going to let your girlfriend do everything."

I sighed, shaking my head as I pulled the blades from my hips and stepped out into the pathway.

CHAPTER 27

Most of the guys on the front line saw me and immediately directed their fire my way.

I growled so loudly it vibrated the metal roof to my left. Bullets sprayed around me, some finding purchase on my armor only to be reduced to an unrecognizable, dented hulk by the impact against superior technology.

I spun and flung the first blade at the mob, then the second. Before I saw the impacts, I disappeared behind the shanty again, sprinting around the corner and into the next path. I ran face-first into six guys who thought it was a good idea to try to flank us.

"That was actually a really good plan," I said to the first two who bumped into me. "Emphasis on was."

I snapped my teeth through the first one's neck then slashed the second while the other four aimed their weapons.

I held up my second victim, letting go of the first, and marched toward the remaining four terrorists. They opened fire, peppering their dying friend's back with hot rounds. He screamed with every bullet that hit him until there was no life left.

I tossed the body at his comrades, knocking two of them off

balance and onto their backs. The bloody corpse weighed them down as the mist began its work. I jumped into the air, peaking around twenty feet before I descended at the two men trying to free themselves from the dead guy.

They almost made it too. One on the right had wriggled away from his partner and nearly got clear.

Nearly.

I spread my legs to shoulder width and drove my knees into their faces.

The momentum behind the drop killed them instantly. I'll spare the details on this one. It was pretty messed up. Seriously. It reminded me of a 1980s movie where this gym teacher sees one of his students get hurt on a vault and asks for a first aid kit—and a mop.

It was like that. Except, I guess I wouldn't use a mop out here.

Of the last two gunmen, one stood his ground and fired a shot at my head. It hit me too, on the helmet obviously. I think he was aiming for my eye, which was smart on his part given he didn't know how to kill me.

I stalked to him in a single, long stride, ripped the gun from his grasp, and kicked him so hard in the chest that he flew into his buddy who was trying to run away.

They scrambled to their feet and looked at each other in a panic. I held out both hands, as if ready to catch a Frisbee. They must have figured this was my way of telling them to fare thee well, run, be free. The two goons never saw the spinning blades flying at them. Perhaps one of them might have caught a glint of metal. I really don't know. What I do know is they ran headfirst into the sharp spirals. Funny choice of words, given what happened.

The momentum of their bodies carried the men a few more steps as their heads fell backward into the dirt.

Gunfire continued to thunder from the other side of the row of tents and shanties. I rushed ahead then cut left at the next thoroughfare. Straight ahead, the middle of the seething mass of attackers continued pouring toward Vero.

I saw two bodies surrounded by crimson fog, victims of my blades. I think. Maybe Vero did it. There was really no way to keep a tally when I threw those things and then slipped out of view.

I roared at the enemies, turning more than a few heads my way. Then I charged, barreling between the outer buildings and into the midst like a deranged, furry bowling ball.

I slashed back and forth with the blades, cutting through the men, their weapons, everything.

Completely surrounded by the terrorists, I again spun in a circle with the blades extended. I figured the move worked before. Why reinvent the wheel? A spinning wheel of death.

It sounded cool, but unfortunately the men around me were savvy enough to back up this time. Bullets found openings in my armor and cut through flesh. A round zipped through the back of my neck and out the front.

I dropped to the ground, my body burning like I'd been stung by a dozen hornets. I knew the wounds would heal quickly, but the bombardment was too much, and I struggled to get up.

The men moved closer, some raising old swords as they approached, all shouting like they were demon possessed.

Even on my knees, they were going to have trouble getting to me. I threw one of the blades to my left. It cut down the first victim in its trajectory as I flung the second one.

A line of men dropped as the weapon pierced through the lines and out the other side.

I tried to stand, but the hamstring was still healing. It must have been torn by a bullet.

What luck.

I saw Vero in the tower, firing arrows down at the men. She took out one who stepped close toward me with a sword raised. He fell just to my right with an arrow sticking out the back of his head.

More of them rushed me, attempting to pile on to keep me

pinned down. That wasn't smart. I extended my hands in both directions, and the blades returned, cutting through another line of terrorists.

I crouched down as they jumped on, all screaming something I'm pretty sure weren't warm fuzzies. Some stabbed me with knives. Others continued shooting as they pressed their weapon's muzzles into the few gaps in my armor.

I growled and whipped the blades around, cutting away the men nearest me.

Then I caught a flash at the far tower. It came from a rifle, though I couldn't hear the report over the mayhem around me. I saw the outline of the figure holding the gun and realized it was Asim.

He fired again, and again, hitting some of the men at the back of the mob.

As another fell, taking a round to the lower back, the others around him spotted the sniper and broke away from the group.

"Asim," I grunted.

Another blade struck the back of my neck and dug deep. Not enough to do the deed, but it nearly reached bone.

I snarled and swung backhanded at the attacker, hitting him on the side of the head and sending him flying against the fence. More started falling around me. The thump of the arrows hitting the men came in rapid staccato. The mob rushing me dwindled with every deadly strike from Vero's bow.

My hamstring felt better now, and I stood, shedding the two men who'd climbed on my back to weigh me down. I clipped the blades to my hips, and reached back with both hands. Grabbing them by the necks, I slung them down to the ground repeatedly until they both went limp.

I dropped the bodies and peered beyond the last few of Adisa's men standing between me and the ones rushing toward Asim's position. To his credit, our young guide managed to take out one more enemy before his magazine was done.

When the gunfire ceased, I knew he was in trouble.

The men on the ground shot up at him, forcing Asim to duck for cover behind the wall. I eliminated ten more men in a blur of devastating blows, slashes, and one more bite for good measure, while Vero continued eliminating those behind me as they tried to return fire.

I took off running after the men closing in on Asim. One had already reached the ladder and was scaling up the side. Five more waited at the base of the ladder. When the first climber was ten feet above the ground, the second started after him.

I barreled forward toward the base of the tower. The three remaining men on the ground braced their weapons and started firing.

Seven more appeared around the corner and immediately skidded to a stop, probably at the sight of a huge beast charging toward them. Three fell back, almost as if to flee. But one who I figured was the leader, started shouting at them to hold their positions. I only guessed he was telling them to hold the line. It's what I would have done if I were a psycho terrorist lieutenant.

The men took their positions and started shooting with the other three.

"So many bullets," Xolotl said. "I guess these guys won't learn."

I ducked into an alley on my left to avoid the onslaught and leaped up onto the roof of the next building. Using the corrugated metal for a boost, I launched myself the rest of the way to the seven men in the path. I soared a good seventy feet before gravity won and brought me crashing into two of the men before they could adjust their aim.

I rolled to my feet and jerked the rifle from the next guy, spun the weapon around as my hands shifted to human, then pulled the trigger, firing two rounds into the guy's chest. Then I shifted my aim, bracing the stock against my shoulder, and gunned down the remaining men on the ground.

The two I'd hit on the jump writhed on the ground, groaning.

With one hand, I aimed the rifle down at one, pulled the trigger, then repeated.

Now there were only the two climbing the ladder. The first was nearly there. I raised the rifle, put the leader's head in the sights, and squeezed the trigger.

The weapon boomed, kicking back against my armored shoulder. The top climber instantly let go and fell to the ground. The shot to the head had killed him before he fell.

The second hurried his pace, desperate to get over the watchtower wall. I lined him up with the rifle, calmed my breathing, and squeezed the trigger.

Click.

"Oh come on," I complained.

"Are you being lazy?" Xolotl asked.

"Shut it."

I rushed forward to the ladder, pulling a spiral blade from my right hip. I swung my arm hard at the target, letting the weapon fly. The man saw my attempt and somehow let himself drop one step down, catching himself on the rails of the next rung as the spiral blade sailed by, narrowly missing his head.

I grunted in frustration and drew the next one, but more gunfire erupted behind me between a drab brown tent and a shanty.

One of the bullets sliced through the back of my knee and hit the bone from the rear. The joint gave out, and my leg buckled. I tumbled forward, my balance lost, and rolled to a stop on the hard ground.

I glanced up and saw the second climber reach the top and vault himself over. Without him in view, I had no idea what was happening. With the blade still in my left hand, I whipped it toward the four men shooting at me, while I reached out to catch the first one.

I caught the weapon and held it for under a second before I sent it to join the other. The two blades burrowed through the chests of the two men in front then the abdomens of the men behind them.

I picked myself up off the ground and dragged my feet over to the ladder, where I caught my two blades and clipped them to my waist. I heard a commotion above but couldn't tell what was happening.

Hurrying, I reached up and pulled my weight onto the ladder. Using my right leg, I boosted upward, leaping three rungs at a time and only using my hands for support. Within seconds, I reached the top and surged up and over the wall.

Asim knelt over the body of the climber. A knife handle protruded from the man's chest just below the neck. His wide eyes stared lifelessly up at the ceiling.

Asim spun around, ripping the knife from the dead man, and brandished it at me. He relaxed when he saw who, or what, I was. He was probably the first person who'd ever relaxed upon seeing me in this form.

I held up both hands, shifting into my human body. "You okay?"

Asim nodded. "Yes. What about my sister? Where is she?"

My heart sank. I knew I'd have to answer that question. I'd hoped, foolishly, I could put it off for an hour, maybe longer.

I took a deep breath and exhaled. "She isn't here, Asim. Kofi Adisa took her and the others to Dongola."

"What?" He looked around in no direction in particular, as if he might find his sister somewhere in the darkness beyond the ruins.

"Just take it easy," I said, trying to calm him down.

"We must find her," Asim said. "What are we waiting for? We need to get to Dongola."

It was the first time I'd seen the guy lose his cool, but he was dumping it like a bad stock.

"Listen," I urged, reaching out to take the knife from him. "It's going to be okay. We're going to find your sister. But we don't know where in Dongola Adisa may have taken her."

Asim continued to search the desert for answers. But it yielded none.

I heard the sound of someone ascending the ladder and looked down, ready to slash whoever it was. I stood down the instant I saw it was Vero.

"Hey," I said, reaching out a hand to help her the last few feet over the top. Not that she needed it.

She obliged and took my hand. I pulled her up to the railing, where she dragged herself over the lip and onto the floor.

"You guys okay?" she gasped.

"He just found out about Dongola and Adisa's caravan."

"I'm so sorry, Asim."

He shook his head, a dark shadow falling across his face as if it bloomed from within.

"Do you know anyone in Dongola?" I asked. "Anyone who might know something about Adisa, where he does his business there? Anything at all would be helpful."

Asim thought for a minute. I knew it had to be difficult. He'd come here expecting to rescue his sister and instead had come up empty-handed. At least we'd struck a serious blow to Kofi Adisa's little army.

"I sense some have escaped," Xolotl said.

Let them go, I thought. *The desert can take them. And if it doesn't, they'll tell the story.*

"Indeed. Fear goes a long way to keeping a certain type of villain in line."

Asim paced to his left then back. It was obvious he was a ball of anxiety with legs. It was difficult to imagine what I would feel like if I had a sister and this happened to her.

"I know someone," Asim said. "They are from my village but moved to Dongola to open a bar."

"A bar?" I asked, curious.

"Yes. While many here do not consume alcohol for religious reasons, there are still many who do."

"My kind of guy," Vero said.

"Girl. It is a girl, well, a woman. We were friends. But I haven't seen her in two years."

I glanced over at Vero with a knowing expression. I didn't say anything, not yet, but from how Asim sounded when he talked about this bar owner, it seemed like maybe there was more to these two than he was letting on.

"My kind of girl then," Vero corrected.

While Asim's contact could prove useful once we arrived in Dongola, there was also the possibility that we were already too late.

"Time is critical," I said. "We need to get to Dongola as soon as possible, find out who the buyer is, and where the transaction is going to take place."

"We'll need to fuel up the truck before we go anywhere," Vero said. "We have more than enough to get back to the village, but I'm not sure about getting to Dongola."

On top of that, the mission to find the Apedemak Medallion still loomed over us. I felt like that was also on a timer and that if we abandoned it to go to Dongola, we might not find it before someone else did.

"There is a fuel tank on the other side of the camp," Asim said. "They use it for their patrol trucks."

"That's convenient," I thought out loud. "So let's get moving. The sooner we can get out of here, the sooner we can find your sister and the others."

CHAPTER 28

We drove into Dongola under the cover of darkness, which was broken only by our headlights and the occasional flicker of light from the town ahead. If not for the air conditioning in the SUV, the journey would have been abysmal with the three of us dirty and sweaty from the battle at the ruins.

I rolled down my window as we entered the outskirts of town, where the paved road gave way to a rutted dirt track. The air here was still warm and thick with humidity, a surprising change from the dry, chilly desert from before.

Our old SUV bounced and jolted, the suspension groaning in protest. The headlights raked across half-finished buildings and piles of rubble, casting long, eerie shadows. The smell hit me first—a mix of dust, rotting garbage, and something acrid I couldn't quite place. I immediately regretted rolling down the window and turned the hand crank quickly to block out the odors, though I knew that was probably too late.

The darkness was nearly complete, broken only by a few dim streetlights that buzzed and flickered, barely illuminating the road.

These were even fewer and farther between on the dirt side streets that extended out in both directions. Mounds of dirt decorated a few front "yards" as though they were being kept there to repave in case the avenues washed away in a rare monsoon.

Most of the town seemed to be without electricity, even though rickety power poles and electrical lines ran along the streets. Here and there, the warm glow of kerosene lamps seeped through cracks in shuttered windows, hinting at life inside the colorful homes that lined the street.

We slowed to a crawl, careful to avoid a few deep potholes that pockmarked the road. In the beam of our headlights, I saw a pack of emaciated dogs scavenging through a pile of trash. They scattered as we approached, their ribs clearly visible beneath mangy fur.

The town was quieter than I had expected. Not that I'd anticipated a bunch of parties. Still, even in this place that civilization seemed to have forgotten, it was strange to hear no TVs blaring, no music playing, no signs of traffic—just the low murmur of voices carried on the still night air, punctuated by the occasional cry of a baby or bark of a dog. Somewhere in the distance, a generator chugged away, its drone a constant backdrop to the night sounds.

As we neared what seemed to be the town center, a few people were still out on the streets. Men in long, loose robes sat on plastic chairs outside a small shop, the glow of their cigarettes pinpoints of orange light in the darkness. They watched our car pass with mild curiosity, their conversation pausing briefly.

The headlights swept across a group of children playing in the dirt by the roadside, their bare feet and ragged clothes indicative of the poverty that gripped the region. They stopped their game to stare at our car, some waving excitedly, others just watching warily as we passed.

"Little past their bedtime, wouldn't you say?" the voice in my head said.

I nodded.

"Her place is just ahead on the right," Asim said, breaking the long-held silence in the cabin.

We pulled over near what looked like a market square, now deserted save for a few stray cats picking through the leavings of the day's trade. The stench of rotting produce and animal dung was strong here, making me gag slightly as I stepped out of the car.

My feet sank slightly into the soft sand of the street, and I could feel the heat of the day still radiating from the ground. The dense humidity, combined with the pungent odors, made it hard to breathe. Mosquitoes immediately began to whine around my head, drawn by our movement and the carbon dioxide we exhaled.

In the dim light of a nearby streetlamp that actually worked, I could make out the shapes of market stalls—rickety wooden structures with corrugated metal roofs. Torn tarps fluttered in the slight breeze, creating an unsettling rustling sound in the quiet night.

As my eyes adjusted to the darkness, I noticed more details of our surroundings. The buildings were a mix of crude mud-brick structures and more modern but poorly maintained concrete blocks, some painted in bright, cheery colors that contrasted with the gloom that hung over the town. Many had unfinished upper stories, with rusted rebar sticking out from the tops like strange metallic plants.

A public water pump stood in the corner of the square, surrounded by a muddy patch of ground. Even at this late hour, a few women were gathered there, filling large plastic containers with water to carry home. The creak and splash of the pump carried clearly in the still night air.

As we stood there, taking in the scene, a man approached us. He was thin to the point of gauntness, his clothes hanging loosely on his frame. He spoke rapidly in Arabic, gesturing toward our car and then down the street. I shook my head, not understanding most of it, and he switched to broken English, offering to guide us to a place to stay for the night.

Asim took over. He stepped forward and spoke rapidly to the man, pointing in a few directions.

The stranger seemed to accept whatever Asim said and ambled away down the street to bother some other passerby.

"What did you tell him?" Vero asked.

"I told him you two were monsters, and that he should run away before you changed."

"And he believed it?" I wondered, looking after the guy as he disappeared around a corner.

"People around here can be superstitious," Asim explained.

I was surprised the stranger hadn't asked why he was with us, but apparently some of the folks around here were a touch simpler than most.

"This way," Asim said, motioning toward a concrete building up ahead to the right. Graffiti in bright, fluid colors adorned the walls. Some of the artwork was genuinely good, painted by young hands with spray paint and a vision for beautiful scenery. Some was nothing more than a word or two staking their claim to the wall.

As we followed Asim down the street, the sounds of the town settling for the night surrounded us. Another baby cried somewhere nearby, quickly shushed by its mother. The call to prayer echoed faintly from a distant mosque.

"A little late for that too," Xolotl said.

Underneath it all was the constant hum of insects, a reminder of the unseen life teeming in the darkness around us.

Dongola at night was a town of shadows and survival, far removed from the comforts we'd left behind a few days before. As we picked our way carefully along the darkened street, I couldn't help but wonder what the light of day would reveal. Or if I even wanted to be around for that. It probably looked like Brooklyn in the 1970s—a wasteland. I didn't need to see that.

Asim led us to the entrance of the cantina, where a black sign hung out over the doorway. It read, Urdu Outpost.

I knew the name *Urdu* from my quick research into the region. Urdu was one of the other names for Dongola.

The area had a fascinating history in its own right. Along with ancient ruins from the early days of Egypt through the Roman Period, the land had played a significant role in several major battles that most world history classes skipped over.

The current location of the town was actually called New Dongola. The place known as Old Dongola was an abandoned medieval town about two hours south, and on the other side of the Nile.

That spot had initially been built as a fortress and grew into a village, then a town. Time, however, rendered the location unsustainable and basically useless, until everyone had relocated.

Asim paused at the wooden door, hesitating to open it.

"What's wrong?" I asked. "Religious restrictions?"

"No. I am not Muslim."

I knew what he referred to. Part of my research into Dongola, and Sudan in general, was their cultural customs. Alcohol had been legalized in Sudan for all non-Muslims. But it remained illegal for Muslims to the point that it was also against the law for a non-Muslim to drink with a Muslim.

I wasn't sure how they policed that, but I guessed places like this one that were openly bars, were probably watched by the local authorities.

"I just haven't seen her in a long time," Asim said.

Someone laughed out loud inside the building. Light snuck out through the closed shutters covering the windows, but other than that I couldn't see anything within.

"It'll be fine," I reassured him. There was no way I could know that. Maybe Asim and his friend had a big falling out before, one of those hard-to-forgive situations. But if I had to guess, I'd say he had feelings for her, and they were either not reciprocated or she simply chose a new life over living in that forsaken village in the middle of the desert.

Not that Dongola was a huge upgrade, but it was perched on the edge of the Nile, so at least there was a dependable water source nearby. Maybe a chance for a boat day now and then.

Asim swallowed back his apprehension and pulled the door open.

Immediately, a cloud of cigarette and cigar smoke wafted out of the cantina, billowing up into the night.

"Ah, I miss the old days where people could smoke indoors."

"Really?" Vero asked, looking at me like I was nuts.

"No. Not really."

She chuckled as Asim entered the building. We followed behind him into what I could only describe as the perfect adventurer's saloon.

It was like something out of one of my favorite archaeological thriller movies. Old pictures of explorers hung from the walls, along with images of antiquated cargo planes—pilots standing next to some—weathered maps, rugged netting draped in the corners, antique chests propped up in various places along the walls, and round, wooden tables in the main area.

The bar counter was made from steel and looked like it had been here since the building was constructed. No idea how long ago that was. Beneath the counter, the façade was made of faded wood, though I couldn't tell which kind, and because we were in the desert without a ton of trees other than palms, I couldn't even venture a guess other than it was imported way back when.

Four black chandeliers provided dim light from faux candles, and black sconces along the walls added their own modest glow.

Behind the bar, a young woman—I guessed about Asim's age—busily rinsed glasses and set them in a plastic tray to be washed later.

Asim paused, but I nudged him forward. I didn't care to be noticed by the six patrons sitting around the room.

Only one sat at the bar—an old guy with long gray hair, a brown leather bomber jacket, and faded blue jeans—hunched over his drink.

The door closed loudly behind us, and everyone except the guy at the bar looked up from their conversations at the newcomers.

They weren't exactly the friendliest lot, and I got the feeling some of the guys in here were available for hire for less-than-legal jobs, which was on brand—the joint reeked of being a smuggler, mercenary den.

"Keep moving," I whispered to Asim, who still seemed to struggle to make his legs move.

I took the lead and made my way between two rows of tables until I reached the bar. I found three stools a couple down from the old guy, and pulled one out for Vero.

She smiled and thanked me, sitting down to my right. I sat in the middle while Asim reluctantly took the stool on the left.

No sooner had he sat down than the bartender turned and faced us.

She moved with quiet grace behind the worn metal counter, her dark eyes alert and watchful. She couldn't have been more than twenty-three, but there was a weariness in her gaze that spoke of a life lived hard and fast. Her skin was the color of burnished copper, smooth save for a thin scar that traced her jawline, a reminder of some past struggle.

Her hair was pulled back in a series of intricate braids, revealing high cheekbones and full lips that probably rarely smiled, but longed to. If she did smile, it was a fleeting thing, gone almost before you noticed it, like a mirage in the desert.

She wore a long colorful skirt that swished softly as she moved, paired with a simple white blouse. A delicate silver necklace glinted at her throat, incongruous with the harshness of her surroundings. Her hands, strong yet supple, spoke of a life of labor that belied her beauty.

There was an air of resigned determination about her, as if she'd seen too much to be surprised by anything anymore. Yet beneath that hard-earned toughness, a spark of intelligence and curiosity seemed to linger in her eyes, hinting at dreams not yet extinguished by the harsh realities of life in Sudan.

She gave off the impression that no one should mess with her, and if they did, they'd be sorry.

Her eyes swept across our faces, and for a second, it seemed we were just three new patrons here for a drink, probably about to head out for a tour to the nearby ruins, or perhaps to Old Dongola.

Then she did a double take, snapping her focus back to Asim.

"Asim?" she said, leaning closer toward him to get a better look.

"Yes, Magali. It's me."

She smiled from ear to ear. "What are you doing here?"

It seemed she wanted to embrace him, but the counter separated them, and neither made a move to get around it.

"We need help," Asim answered, cutting straight to the point. "My sister was taken by Adisa. She and the others he took from our village have been brought here to Dongola. We need to find out where they are."

The smile on her face melted to a look of deep concern. She crossed her arms and glanced at me and Vero.

"That's a dangerous thing to ask about," Magali said. "Adisa has eyes and ears everywhere in this region. Including here in Dongola."

"But not in your bar, right?" I asked.

She looked at me without answering, so I continued. "Hi. I'm Gideon. This is Vero." I nodded at my girlfriend. "Any information you could give us would be greatly appreciated."

Magali turned away and picked up three empty glasses near the beer tap. She poured until the three pint glasses were nearly full to the rim with a thick, foamy head and an amber body. Then she placed the beers down in front of us and nodded.

"First we drink. Then we talk."

"Where's yours?" I asked.

She flipped up a bottle of Jack Daniel's, twisted it in midair, then started pouring the whiskey into a glass sitting at her waist near the ice bin. She filled it halfway then returned the bottle to its station with a flourish.

"I don't do beer," she said. "I'm a whiskey girl."

I nodded. "I admire that," I said. "What are we toasting to?"

"Not what," Magali corrected. "Who."

I frowned, not understanding.

The bartender looked over at the old man sitting hunched over three glasses. One was a half-empty pint glass; the other two were empty tumblers.

"To him," she said.

CHAPTER 29

I didn't understand.

"Sorry, who's that?"

"The name is Starnes," the man answered in a gruff tone. His accent was Southern, but I couldn't place which state.

"Okay," Vero said, raising a glass. "To Starnes."

Asim reluctantly raised his beer with the rest of us, but he kept his eyes on Magali, who was carefully watching the old man.

"Don't toast to me," Starnes ordered. "I didn't say I was going to help you. You're crazy if you think you can get those people back from Kofi Adisa." He raised his beer to his lips and took a sip, then set the glass back down. "They're as good as gone."

Asim barely touched his drink. "Can you help us or not? I am not going to give up on getting my sister back."

Starnes nodded. "Yeah, well, if that's the case, I hope you're prepared to die trying."

"I am." Asim didn't hesitate to say it.

The old man shook his head, looking down into his drink.

"Please, sir," Asim continued. "If there is something you know that can help us, tell us."

"You're always so stubborn," Magali said to Starnes. "It's not your problem if they die trying to get his sister back. I know you know something. You know everything that goes on in this town."

"It's my business to know," Starnes replied. "Helps me stay away from trouble. Helps me stay alive."

Magali lowered her voice to a conspiratorial tone. "Starnes here is a smuggler. You want something, almost anything; he can get it."

The old man looked up from his drink, peering at her as though he wished she hadn't said any of that.

"Don't give me that look," she said. "Your profession isn't as big a secret as you'd like it to be."

"Secret enough for Adisa to leave me alone."

"True. But how much longer do you think that will last? He comes into town more and more often, recruiting more to his side, terrorizing the people."

"You seem to be doing just fine," he argued.

"I know how to stay out of trouble." Magali shifted uncomfortably, and for a second, her eyes met Asim's again. "But I'm not immune. You know that."

"Yeah, I know."

I had to reenter the conversation. "What do you mean, you're not immune?" I hoped nothing horrific had happened to her, because if it had, I just ripped the scab off.

"Now and then, he comes here with some of his men to drink. Usually, they don't cause too much trouble. Now and then, though, they start something with another customer. It always ends the same. They're bullies. They gang up on a single person and beat them until they're unconscious. One nearly died."

"But he has done nothing to you, right?" Asim asked, his voice brimming with desperate concern.

"No," she said, her tone bashful. "I know he would like to. But no, he has left me alone, except for forcing me to give him and his men free drinks when they come by."

Asim turned to the old American. "Mr. Starnes. If you know

anything, anything at all about where my sister might be, please, tell us."

Starnes tipped the glass back and finished his beer. He set the glass down hard on the counter with a thud as he exhaled. He twisted his head slowly until he faced Asim.

"If you want to get yourselves killed, that's no problem for me. I just don't like sending people to early graves."

I grinned. "We'll be all right."

"You think so? Because from what I hear, it isn't just Kofi Adisa and his crew of bandits you're going to have to deal with. They're doing a deal with a group from China at midnight, down by the river. So, you'll have double the trouble."

"What can you tell us about the Chinese?" Vero pressed.

Starnes shrugged. "Not much. I know they brought weapons with them. Part of the deal they brokered with Adisa. They've been supplying them for over a year now. I hear Adisa keeps a weapons cache at his little compound in the desert."

"Yeah," I said, resisting a coy grin, "he doesn't have those anymore. And most of his men are dead."

Starnes frowned at the statement. "What are you talking about?"

I inclined my head slightly. There was no way I could give up all the goods with this guy. One, I didn't know if I could fully trust him. Maybe Magali had bad judgment. And two, revealing my alter ego would probably freak him out more than anything else. Not to mention Magali. That was the kind of thing you had to ease people into. Although I guessed there was no way to ease someone into that.

Hey, by the way, check this out. I can shape-shift into a terrifying monster. Cool right?

I decided a more clandestine approach was probably best.

"Word is his compound was attacked earlier. Almost no survivors."

Starnes chuffed. "That would make things interesting. Where'd you hear that?"

I shrugged. "I have sources."

He peered at me, clearly trying to assess if I was full of crap or not.

"He has a small army. It would take a massive assault force to do what you're saying."

The assessment wasn't wrong. It really would have taken a large force—under normal circumstances. But normal had taken the last train to Clarksville a long time ago. And yes, I liked The Monkees.

"Nevertheless, we're going to stop Adisa. Can you tell us exactly where this deal is going down or not?"

Starnes kept looking at me like I was a few bottles short of a six-pack. "You three? That's it?"

"Let's just say we have an unusual set of skills."

He snorted derisively. "Sure. I can tell you where it is. People die every day doing stupid stuff. Why should you three be any different?"

I appreciated his callous honesty. I'd already noticed the man didn't have any red mist hovering around him. So that told me all I needed to know. Scoundrel? Probably. Done some bad things in his life? Who hadn't? But he wasn't evil. That I could trust.

"That's no way to talk to my guests," Magali said.

"Just telling the truth," Starnes replied, casting her a wayward glance. "There'll be at least two dozen Chinese at the rendezvous. You can count on that. Plus, however many Adisa brought. I heard his caravan pulled in just over an hour ago. I'd assume he has at least a few dozen guys with him. So, you're going to be heavily outnumbered."

"I like those odds," I said.

Magali stared at Asim with worry in her eyes. "Are you really going to do this?"

Asim nodded. "It's my sister. We're the only ones who can save her and the others. If we don't stop Adisa, I'll never find her again. She'll disappear forever."

"Yep," Starnes agreed, holding up his empty glass in a silent request for a refill.

Magali ignored him for the moment.

The old American sighed. "There's a port on the river. It isn't used much anymore, except for moving illicit goods... and people. Adisa uses it to get his shipments, usually weapons, opium, that sort of thing. It's easy enough to find. Just head due east from here, and you'll walk right into it. Although I don't advise just walking up to the gate and asking if you can come in. There'll be guards."

"I would expect that. And patrols sweeping the area."

"Yep. The second you show your face, they'll sound the alarm and bring hell down on you."

"Then I guess it would be a good time to employ the oldest tactic in warfare."

He and the others waited for me to say it.

"Divide and conquer. Turn them on each other. These sorts are usually extremely suspicious. They may be doing business, but they won't trust each other. We just have to light that fire."

Starnes thought about it for a moment before responding. "Sure. In a perfect scenario, that could work. But the prisoners could be in danger too."

"Not if Adisa and his men turn on the Chinese. They'll be so focused on each other they won't notice us freeing their captives."

"Again. In a perfect scenario. But hey, go for it. Maybe you'll take a few of them with you. And the less people that scumbag has in his little army, the better."

The front door burst open. All of us turned to see who'd just interrupted the relatively quiet bar.

A man stood in the doorway, a rifle hanging from his shoulder. He breathed hard like he'd just run a mile or three. Sweat stained his tunic, adding to the overall grimy appearance of his skin and beard. His eyes were full of fear, or desperation, or both.

"No guns allowed in here," Magali said.

The guy ignored her and stalked over to the bar. He found an empty seat a few spots down to Starnes' left and sat down.

The old American turned his head to face the man. "Did you not hear what the lady said, amigo? No guns in here."

I'd already noticed the sidearm tucked away in a shoulder holster within the American's jacket. But I figured Magali gave him a pass, maybe because he was a regular, or maybe because she knew it wasn't worth the fight.

The newcomer stared straight ahead, ignoring the comment.

His breath slowed, but he said nothing.

Magali looked at Starnes, then me, then back to the stranger.

She said something to him in a Bedouin dialect I didn't understand, presumably telling him again that his firearm wasn't welcome here.

He looked up, his eyes moving from her, to Starnes, then down at his rifle.

What none of the others noticed, except for Vero, was the red fog swirling around the guy. It was the first thing I saw when he walked in the door. At first, I just figured he was some crazy local. But then I spotted splotches of blood on his tattered clothing. It was relatively fresh.

One of Adisa's men.

"Brilliant deduction," Xolotl said, laying on the sarcasm thick as sorghum.

"You okay, man?" I asked, not concerned about his well-being in the least. I wanted to get him talking.

The guy shook his head, still staring forward.

"You look like you've seen a ghost," I added, poking the bear.

He snapped his head around and stared into my eyes. For a second, I wondered if he could possibly recognize me, but that was impossible. If he'd been there, he would have only seen the monster.

"They came out of the darkness," he said, lips trembling. He looked at Magali. "Drink."

"You could say please," Starnes interjected.

Magali swallowed and found a bottle of Jim Beam, poured him a short glass, and slid it over to the man.

He gripped it with his right hand, tipped it back, and swallowed the contents. "More," he said, slamming the tumbler back on the counter.

Magali glanced at Starnes and me. I nodded.

She refilled the glass, this time making it a double.

The man raised the drink to his lips again and chugged the whiskey.

This time, he set the glass down more slowly, and visibly calmed.

"Who came out of the darkness?" I asked, already knowing the answer. "Where did you come from?"

"Jebel Barkal," he answered, tipping his hand.

Starnes immediately connected the dots and let his jacket fall open a little wider to give easier access to his hidden pistol.

"Kofi Adisa's compound?"

This snapped the man out of his haze, and he looked over at Starnes with fire in his eyes.

"They killed everyone."

"Not everyone," I corrected. "You're still alive." I was just glad the guy could speak decent English.

He barely acknowledged me before Starnes spoke up again. "Who killed everyone?"

"Demons," he answered and pointed to his empty glass.

Again, Magali glanced at me for confirmation, and I approved with another nod. The looser this guy's lips, the better.

She poured another single. This time, the guy sipped it slower than the first two.

"Demons?" Starnes asked. "That's a first."

The stranger's head whipped around again. "They came from the desert, two... monsters." He struggled to find the word. "We tried to fight them. But our bullets... they... they did nothing to the demons. They cannot die."

Every word flowing from his mouth grew more desperate, more fearful, like he was talking about a real-life boogeyman.

"I think maybe the desert has gotten to this one," Starnes said to Magali with a jerk of the thumb.

"How did you get here from Jebel Barkal?" I asked, cutting through the old American's skepticism.

"I ran from the mountain and waited until the demons left. I saw them leave in a truck."

"What kind of truck?"

"I don't know. I only saw the lights. I waited, then I took one of our trucks and drove away as fast as I could."

"If you drove here, why are you so out of breath?" Starnes asked with a chuckle.

The terrorist turned and raised his rifle, pointing it at the older man.

"You think this is funny, American? I know what I saw."

The other patrons in the bar watched with intense interest, but were now carefully leaving their seats and making their way toward the exit.

Starnes remained stoic, starting down at his empty glass.

The man had ice running through his veins, at least from my view. The gun pointed at him didn't seem to faze him in the least. It made me wonder how many times he'd been in that position. I guessed several because he was a smuggler, though what goods he moved from place to place, I had no idea.

"Put the gun down, son," Starnes said, his voice cool like the other side of the pillow.

The gunman didn't comply.

"They were real," he said. "I know what I saw."

"I believe you," I cut in, stepping away from my barstool.

The gunman tore his gaze from Starnes and focused it, and his weapon, on me.

"Don't move," he snapped. "I will kill you right here."

I sensed Vero just behind me, probably thinking the same thing as me.

"You're going to kill this guy, right?" Xolotl asked. "Because between you and me, he's got it coming."

I agreed silently and took a cautious step toward the gunman. If he was going to fire that weapon, I didn't want the bullet accidentally hitting one of the other people in here. I didn't want it to hit me either, but at least I wouldn't die from it.

"Stop right there!" the gunman ordered, retreating a step. "I've killed people."

"I know," I said. "You have the mark on you."

The statement puzzled him, and he took another step back.

I held out my hands, an unspoken request for him to hand me the weapon.

"You don't have to do this," I continued, passing Starnes and putting my body between his and the crazed gunman.

The men near the door paused for a second. Then one of them reached out and pushed it open. The hinges creaked, startling the terrorist.

He turned his head to see what was happening, and I took a big step toward him. He saw the movement and instinctively pulled the trigger.

The room shook from the deafening report of the rifle. My ears rang first. Then I felt the familiar pain from where the bullet hit me in the chest.

I winced, doubling over for a second.

"No!" Magali shouted.

The gunman twisted to aim the gun at her, a reaction born of fear and uncertainty.

Then I shifted into the monster, towering over him within seconds.

His focus switched back to me, and his eyelids widened.

"Demon," he muttered.

I ripped the gun from his grip, jerking him toward me in the same move.

He stumbled forward and I caught him with my furry, clawed left paw, wrapping my fingers around his neck.

I squeezed, feeling his throat tighten in my grasp. "You're going to help us get into the port where your boss is doing this deal. Understand?"

He shook his head. Well, tried. I was holding his neck pretty tight.

"I'll say it again, then. We are going to break up Adisa's little deal tonight. And you're going to help us. Or I'm going to rip your body apart one limb at a time. You saw what we did to your friends back at the ruins. So, you know I mean every word."

The man attempted to nod, but all he could manage was a few twitches of his head up and down.

"Good," I said. I held on for a few more seconds, watching his eyes bulge. Then I released him and shoved him down to the floor.

I shifted back to my human form and took a deep breath. The wound in my chest had already started to heal.

The stranger coughed, desperately trying to fill his lungs with air.

I turned toward Magali and found both her and Starnes staring at me in disbelief. The old American had drawn his pistol and now held it firmly pointed at the guy on the floor.

"You heard someone took out Adisa's men, huh?" the old American asked.

"Something like that."

Confusion and disbelief was written all over his face.

"Look," I added, "I wasn't trying to lie. It's just that—"

"There are real-life monsters roaming around, and you thought telling me that you were one of them wouldn't help out your mission?"

"Something like that."

Starnes twisted his head and looked at Magali. "You know what? I think I'll pass on that next beer. I've probably had enough for one evening."

"I know. It's a lot to take in."

"How? Why? What are you?"

"I'm a person, just like you. So is she," I pointed at Vero.

"She can do that too?" Starnes' and Magali's jaws might as well have had brooms attached to them to sweep the floor.

"Short story, these medallions give us that ability. Along with incredible strength. Our job is to eliminate guys like Adisa. To take out the trash the world governments won't, to put it another way."

Starnes laughed. "No money in taking out regional warlords. That's all the governments care about."

"True. So now you see what happened at Adisa's compound. That's how we were able to take them down."

"And we inadvertently destroyed most of their weapons too," Vero added.

Starnes holstered his pistol and crossed his arms. "So now you're here to rescue this guy's sister, and kill Kofi Adisa."

"Yes. And we can do that a lot quicker if you'll show us the way."

The old American inclined his chin, peering across his nose at me. "All right. I'll take you to the port. Not sure what your plan is for this one, though. If you ask me, he's a loose end you might as well cut right now."

I looked over at the cowering man on the floor. I couldn't tell if he'd pissed himself or was just sweaty.

"I have a plan for him. Just get us to the port. We can take it from there."

CHAPTER 30

J ust as Starnes said, the port near the river was due east from the cantina. The street ran straight into it.

We killed the lights two blocks up, per Starnes' suggestion, and then parked along the edge of the street in front of an empty lot between two derelict buildings.

The old port sat on the banks of the Nile, a dark and forgotten place on the outskirts of Dongola, itself a dark and forgotten town. In the pale moonlight, the port's abandoned structures threw long shadows across the dusty ground. The air was thick with the smell of the river—a mix of mud, rotting vegetation, and fish.

A rusty chain-link fence surrounded the entire area, stretching as far as the eye could see in both directions along the riverbank. The fence swayed slightly in the night breeze, the metal links clinking softly against each other. In places, the fence had collapsed or been pushed down, creating gaps that had been hastily repaired with strips of barbed wire.

The main gate was a patchwork of welded metal and more chain-link, barely hanging on its hinges. Two men stood guard, their forms bulky with body armor and weapons. They were alert, eyes scanning the darkness beyond the fence, hands never far from their rifles. The weak light from a single bulb above the gate cast their faces in harsh shadow, making them look more like creatures of the night than men.

Beyond the gate, the port spread out in a maze of crumbling concrete and rusted metal. Old cargo containers were stacked haphazardly, creating narrow alleys and hidden corners. Many of the containers had been pried open, their contents long since looted. Now they served as makeshift shelters, judging by the dim glow of fires visible through some of the gaps.

The wharf itself was in a state of decay. Wooden planks, warped and rotting from years of exposure to the elements, creaked and groaned with every slight movement of the water. Several small fishing boats were tied up, bobbing gently in the current. Their peeling paint and frayed ropes spoke of years of neglect.

A large warehouse dominated the center of the port. Its metal roof was partially caved in, creating a jagged skyline against the star-filled sky. The walls were covered in graffiti, a mix of Arabic script and crude drawings. Most of the windows were broken, the remaining glass glinting dangerously in the moonlight.

Parked in front of the warehouse were a dozen military-style trucks. Their drab beige paint was chipped and faded, but they looked well maintained and ready for action. The trucks were arranged in a loose semicircle, their front ends pointing outward as if ready to drive off at a moment's notice.

Contrasting sharply with the rugged trucks were ten high-end SUVs. Their sleek black bodies reflected the moonlight, the chrome details gleaming. These were clearly new vehicles, their presence incongruous in the run-down port. Mercedes G-Wagons composed the majority, their boxy shapes unmistakable even in the dim light.

Deeper into the port, more armed guards patrolled in pairs. They moved with purpose, their paths crisscrossing the open areas between buildings and stacks of containers. Each pair kept a careful distance from the others, ensuring maximum coverage of the area.

Their footsteps crunched on the gravel and broken concrete, a constant reminder of their vigilance.

The Nile flowed silently past the port, its surface a dark mirror reflecting the night sky. The water lapped gently against the wharf and the hulls of the moored boats, creating a constant, soothing background noise. Occasionally, the splash of a fish or the call of a night bird would break the relative quiet.

Toward the river's edge, old loading cranes stood like silent sentinels. Their once-bright paint was now faded and peeling, streaked with rust illuminated by the moonlight. Thick cables hung limply from their arms, swaying slightly in the breeze. These machines, once the lifeblood of the port, now served only as perches for the occasional bird.

The moonlight cast everything in a silvery glow, softening the harsh edges of decay but also deepening the shadows. It created an eerie landscape of light and dark where shapes seemed to shift and move when viewed from the corner of the eye.

Near one edge of the port, a small office building hunched low to the ground. Unlike the other structures, this one showed signs of recent use. Light spilled from its windows, and the hum of a generator could be heard nearby. Shadows moved across the blinds, suggesting activity inside.

The entire port had an air of tension about it. Despite the late hour, there was a sense of alertness, of waiting. The guards' movements, the idling engines of some of the vehicles, the lights in the office—all hinted at some imminent action.

From outside the fence, the port appeared to be a hub of clandestine activity. The contrast between the old, decaying infrastructure and the new, high-end vehicles was stark. It spoke of a place caught between its past and some new, potentially dangerous future.

Here in the port, it was eerily quiet save for the patrols and the river. It was as if this place existed in its own bubble, separated from the world around it by more than just a fence.

"This is where we part ways," Starnes said from the back seat. "I don't want the kind of trouble you three are looking for."

"Are you going to walk back?" Vero asked, her question laced with guilt.

"Well, I'm not taking your ride. Besides, it's less than a ten-minute walk from here. I'll be fine. No one messes with me in this town. Probably because they think I'm just a broke, old has-been."

I sensed he played that role on purpose, but there was more to Starnes beneath the rough, devil-may-care exterior.

"Thanks for getting us here," I said. "I guess we really could have found it on our own."

"Better safe than sorry, I suppose. Good luck. Although based on what I saw back at the bar, I don't think you'll have much trouble taking out the bad guys. Protecting the prisoners, though; that's a different matter."

Starnes opened the back door and stepped out onto what passed for a sidewalk—a beaten dirt pathway that led from the street corner back down the way we had come.

He eased the door shut and without a goodbye, walked away.

I watched him for a minute until he disappeared in the shadows a block from our position.

"He is an interesting person," Asim noticed.

"Very."

"I wonder what his backstory is," Vero said.

I'd considered the same thing, but I had a feeling if we were going to ever find out more about the enigma named Starnes, we'd have to get the info from someone else. He struck me as the type to keep his secrets buried deep within, locked in a vault with no key.

Peering through the windshield, I watched the guards at the gate. They barely moved, except turning their heads and occasionally speaking to each other. They hung onto their rifles in a casual but ready manner—definitely not military trained. Not that I would have expected that. These weren't the usual mercenaries who'd left the military to pursue a life in private security. These men were either zealots who rallied to Adisa's so-called cause, whatever that was, or they'd been captured as young men and brainwashed into service.

I was fifty-fifty on which it might be.

The next patrol sauntered by inside the fence. One of the men said something to the gate guards, and the four laughed as the patrol continued past and into the shadows of the corner to our right.

I heard movement in the cargo area of the truck and remembered our prisoner. We'd zip-tied his wrists and slapped a strip of duct tape over his mouth to keep him quiet. He'd moaned a little, made some other noises, but eventually shut up—probably from exhaustion. After all, he'd had a long night.

I stepped out of the truck and walked around to the back. Vero and Asim joined me, and I opened the back door.

The man was curled up in a fetal position with his hands behind his back.

"Now," I began, "I can't trust you enough to take the duct tape off your mouth. Or the zip ties off your wrists. You might do or say something stupid."

The man stared at me with the same horror he'd felt back in the cantina.

"So, you're going to walk over there to that gate. The guards are going to wonder who you are, and what you're doing there. You won't be able to answer right away. You know, because of the tape on your mouth. If they don't shoot you on sight, they'll take the tape off. That's when you tell them what happened at the compound, and that the monsters who took out Adisa's men are right here, in this truck, waiting to attack."

Surprise streaked the man's eyes, narrowing them slightly.

It was obvious he didn't understand why I would want him to give away our position and our intention. For all he knew, we were going to use the element of surprise, and if he followed my instructions that would be thrown out the window.

"Do you understand?" I asked.

He nodded, probably out of sheer desperation to get out of the back of the truck.

"Good."

I pulled on his ankles and dragged him out until his feet touched the ground.

He looked at me with uncertainty oozing from his eyes. The guy probably thought the second I let him take a step away I'd turn into the beast and kill him on the spot.

I ushered him around the back of the vehicle then nudged him forward.

He took a few reluctant steps before looking back over his shoulder, probably expecting to see the monster from before.

I waved at him with a fake, crap-eating grin on my face. "That's it. Shoo. Go. Fly free, little birdie."

He shuffled forward then walked faster, picking up his speed to a brisk pace.

I gently closed the back of the truck and turned to Asim. "Take the truck back around that corner and down to the other end of the street. Then make a left and get into position near the southwest corner of the port."

Asim nodded, accepting my orders without question.

"We'll stay in the shadows over in this cluster of trees and shrubs." I pointed to the gap between abandoned homes where nature had taken over. "He'll be more than happy to tell his comrades where we are so they can come have a look."

"But the truck will be gone, and they'll think he's lying or insane," Vero said.

"Yep. Either way is fine. I just want to draw the guards out from the gate."

"That will cause suspicion from the next patrol," Asim said.

"Exactly. And we're going to play off that."

Our bait passed the corner of the street and kept walking toward the port.

"Time to go. Don't start the engine until you're out of sight."

Asim nodded, though I could tell he was wondering how he'd move the truck at all without starting the motor.

"We'll push you," I said with a grin at Vero.

Asim climbed into the driver's seat, turned the key to unlock the wheel, and waited as Vero and I leaned into the hood.

With our strength, pushing the heavy truck was as simple as moving a child's Power Wheels car.

Within fifteen seconds, the truck was around the corner and out of the line of sight to the port gate.

We kept it rolling for a few more seconds then let go.

I waved at Asim before Vero and I hurried back around the corner to watch our bait.

The man slowed down as he passed the last corner across from the port. I could only figure that he thought someone approaching the gate quickly might cause the guards to shoot first and ask questions later.

The glow of the twin lights hanging above the gate reached the man, which meant there was no way the guards didn't see him.

As expected, both gunmen raised their weapons, dumping their nonchalant stances in exchange for a high alert attitude.

They were saying something to our bait guy, but we were too far away to hear in detail. With our heightened hearing abilities, I could detect syllables and sounds, but nothing specific.

"Come on," I said to Vero.

She followed me into the brush and over to the edge of the building closest to the port. There, we peeked around the corner, concealed by shadows, and watched as our bait continued to approach the two gunmen.

It probably didn't help him that his hands were tied behind his back. The guards were probably telling him to put his hands up over his head, which was impossible unless he had some kind of weird joint problem.

The guy got down on his knees about thirty feet from the two guards. As they approached him, both keeping their weapons trained on him as they drew near.

One of the gunmen stepped close and knelt down, checking the zip ties binding the man's wrists. He looked up at the other, probably questioning what he should do or why this guy was bound.

They dragged him up and continued speaking. The guards appeared angry, and we could hear their voices as they shouted, demanding answers.

I wondered if our bait would do what he was told. I really only gave it about a 30 percent chance he'd obey my orders and direct the guards to where the truck had been parked a few moments ago.

It was far more likely he'd try to explain what happened at Adisa's compound, the attack by terrifying monsters, and how he'd narrowly escaped only to be found by one of the beasts who sent him here.

The guards, of course, wouldn't believe the story. Which would then, logically, bring our bait man back to his original orders— sending the two guards our way to prove it.

In theory.

In reality, they might just shoot him dead right there on the spot and return to their usual duties. If that happened, we'd just have to be a little more direct with our approach. I hoped to avoid that because doing so could put the prisoners at risk.

We watched for several more seconds until the two guards glanced at each other as if wondering if they should check it out or not.

Then the one on the left nodded, and the other guard plus our bait guy started walking toward us, while the remaining guard returned to his post.

"Only one of them is coming," Vero whispered.

"Yeah. I didn't think about that possibility. They're playing it safe. Never leave your post abandoned."

"What do we do?"

I retreated back into the shadows.

"We stick to the plan. Pull those two into the brush here, and eliminate them. The other guy will start to wonder what's going on. He'll have to check."

"Or call for backup"

She had a point.

"Yeah. That could happen. I guess we'll cross that bridge when we get to it."

We hid behind a stand of four palm trees, skirted by a collection of dense shrubs and tall grass.

It was really amazing how much life the Nile river provided to the land surrounding its banks. I hadn't seen much flora since we'd arrived in Sudan, and it felt good to be around plants again—I came from the state of Tennessee where we had tons of forests and plant life.

I breathed steadily as we waited behind the tree trunks, crouching low to peek through the long strands of grass and the foliage of the shrubbery.

Two minutes passed before the men appeared around the corner of the abandoned house to my right.

The gunman stood behind the bait, keeping his rifle leveled at the man's back. Apparently, they didn't know each other even though they were on the same team. That wasn't all that surprising. Adisa ran a big operation. How many kids did you not know when you were in high school?

"Where are they?" the guard demanded.

"They were here. I swear. They were right here. The truck..." The bait spun around in all directions, which caused the guard to tense, raising his rifle.

"You're lying. I knew you were lying."

"No. Please. This is where they were."

"Yes. These monsters you talked about. I should shoot you right here."

Time to set the trap.

I reached out and grabbed the nearest shrub in front of me and shook it. The branches and leaves rustled loud enough for the two men on the edge of the street to hear.

As anticipated, they both twisted our direction to see what had caused the noise.

"What was that?" the guard asked.

"I told you. They're—"

"Do not say monsters again. Do you understand?"

His captive nodded, but through the undergrowth, I saw the fear in his eyes.

"It is probably just an animal," the guard reasoned. "A stray dog. Many of those here in Dongola. Come. We will see what Kofi says we should do with you."

"Kofi?"

"Yes. I doubt he will be as understanding as I have been."

"But you have to—"

I shook the bush again. Vero followed suit, rustling the tall grass near her.

The men snapped to attention again, and this time, the guard took a wary step forward. He swept the gun toward us, easing it from left to right in case something jumped out at him.

"Don't move," the guard ordered his charge. "If it's a dog, it won't bother us anymore."

He took another step forward, his eyes peering into the vegetation to spot the cause of the noise.

CHAPTER 31

It would only be a matter of seconds before he spotted us. Even in the dark, the moonlight would give us away when he got close enough.

Still, we had to wait for the perfect time.

Unfortunately, the bait started backing away, turning to walk back down the street toward the cantina.

I couldn't worry about him. Not now.

The guard moved closer. Tall grass brushed against his pants as he continued deeper into the shadows. Red fog swirled around him, begging me to render judgment upon him.

"You thinking one more step?" Xolotl asked. "Because I would have already jumped the guy."

I stayed silent and waited. To spite my invisible friend, I waited two steps.

Then I summoned his power and shifted into the beast.

I imagine the first thing the guard saw in the shadows of the undergrowth was the red glow of my eyes a split second before I rose from the darkness to tower over him.

He took an involuntary step back and tripped on a rock or a root.

The man fell backward, landing so hard on the ground that the jolt twitched his trigger finger. The rifle boomed, firing a round impotently into the night sky.

I moved in a blur, so quickly that he couldn't even lower his weapon toward me before I tore it from his hands.

"I really wish you hadn't done that," I snarled.

I opened my jaws and snapped down onto his neck, twisted, then pulled.

I still wasn't into the taste of blood. But there was no denying how it seemed to feed the power rushing through me.

I dropped the soon-to-be-dead man down to the ground to let him bleed out and for the mist to consume. I looked into the street, focusing on the bait. He'd already started running away, his stride awkward due to having his hands bound behind his back.

"Should I get him?" Vero asked. She held the bow at the ready.

"I think that gunshot probably got the other guard's attention. Give it a second."

We waited, standing over the first guard's body, then heard shouts coming from the direction of the gate.

The other guard was yelling at the bait guy to stop. Then shots rang out from around the corner of the building to our right. We turned and watched as our bait received multiple rounds to the back, dropping him to the ground in midstride.

We ducked back into the shadows, waiting for our next victim.

"Well," I said, "there goes the element of surprise." No doubt multiple patrols were on their way to the gate to find out what was going on.

Nine seconds later, the second guard appeared around the corner. He looked around for a second before noticing the body of his partner slowly disappearing from his clothing.

He touched his radio earpiece and started barking in Arabic. When he was done, he raised his rifle, planting the stock against his shoulder, and took a brave step forward off the street.

He moved quietly, deliberately toward us. Again, I reached out and shook the bush nearest me.

The gunman reacted instantly, firing a flood of bullets around the area. Some of them struck the trees between us and him, but none found their mark. When his weapon fell silent, I stepped out of the shadows once more.

He screamed, touching his earpiece to call for help. The last four rounds spat from his rifle's muzzle, bouncing harmlessly off my armor.

I leaped toward him. He tried to turn and run, but I caught him by the arm and jerked him back.

Vero emerged from the shadows, still carrying the bow in one hand.

The man looked at her then at me, abject terror blazing in his eyes. He was mumbling prayers over and over again. He mentioned Allah several times.

I shook my head and lifted him off the ground, pulling him close so he could feel my breath on his skin as I spoke.

"He's not on your side."

The man trembled as if he was having a spasm, shaking his head, begging me to let him go.

The mist, however, told me not to oblige.

I stepped toward the street, spun around in a circle, letting my arms extend to increase the momentum, then let the man go.

He sailed through the air, his body spinning horizontally as it climbed into the night. His screams faded as he flew higher; at his peak reaching nearly seventy feet up.

Vero and I moved around the corner to see where he would land and to watch the reaction of the men inside the port.

The guard fell from the sky in a dramatic arc until he hit the ground violently about twenty feet from the gate.

Six more gunmen had already run to the entrance and stepped out from the port's interior to find out what had caused the gunfire.

Their reaction to their comrade splatting on the broken asphalt a few yards away from them was borderline hysterical. Maybe hysterical was a little dark. Five of them turned their guns outward, aiming down the street to find whatever or whoever had done this. The last guy stepped over to the dead man's body, I guess to see if he was okay. Which he was not. It probably should have been pretty obvious, but there's always one in every crowd.

The other five immediately pushed out and down the street toward our position. Headlight beams raked across the buildings across from us, casting long shadows of the gunmen along the road and on the façades.

More headlights followed, and a terrible epiphany hit me.

We'd botched the entry, and now everyone inside the port was making a run for it.

"Looks like they're running," Vero said, thinking the same thing.

"Yeah," I agreed. "We can't let them get away."

Angry shouts filled the air, drawing closer by the second. Those sounds were drowned out by the revving of engines.

"What should we do?" Vero asked.

I glanced over at the nearest palm tree, and an idea sprang into my head.

"You ever played baseball?"

She arched an eyebrow, obviously wondering what I had in mind.

I moved quickly over to the tree and wrapped my hulking arms around it. Then I leaned back, pulling on the trunk as hard as I could. I felt it shift a little, but the roots were strong.

Vero saw I was struggling and quickly shifted into the bear to push on the trunk from the other side.

Every second ticked by like a slamming gavel. I felt the tree shudder more, but it was taking too long.

"Step back," I said, releasing the trunk. "Should have tried this first."

Vero moved away, and I produced one of the blades again and flung it at the tree.

The trunk severed four feet off the ground, and fell into the road. It only blocked part of the street, but that wasn't my plan.

The blade returned to me and I caught it, clipped it to my waist, and hefted the huge trunk.

"We're going to swing this at the oncoming vehicles," I said.

Vero understood and lifted a few feet away from me.

We held up the tree, waiting until the first vehicle was just around the corner. "Now!" I barked.

We reared back, and swung the palm hard toward the oncoming traffic.

Our timing was perfect. Just as a black G-Wagon appeared and tried to swerve out of the way, the top of the tree smashed into the grill. Combined with the driver suddenly slamming on the brakes, the SUV's inertia flipped it over onto its top with a violent crunch, effectively blocking off the center of the road.

"Now what?" Vero asked.

"I'll take these guys. Get into the port, and find the prisoners."

She nodded and disappeared through the bushes behind the buildings.

More angry shouts filled the air.

Then the gunmen appeared, their figures silhouetted by the headlight beams.

Two of them turned toward me with their rifles raised, while the other three hurried to the felled tree to move it out of the way.

Four more men appeared to help them, none of them realizing they'd just stepped right into my trap.

I stepped forward like a killer in a horror movie: slow, deliberate, menacing.

The two gunmen opened fire. The bullets bounced off my armor in quick succession as I continued stalking toward them.

The men attempting to move the tree saw me approaching and left their task to assist.

More rounds flew my way, a few catching my flesh.

I ignored the pain and dove to the right, flying through a barri-caded window in the building next to me.

I knew the men would come after me to "finish the job," but they hadn't even begun. Inside the run-down home, I sped across the dusty floor and barged through the boarded back door and out into a dense patch of shrubbery and palm trees separating the property from another home on a parallel street. I cut to the left and skirted through the brush until I reached the next side avenue, then turned left again.

A line of the same SUVs, as well as several trucks I figured were from Adisa's caravan, sat parked in the road, waiting for the tree to be moved. For a brief second, I wondered why they didn't just drive over it. Maybe they were afraid to keep going after what had just happened to the first vehicle.

Just as I reached the corner, one of the SUVs backed up and turned as if the driver meant to detour onto a side street.

I charged toward the vehicle, and before the man behind the wheel could accelerate, I flung the blade in my right hand at the driver. The metal spiral sliced through the windshield, the driver's neck, and out through the back window, taking out the guy in the back seat on that side as well.

Without anyone controlling the brakes, the vehicle idled back-ward until it bumped into the one behind it.

Men spilled out of multiple SUVs. More jumped out of the cargo trucks, all of them armed with guns—some rifles, many with pistols.

They opened fire, sending a wall of bullets my way. I jumped and landed on the other side of the street then reached out my right hand to catch the blade before diving behind another derelict building.

The gunfire continued, but I was too fast.

I sprinted hard, running past the buildings on the last block near the port. When I burst into the open again, I found the end of the line of trucks. The drivers of most had stayed behind the wheel, while their occupants had hit the ground to hunt me down.

But they were all looking at the house I'd gone into up the block as their Chinese comrades and some of their own continued to pour rounds into the crumbling building.

I charged forward at the last cargo truck, catching the eyes of two men on the near side a moment before I snatched them in my claws and slammed them into the side of the truck.

Something in their backs cracked. I assume it was their spines. Their bodies simultaneously went limp, and I dropped them to the street. The driver saw what happened and threw open the door, extending a pistol my way. He managed to get three shots off before I grabbed him by the forearm, jerked him out of the cab, and slammed him down onto the road.

He writhed around, dazed, probably concussed, and definitely in significant pain. But I eased that suffering by shifting my hands into human form, picking up one of the other men's rifles, and putting a round through his head.

The attack drew the attention of everyone else in the line up ahead, which was fine by me.

I raised the rifle and fired, taking out two gunmen before they knew what hit them. Another driver exited his cab and caught a round through the neck as I stalked up the line. More men spilled out of the back of the cargo hold, none of them thinking for second that maybe they should have remained hidden, or perhaps tried to find cover.

I cut them down with the remaining rounds in my magazine and then pressed ahead, dropping that rifle to scoop up another one.

I'd never really been keen on AK-47s. The recoil always seemed to ride up when I'd try them out at a friend's gun range on his farm. But with my additional strength, I found it easier to control and continued picking off enemies as I marched toward the front of the line.

More bullets zipped past me as I reached the second truck, and I ducked in behind it for a second. I stole a glance into the port, checking to see if Vero was in sight, but she was nowhere to be found.

Even with her considerable power, I still worried about Vero. It was natural, I guess, to feel that way about someone you loved.

"You don't have time for that nonsense," Xolotl said. "There are eight guys coming your way."

"You've been quiet for a few minutes," I snapped back at him.

"Seemed like you had things under control. Although I was wondering why you didn't just work your way down from the front of the line until they were all dead."

"I blocked the road."

"Yeah, sort of."

I spun around the corner of the truck and opened fire on four men rushing my way. The spray of bullets tore through them, dropping each one in midstride before they could reply with their weapons.

"You're pretty good with that," the voice in my head noticed.

"Yeah, well, I am from Tennessee."

I dropped the weapon and leaned into the side of the truck, squatting down to get my shoulder under the cargo area. Then I pushed hard with my legs and flipped the truck up and over onto its side. The shouts of the other four attackers snuffed out immediately as they were crushed under the weight of the heavy vehicle.

Now, every guy in the escaping caravan seemed to be charging toward me, guns thundering, bullets cracking past or striking my armor.

The thick air filled with the lingering, bitter smoke of spent powder. Clouds of it hung all around, with no breeze to shift it into the night.

I ducked back behind the flipped-over truck, letting the hordes of gunmen get closer. After waiting for a second, I glanced at the building to my left, turned, took one step, and jumped.

The men approaching the truck opened fire again, but I was too fast. I flew through the night and over the building, landing behind it on my feet at a run. Cutting left, I sprinted hard behind abandoned homes. The air blew through my fur—yes, that was still weird—as the structures and plant life blurred by.

I reached the next street and jumped high again, maintaining my speed as I flew over the side alley and landed again behind a series of worn-down buildings. When I reached the front of the column again, I veered back into the main road and took cover behind the SUV I'd smacked with a tree.

Steam billowed out of the hood and into the night. One of the men inside wasn't moving. The other three had left the vehicle and moved back with the rest to eliminate the threat.

It would have been better for them if they'd just turned around and tried to escape down one of the other thoroughfares, though the driver who'd attempted that had lost his head, so maybe it wasn't a great idea. Then again, every one of them was in a killing lane, and there would be no escape. To make matters worse, the entire group of combined forces were clustered around the truck where I'd been hiding, and moving toward the house I'd jumped over, surrounding the place to try to hem me in.

I really don't like to use clichés. But the old saying about fish in a barrel came to mind. And they were the fish.

"You going to keep running around in circles, or are you going to finish them off?" Xolotl asked.

I sighed. "You know, you can really be a pain sometimes. Of course I'm going to finish them off."

"Well, do it already. We haven't got all night. And we still need to get to Naga."

He was right about that. There was still the journey to Naga, to the ancient hidden temple.

I slipped back up the street, sneaking past the empty vehicles. Every single guy with a gun was focused on the worn-down house.

"You'd think at least a few would watch their rear," the voice said. "How dim are these guys?"

I didn't answer, instead moving quickly back toward the mob until I was nearly within striking distance.

"How you going to do this one?" Xolotl asked. "Spinning blades of fury? Leaping hero slam? Or just tear your way through all of them?"

"Okay, I don't know what a leaping hero slam is, but you're not helping."

"Feels like I—"

"You're not. Just tell me if someone is sneaking up behind me. Okay?"

"Yes, sir. Jeez."

I crouched behind the last G-Wagon in the line and peeked around the corner. The men were closing in around the house.

"Oh," the voice said.

I ducked back down. "What is it now?"

"Nothing. You told me to stop talking."

"First off, I didn't say that. I said just tell me if someone is behind me."

"Well, okay. Then, still nothing."

"You're exasperating. What is it?"

"I just thought you might want to know there's a bag of grenades in the back seat of this one."

I grinned. "Yeah, so that is definitely helpful."

I moved over to the open driver's side back door and found a black duffel bag sitting in the center of the seat.

What were they planning to do with these?

"Who cares?" the voice asked. "I say use 'em."

I snorted quietly, removing the bag from the cabin. I knelt down near the back of the vehicle and opened the bag.

One of the men shouted from near the house, and the entire group opened fire. The deafening cacophony roared through this section of town.

I picked up two grenades, pulled the pins, and hurled one at the group on the right and one to the left, then repeated with two more.

"This'll be a blast," I muttered, ducking down behind the vehicle.

"Seriously? Come on, Gideon. You're better than—"

The explosions cut him off before he could finish his insult. The ground shook under me. Shrapnel zipped by, some of it pelting the other side of the vehicle.

The gunfire stopped instantly.

I stepped around the rear of the SUV and stalked toward the carnage. Clouds of acrid smoke hovered over the teams of gunmen. Some of them were still alive. For now. But they wouldn't be a threat. Every one of them was injured or mangled in some way.

"Better finish them off," Xolotl said in a grim yet satisfied tone.

I nodded. "Yeah."

CHAPTER 32

After eliminating every single guy from the Chinese forces, and from Adisa's side, I hurried through the open gate and toward the warehouse. I saw movement near one of the big bay doors and recognized Vero immediately.

I shifted into my human form on the run and slowed down as I neared the building.

"Did you find them?" I asked, panting.

"Yeah," she said, turning to point into the warehouse. "They're all okay."

Dozens of young women and girls stood inside. Most of them still looked tired and afraid, but also confused. I had no idea what they'd seen Vero do once she got inside. That was a story I'd have to get from her later.

A wave of relief rushed over me. "And Asim's sister?"

A young woman walked toward me, stepping away from the others.

"I am Asim's sister," she said. "My name is Korisi."

She wore a tattered blue dress. Her hair was matted, and her face was dirty, but underneath it I detected beauty, like a desert rose bursting from the parched soil.

"This is Gideon," Vero said.

"Nice to meet you. We're going to get you all out of here and back to your village."

Korisi nodded, tears streaming down her face. "Thank you. I do not know who you are or how you found us, but thank you."

"You're welcome. Your brother is going to be happy to see you're okay."

"Where is he?"

"He's waiting nearby." I looked at Vero. "I eliminated the guys who tried to escape."

"How are we going to get all these people back to the village?" she asked.

Sweeping my gaze across the roomful of people, I did a silent count. "There are a couple of cargo trucks out there, and some G-Wagons still intact. Probably only need two or three to get everyone back to the village."

I met Vero's eyes and lowered my voice. "We need to hurry. The sooner we get them all back to the village, the better."

I led the group out of the building with Vero taking the rear. I turned my head back and forth, constantly sweeping the area for any signs of trouble. If bullets started flying now, it would be nearly impossible to keep all of the young women safe.

So far, I didn't see any sign of trouble.

"Nothing on my end," Xolotl said.

His reassurance eased my tension. I knew he could somehow sense things better than me, which had bailed me out of trouble more than once.

We kept moving, ushering the group through the gate, then down the street.

By the time we arrived at the column of vehicles, the crimson mist had done its job, consuming every trace of the men who'd died there. Only their clothes and weapons remained.

"Any of you comfortable with a gun? I suggest you pick one of these up," I said.

To my surprise, a dozen of them broke out of the group and scooped up weapons. "Those of you who don't know how they—"

"We grew up in Sudan, Gideon," Korisi interrupted with a cool, grim grin, "we know how these work."

"I like her," the voice said.

"All right. Those of you who can drive, pick a truck and load up. Leave the SUVs. They can be traced."

The converted military trucks, however, didn't have that issue unless Adisa had installed some kind of homing device on them. I doubted they had LoJack out here.

The women split up into smaller groups, the drivers organizing them quickly before heading to their trucks.

There were four left, with three drivers.

I looked to Vero as she watched the rear to make sure no one snuck up behind us.

"You okay driving one of these?"

She nodded. "Yeah. No problem. What about you?"

I'm going to go get Asim. "We'll catch up to you and take the rear."

"Sounds good."

Vero looked out at the rest of the girls. "Y'all are with me," she said. "Front truck."

They followed her down the street to the last vehicle standing. She watched until everyone had loaded up in the cargo hold then hurried to the driver side door and climbed in.

Vero made a sharp right-hand turn onto another street then drove away. The other three followed behind, keeping a safe distance between them.

Once they were out of sight around the next corner, I whirled around and sprinted down the street in the other direction. I didn't see our Toyota, but I knew it had to be there in the shadows, probably just around the next corner.

I reached the next intersection quicker than any human could have then slowed to a walk. I looked to the left and spotted the old SUV.

"Gideon, wait," Xolotl said.

Then my heart dropped into my gut.

Standing behind the Toyota were five armed men—and one hostage.

"Crap," I muttered.

A man in a dark green beret, a matching vest and trousers, and tall black boots held a pistol up to the head of a familiar face.

The four other gunmen surrounded our friend and his captor, each armed with the same rifles everyone else had held.

I couldn't be sure, but I thought I saw a figure in a black suit melt into the shadows down the street. Either my mind was playing tricks on me, or it was a Sector agent.

"Ah, there he is," the man in the beret said. His face bore a scar on the right side that ran from his temple to the middle of his cheek. "I was beginning to think you weren't going to come back for your friend."

I stood there, peering through the man's eyes. He held Asim so close there was no way I could risk throwing one of the blades at him. Not that it mattered. By the time I took one from my side, they could kill him.

"Let him go, Kofi," I snarled, tempted to shift into the monster.

"No, I don't think so. I know what you are. I know the legends."

"Glad to hear you can read."

Kofi snorted in derision. "These stories aren't only read. They've been passed down orally for thousands of years. But you already know that."

"So that's why you set up your base at Jebel Barkal," I realized.

"Of course. I've spent over a year trying to unlock the secret of that mountain. Then you came along and did it for me."

Asim squirmed as if trying to free himself, but Adisa squeezed

273

him harder. One of the men to his left pointed his rifle at Asim's head. Now there was double trouble.

"What do you want, Kofi?" I spat his name with obvious disdain.

"I want your medallion," he said.

"Yeah, that's not going to happen."

"Then your friend dies." He clenched the gun to prove he would do it.

"Right. Except if you do, then you'll have to deal with me. If you really know what I am, what I can do, then you also know I will kill you and your little minions within thirty seconds. Although I'd probably make it last for you. I bet I could get at least fifteen minutes of agony before you finally gave up the ghost."

Kofi considered my words in silence for several seconds.

"I guess you didn't think of that, huh?" I taunted.

"Shut up."

I held out my hands wide, as if surrendering.

"I know why you're here."

"You said that."

"Shut! Up!" Kofi's temper took over.

I watched the crimson mist swirling around the five men, begging me to end them, but at the moment, there was nothing I could do. We were in a stalemate, a Mexican standoff without the guns. Well, they had guns.

"You are going to take us to the hidden temple of Apedemak. And you will lead me to his medallion."

"No!" Asim shouted, wriggling harder. "Don't do it, Gideon. Let him kill me. He can't get the—"

Kofi and I both knew I wasn't going to let that happen. Just like we both knew he wasn't going to do it. The man wanted a medallion. And I had no choice but to lead him to it.

"No, you have a choice," Xolotl said. "This can end right here. Right now."

What, and let Asim die? Not an option, compadre.

274

"In the greater scheme of things, many more could suffer if this man retrieves the medallion."

I'm aware of that.

"Then eliminate them."

I shook my head.

I'm not going to do that, X. He's a good man.

"You realize that if you lead Adisa to the medallion, you'll have to fight him, right?"

I actually hadn't considered that, but the statement didn't change my mind. *I can take him.*

"You're used to fighting humans. If he dons that amulet... fighting a dark guardian is way more dangerous."

"Well?" Adisa asked, cutting off my internal conversation. "Are you just going to stand there in silence until the sun rises?"

I could, but I knew that wouldn't change anything.

If I could get his men to turn on him, maybe I'd get a chance to save Asim.

"You abandoned all your men back at Jebel Barkal, Kofi. You let them all die so you could lure me here."

"Correct."

I watched the four guards around him, but they seemed unfazed by the confession.

I'd really hoped one of them might have turned on their leader. Apparently, they were in on the plan.

"Nice try," the voice said.

"How do you propose we do this?"

"You drive," Kofi said. "I ride in the back with him," he shook Asim.

"That SUV only seats five. What's your other guy going to do, assuming one will ride shotgun and one in the back seat."

"The other can ride in the back. There's room."

"You sure treat your loyal followers great."

Again, the barb didn't seem to goad any of his men to mutiny.

Adisa nodded his head sideways at the truck. The man to his left standing behind the other turned and opened the fifth door and climbed in.

"Let's go," Adisa said. "Behind the wheel. And if you try anything—"

"Yeah, I got it, you kill him, I kill you. I live the rest of my life with immense guilt."

I moved slowly forward, toward the SUV. The two guards to Adisa's right kept their weapons on me. Those things wouldn't do anything other than piss me off more. But I knew they weren't going to shoot.

I climbed into the driver's seat and started the engine while the rest of the men climbed into the truck. The one in the seat next to me smelled of abject poverty and like he hadn't had a shower in a week. I hoped it was less than that.

They closed the doors once everyone was inside.

"Drive," Adisa ordered.

I shifted the truck into drive and accelerated down the street. This was going to be a long drive. And I wondered if it would be long enough for me to come up with a way to get Asim and myself out of this.

CHAPTER 33

I drove through the seemingly endless expanse of the Sudanese desert, the SUV's engine humming steadily as the tires crunched over the sandy terrain. The night enveloped us, a vast canopy of stars stretching infinitely above, each one shimmering like a distant gem against the velvet darkness. The moon hung low on the horizon, a luminous half-orb casting a silvery glow over the landscape. It was a serene yet haunting beauty that only the desert night could offer.

As I approached the edge of Naga, the ancient ruins emerged from the shadows, their silhouettes etched against the starlit sky. I eased off the accelerator, allowing the vehicle to coast to a gentle stop. The headlights cast elongated beams across the sand, illuminating fragments of history that had stood silent for millennia.

I turned off the engine and looked back in the mirror at Adisa. "What now?"

"Get out, obviously," he spat.

The guy riding shotgun had kept a pistol on me the entire time. He'd braced it on his thigh, pointing it at my abdomen for hours. I thought surely at some point one or two of these guys would get sleepy. It was an exceedingly boring drive to get here, after all.

The gunman in the front with me waited while the three in the back seat and the goon in the cargo hold exited the vehicle and surrounded my door. Adisa stepped back with Asim pulled tight against him once more, the pistol's muzzle pressed to his head so firmly the skin dimpled from the pressure.

The same guard who'd pointed his weapon at Asim's head before resumed that position as well, while the others watched me closely as I opened the door.

Stepping out of the SUV, I felt the cool night air brush against my skin, a stark contrast to the sweltering heat of the day.

In the quietude of the night, the Temple of Apedemak stood prominently, its sandstone walls bathed in the ethereal glow of the moon. The temple's façade was adorned with intricate carvings, though time had worn them, leaving only traces of the once-vivid depictions of kings and deities. The lion-headed god Apedemak, guardian and warrior, seemed to watch over the ruins, his presence palpable even in the stillness.

Ahead, a pathway flanked by rows of lion sculptures led toward the temple.

"After you," Adisa said, nodding his head to the side, indicating the temple.

I walked ahead of the group slowly, each step stirring small clouds of sand that settled softly behind me. The lions, carved from the very rock of the desert, sat majestically on either side. Some bore the marks of erosion, their features softened by countless sand-storms, yet they retained an aura of regality. Their eyes, though stone, seemed to gaze forward eternally, guiding pilgrims to the sacred sanctuary.

The silence was profound, broken only by the faint whisper of the night breeze weaving through the ruins. I reached out to touch one of the lion statues, the stone cool beneath my fingertips. It was astonishing to think how artisans from centuries past had crafted such enduring symbols of power and protection. Each sculpture told a story, a fragment of a civilization that once thrived here amid the unforgiving desert.

"Keep moving," Adisa ordered.

Xolotl said nothing, remaining eerily silent. I did the same. There was nothing to say. Not yet.

As we moved closer to the ruins, I felt an energy, something I doubted any of the others detected. It was ancient, radiating from the temple. It was warm and welcoming, but I also sensed something powerful about it.

Surrounding the temple complex, the remnants of other structures lay scattered—columns toppled, walls crumbled, yet all bearing the distinct markings of Meroitic architecture. The fusion of Egyptian and indigenous styles was evident, a testament to the cultural crossroads that Naga had been. The famous Roman kiosk stood nearby, its hybrid architectural elements a curious blend that added to the site's mystique.

The temperature had dropped significantly since we left the humid port of Dongola, the heat dried away to a crisp chill. I wished I hadn't taken off my jacket when we'd arrived at the banks of the Nile.

Overhead, the constellations were brilliantly clear, unblemished by the light pollution of distant cities. Orion's belt pointed me toward the east, while the North Star held steadfast in its celestial anchor position.

I kept moving, the beams of the SUV's headlights casting long shadows that danced across the ruins. The interplay of light and darkness created an almost otherworldly atmosphere. Moonlight caressed the sandstone surfaces, highlighting the textures and patterns carved by ancient hands. It was as if the gods themselves had painted the scene, blending reality with the ethereal.

In the distance, the outline of the temple came into view, its grand pylons reaching upward as if attempting to touch the heavens. Though partially in ruins, the structure exuded a sense of majesty and reverence. I could almost hear the echoes of chants, the foot-steps of priests, and the murmurs of worshippers who once filled these sacred spaces.

The vastness of the surrounding desert stretched to the horizon, dunes undulating gently under the moon's glow. The sparse vegeta-tion, hardy shrubs, and the occasional acacia tree stood as solitary sentinels in this expansive sea of sand. The desert night was alive in its own subtle way; with the distant call of a nocturnal bird, and the scurrying of small creatures adapted to the darkness.

I took a deep breath, the air filling my lungs with the dry, cool scent of the desert. It cleared my mind and woke me up from the lengthy drive to get here. There was a profound sense of connection, a bridge between the past and the present. Standing there, I felt the weight of history, the stories of kings and queens, of gods and warriors all interwoven into the fabric of this place. And the power, the power I'd sensed as I approached, only felt stronger, as if pulling me into its epicenter.

The rows of stone lions on either side led directly to the temple's entrance. As I approached, the grandeur of the façade became more apparent, illuminated softly by the moonlight and the distant glow of the SUV's headlights.

The entrance was framed by two towering pylons, their edges worn but still imposing against the night sky. Carved into the sand-stone were intricate reliefs depicting scenes of kings and deities. I could make out the figures of King Natakamani and Queen Amani-tore, their images engraved with a regal precision that had withstood the passage of centuries. I'd only recently learned a little history about this place and its ancient kingdom, but there was no mistaking the figures I'd seen during my research on Nubia and the Kush Empire. They stood in profile, adorned in traditional royal garments, offering tributes to Apedemak. The lion-headed god himself was depicted with a muscular human body and the fierce head of a lion, a symbol of strength and protection.

Above the entrance, a carved sun disc flanked by cobras spread its wings—a common motif symbolizing divine protection in both Egyptian and Meroitic cultures. The doorway itself was slightly recessed, framed by columns etched with hieroglyphs and Meroitic script. Though much of the writing remained undeciphered to modern scholars, the symbols conveyed a sense of sacredness, an invocation to the gods and an assertion of the temple's holy purpose.

Stepping closer, I noticed the threshold was marked by a raised stone, perhaps intended to remind worshippers of the transition from the mundane to the sacred. I hesitated for a moment, feeling a mix of awe and reverence. The mysterious power radiating from the ruins enveloped me now, begging me to enter.

Crossing into the temple felt like stepping back in time, entering a space where the ancient world remained preserved.

Inside, the temperature warmed noticeably for some reason, the thick stone walls shielding the interior from the desert's extremes, seeming to bottle the energy I thought only I could sense. I looked over my shoulder at the men behind me, but they didn't seem to be affected either way by the shift.

The first chamber was a small vestibule, its walls adorned with faded but still discernible paintings and carvings. The light was dim, but enough filtered in from the entrance and a small opening above to reveal the artistry that covered every surface. Scenes of offerings, processions, and deities unfolded along the walls, each telling a part of the temple's story.

I moved forward into the main hall, a rectangular chamber supported by columns that had been carved to resemble bundled papyrus stalks—a design element borrowed from Egyptian architecture. The columns were decorated with more hieroglyphs and images of Apedemak, emphasizing his importance within these sacred confines. The floor was smooth beneath my feet, worn by the footsteps of countless devotees who had made this pilgrimage over the ages.

On the walls, reliefs depicted Apedemak in various forms—sometimes as a lion-headed man, other times as a full lion, or even a serpent with a lion's head. These images were interspersed with representations of other deities such as Isis and Osiris, highlighting the syncretic nature of Meroitic religion. The interplay between light and shadow in the hall gave life to the carvings, the figures seeming to shift and move as the moonlight flickered across them.

At the far end of the hall stood the sanctuary, the most sacred part of the temple. A doorway framed by ornate carvings led into a smaller chamber. I approached cautiously, aware that I was entering a space that had been revered for centuries. Inside, a pedestal or altar stood, though whatever statue or offering that once graced it was long gone. By contrast, the walls here were even more richly decorated, if that were possible. The reliefs were deeper, the carvings more intricate, perhaps to reflect the heightened sanctity of the space.

One particular carving caught my eye. It depicted Apedemak emerging from a lotus flower, a symbol of rebirth and creation. Surrounding him were images of the king and queen, offering gifts and seeking the god's favor. The level of detail was astonishing—the folds of garments, the expressions on the faces, the delicate patterns on jewelry—all meticulously rendered in stone.

The ceiling of the sanctuary was painted with stars, a reflection of the night sky. Although the colors had faded, hints of blue and gold were still visible. It was as if the room was designed to be a microcosm of the universe, connecting the earthly realm with the divine.

As I stood there, the silence of the temple wrapped around me. I closed my eyes and tried to imagine the sounds that once filled this space—the chants of priests, the murmurs of supplicants, the rituals performed in honor of Apedemak. The air seemed to hold a residual energy; a lingering essence of the devotion that had been poured into this place.

Flashlight beams raked through the darkness. I looked back and saw Adisa's men had attached lights to their weapons.

"Now what?" Adisa demanded.

"I don't know. I've never been here before."

The warlord raised his chin and peered at me. "Then I suppose I'll have to hurt your friend. Should we start with a finger or a toe?"

"Hey, take it easy. I told you'd I get you here. I held up my end of the bargain."

"You know that's not going to work, right?" Xolotl said, finally chirping up. I half wondered if he'd fallen asleep during the last leg of the journey.

I knew he was right, but I had to try.

Adisa shook his head. "You were supposed to lead me to the medallion. Where is it?"

"I have no idea," I said truthfully. "Every one is different."

"Well, perhaps I'll just take yours then."

I grinned like that kid in fifth grade who just got away with the greatest prank in history. "Again, we both know you can't do that. Unless your little gun there is going to fire some kind of bladed round that can take my head off."

He clenched his jaw.

"Back to hurting your friend. I've found it best to work from the bottom up. I'll start with a little toe, then the other, until all his limbs are removed. Then you can kill me and live with that vision the rest of your life."

I didn't like the idea. Obviously. I couldn't let that happen to Asim. But I didn't know what I was supposed to do.

"Crazy idea, kid, but maybe take a closer look at that altar."

Of course. It did seem that the energy I felt all around was somehow coming from that spot.

"Let me look a little closer at the altar," I said, basically repeating Xolotl's words.

Adisa motioned for one of his men to stay close to me. It was a bit of a hollow gesture at that point. I could end the guy in a second no matter how many rounds he put through me.

I walked back over to the altar and asked if I could use my phone light.

"No. You think I'm stupid? Use his light."

He barked an order at the gunman, who immediately removed the light from his weapon and handed it to me.

"Thanks," I said with unfiltered sarcasm.

I pointed the light at the altar and started scanning over the surface. I noticed a few things I hadn't on the first once-over. I hadn't been trying then, hoping somehow Adisa would screw up and I could eliminate him. But the guy kept Asim stuck to him like Velcro.

I moved around to the back side of the plinth and continued scanning. The gunman watching me shifted as I did and stayed close in case I tried to make a move. Not that there was much I could do. Not yet.

Within ten seconds of moving around to the other side of the altar, I found what I was looking for—a round indentation in the stone with the emblem carved into it. The circle and symbol matched the size and design of the necklace we'd found in Portugal. A thought of that adventure flashed through my mind, and it felt like ages since all that had happened even though it was only days ago.

"I have to get something out of my pocket," I said, standing up straight.

"What is it?" Adisa snapped.

"It's a thermal detonator."

The man's face scrunched in confusion. "What?"

"Never mind." I knew he wouldn't get the *Star Wars* reference. "It's a small disc. I think I'm supposed use it here."

"Use it for what?"

It was so hard not to roll my eyes at this guy. How he was able to convince so many to follow him outside of brainwashing was beyond me. I guessed desperate people anywhere in the world would listen to a madman if he offered them something better.

"The entrance to the temple is hidden, as in magically hidden. If it wasn't, the medallion would have been found a long time ago. Does that make sense?" I spoke to him as if he were a child.

He narrowed his eyelids and nodded to the man closest to me. "Watch him."

The guard moved closer, tightening the grip on his weapon. Were things different, it would have been all too easy to end his life right then and there, probably within a few seconds.

I slowly reached into my pocket and pulled out the disc. I stared at it for several seconds before bending down to place it in the cutout.

I had no idea if this would work, and if so, how. Maybe the metal was made of some otherworldly element bestowed with powers we humans didn't yet understand. Or perhaps this sacred location interacted with it by producing a subtle energy, maybe the one I was still feeling all around me.

Of course, it was also highly possible that nothing would happen once I set the disc in place. If that were the case, I'd have to think of something else fast.

Leaning in close to the altar, I pinched the disc between my thumb and index finger, lined up the symbols, and pressed it into position. It was a tight, but perfect, fit.

I raised up again and took a step back, hoping something was going to happen.

"Well?" Adisa demanded. "Why is it not working?"

I didn't know. I started to tell him the same, but suddenly the earth began to rumble under our feet. It was low at first, like a freight train, far away but still charging down the tracks. Every second that passed, the sound grew louder, and the ground shook harder.

The guard nearest me almost lost his balance but recovered by leaning against the altar. Adisa and the other three wobbled, struggling to stay upright.

Oddly, I noticed the temple ruins around us seemed unaffected by the highly localized earthquake. The ancient stones, the columns, the roofing, the walls, all should have toppled over. But they remained perfectly still.

"What is this?" Adisa shouted over the sounds. "What did you do?"

He kept his pistol pointed at Asim's head, but his grip loosened as he tried to stay upright.

I considered producing one of the blades and taking a shot at the leader's throat, but there was no way. Even with a little separation between him and Asim, it was too risky.

The noise around us swelled to a near-deafening level. I felt the energy around me pulsing like a heartbeat.

Just as it seemed the noise would be unbearable, everything around me vanished—the temple, the altar, Adisa and his men, and Asim, vanished, and I found myself standing in a black void.

CHAPTER 34

I looked around for a second to get my bearings before I heard Adisa shouting at his men, then at me.

"Where are you, Gideon?" he yelled. "What have you done?"

I didn't answer immediately. If there was a way I could have snuck up on them without being seen, I could have taken out the warlord and his goons before they ever knew what happened.

The darkness was absolute as we moved forward, the stale air thick with the weight of centuries. My flashlight had gone out, as had everyone else's. The only thing I could figure was there'd been a massive pulse of energy that disabled anything electrical.

I retrieved my phone from my pocket and found it powered off. I pressed the button on the side, but nothing happened. This place, it seemed, was a power sink.

Suddenly, as if responding to an unspoken command, flames erupted along the walls. One by one, magical torches ignited with a whoosh, their golden light illuminating the vast expanse of the temple. The sudden brightness forced me to squint, and when my eyes adjusted, I was rendered speechless by the sight before me.

Towering pillars carved from smooth sandstone stretched upward, their surfaces adorned with hieroglyphs of the Kush Empire. The symbols danced in the flickering light, telling tales of ancient kings and forgotten battles. Along the walls, vivid depictions of Apedemak, the lion-headed god, came to life. In one scene, he led warriors into battle, his mane flowing like fire as he vanquished foes with a mere swipe of his paw. In another, he stood protectively over the people, his fierce visage a shield against all dangers.

The images shifted seamlessly from scenes of war to those of prosperity. Fields of grain swayed under a benevolent sun, rivers teemed with fish, and families gathered in joyous celebration—all under the watchful gaze of Apedemak. The artistry was exquisite, each stroke of pigment preserved as if applied yesterday. The colors —rich golds, deep reds, and vibrant blues—were a stark contrast to the monochrome world above.

"Incredible," Adisa said, looking around at the wonders surrounding us. His men, too, took in the sight of the mysterious chamber. "Where are we?"

"The true Temple of Apedemak," I said.

"Where is the sky? The desert?" He sounded a little panicky.

"The real question that will scramble your noodle is, were those things really there to begin with, or were they merely a part of your imagination projected onto a 3-D screen?"

The warlord's confused expression told me all I needed.

"This place doesn't exist in the same plane or realm as the world you know," I explained. "It could be underground. It could be ten thousand feet in the air. It doesn't matter because it is only real to your perceptions." It was still obvious I was getting nowhere with this explanation. If nothing else, he looked more confused than before. "You know what? Don't worry about it."

"Very well," Adisa answered. "Lead the way."

I trudged past him and his three bodyguards, with the guy watching me following close behind, the rifle aimed at my spine.

The room funneled us into a long corridor, the walls angling subtly inward, creating a sense of being guided by unseen hands. The floor beneath us was smooth, the stone cool even through the soles of my shoes. As we moved forward, the guards' footsteps echoed alongside mine, a steady rhythm.

"Keep moving," the warlord commanded, his voice slicing through the silence.

Like I needed to be told to keep moving. I glanced back at Asim, his eyes reflecting both fear and defiance. Adisa remained directly behind him, now pointing his pistol at the back of my friend's skull. I wanted to offer some reassurance, but I could find none.

We passed through an archway with the image of Apedemak painted over it, as if welcoming us to his inner sanctum. On the other side of the entrance, the passage opened into another vast chamber that took my breath away. At its center stood a pedestal carved from obsidian, and atop it, hovering a foot above the surface, was the medallion—a disc of pure gold attached to a golden necklace. Embedded at its center was a gem that radiated an amber light, bathing the room in a warm glow that pulsed like a drum. The light seemed almost alive, casting intricate patterns on the walls as it refracted through the gem's facets.

Around the chamber, weapons lined the walls on ornate racks: swords with blades that gleamed wickedly, their edges honed to perfection; spears that stood tall, their shafts inlaid with precious metals and capped with razor-sharp tips; and shields that bore the emblem of Apedemak, the lion's head rendered in meticulous detail. Despite the immeasurable age of these armaments, they appeared untouched by time—no rust marred their surfaces, no decay dulled their shine.

The warlord's eyes widened with a mix of greed and triumph. "At last," he whispered.

I hoped he'd be stupid enough to forget his need of a hostage and step forward toward the medallion. That would have afforded me the few seconds I needed to spin a blade through his neck and take out his guards.

Instead, he shuffled to the right, keeping Asim between him and me until he stood at the base of the plinth.

I wanted to tell him not to do it, to offer some made-up warning about how it could kill him. But I knew it wouldn't matter. He was bent on taking it, claiming it as his own so he could harness the power of a god.

Keeping the pistol pointed at the back of Asim's head, Adisa reached out his right hand toward the medallion, but as his fingers neared it, the amber light intensified, forcing him to recoil. A low growl echoed through the chamber, though no creature was visible.

"Perhaps it's not meant for you," I warned, the words escaping before I could stop them.

He turned sharply, his gaze piercing. "You can't scare me," he scoffed.

Ignoring his taunt, I looked back at the walls. More hieroglyphs covered every inch, interspersed with scenes that seemed to tell a prophecy. One image depicted a figure resembling a traveler, standing before Apedemak, the medallion held aloft, light emanating outward to repel darkness.

Asim noticed it too. "Look," he urged softly, nodding toward the wall.

The guards shifted uneasily, their confidence wavering in the face of the unknown.

The warlord's impatience flared. "Enough of this!" he barked. He jabbed his hand out and this time pushed through the burst of light until his fingers touched the amulet.

A voice resonated throughout the chamber—not spoken aloud but echoing inside our minds: "Only the worthy may claim the heart of Apedemak."

The guards looked around, trying to find where the voice had come from.

A deep tremor shook the chamber. The torches lining the walls flickered wildly, their flames contorting into unnatural shapes. An oppressive darkness began to seep from the medallion, swallowing the warm glow that had once filled the room. Shadows stretched and twisted, crawling up the walls like living creatures.

"Asim!" I shouted as a sudden force hurled him away from Adisa. He crashed into a rack of ancient weapons, the clang of metal echoing sharply before he slumped to the ground, seemingly unconscious. Concern and anger surged through me, but before I could move toward him, my attention was wrenched back to Adisa.

His men exchanged uneasy glances, the confidence they had displayed moments before now eroding into palpable fear.

"What's happening?" one of them muttered, stepping back. Another guard gripped his weapon tighter, his knuckles whitening. The atmosphere was thick with dread, a suffocating weight that pressed down on all of us.

Adisa stood at the epicenter of the chaos, a sinister grin spreading across his face. The medallion's light had shifted from amber to a deep, malevolent crimson, casting eerie shadows that danced across his features. Tendrils of dark red mist spiraled around him, seeping into his skin like ink dissolving in water.

The hieroglyphs on the walls began to glow with an ominous black light. The once-noble images of Apedemak transformed—where the lion god had been depicted protecting his people, he was now shown leading armies into brutal conquest, his face twisted into a snarl. Scenes of prosperity warped into visions of destruction and despair.

A low growl emanated from Adisa's throat, growing louder until it resonated throughout the chamber. His body convulsed, muscles bulging unnaturally beneath his skin. His eyes blazed with a feral light, pupils narrowing into slits. Coarse fur sprouted along his arms and neck, spreading rapidly as his humanity was consumed by the beast within.

The guards recoiled in horror. One started to say something, but his words were cut short as Adisa's transformation accelerated. The warlord's jaw elongated, teeth morphing into sharp fangs. Ears shifted upward, reshaping into pointed tufts. Fingers curled into claws, each tipped with razor-sharp talons. Dark, metallic armor now encased him.

Why does he automatically get the armor upgrade?

"Kofi?" a guard whispered, his voice quavering. But the figure before us was no longer the warlord we knew. He had become the embodiment of Apedemak—the lion-headed god brought to terrifying life.

A dark aura radiated from him, the air itself seeming to vibrate with malice. The chamber's light dimmed further, the shadows thickening into an almost tangible form. The medallion was now fused to his chest, its crimson glow pulsing like a heartbeat.

Adisa threw back his lion head and released a roar that shook the very foundations of the temple. Dust and small stones rained down from the ceiling. The sound was a dreadful blend of human agony and animal fury, echoing endlessly in the confined space.

The guards were paralyzed with fear. One dropped his weapon, the clatter startling in the heavy silence that followed. He bowed down to his knees, and the other three followed suit. The men prostrated themselves as if in worship to their leader.

A guttural voice echoed through the chamber, pulling my attention back to the monstrous figure.

"Bow before me, or die!" Adisa ordered, pointing at me.

Xolotl said nothing. I wasn't sure if he was allowed to in this place or if he was just observing. I got the feeling, though, that it was by choice, that he was testing me in some way to see if I could handle this on my own.

"Yeah," I answered, shifting into the Chupacabra, equaling Adisa's height. "That's not going to happen."

He raised his hand, and the shadows around him forged a black spear with an obsidian blade at the top. "I hoped you would say that," Adisa snarled.

The guards looked up at me from their positions of worship, looks of sheer terror filling their faces.

I picked up the closest one and hurled him at my enemy. Adisa swiped his clawed, paw-like hand across his body, knocking the guard away. The man flew to my left and smashed into the wall with immense force. He fell down onto a spear sticking up in a rack, impaled through the gut. The guy didn't feel it. He was dead on impact.

I threw the next guard, and the third, at Adisa, but he was all too happy to kill his own men in the same way, knocking them aside as though they were nothing more than pillows. Each one died the same death—with a violent impact against the wall.

I stole a quick glance over at Asim. He remained motionless on the floor. I had no way to know if he was dead or alive, but something told me he was only unconscious—for now.

"Are you done?" Adisa growled, holding out the spear in front of me as if in challenge.

The spiral blades appeared at my sides. I held them up, turning my body to the side. "Not yet."

CHAPTER 35

I didn't wait for Adisa to attack first. I threw the sharp disc in my right hand, hoping to take off his head in a single move.

Adisa anticipated it, though, and flipped up his spear in time to knock the spiral blade down to the ground.

I quickly threw the second, aiming at his left leg, but again Adisa was too fast. He twisted his body to the side, and struck the blade with the base of his spear, batting it to the wall, where it fell to the floor. For an instant, I wondered why the blades weren't returning to me as before. I didn't have time to figure it out.

"Looks like you're all out of tricks," Adisa said. He rushed toward me, leading with the long spear. I stood my ground for a moment, waiting for him to attack.

Adisa thrust the spear at me, stabbing at my neck, but I spun away and grabbed the shaft. I attempted to rip it from him, but his grip was every bit as strong as mine, and before I could even make it budge, he shoved me backward, using both my momentum and his strength to push me against the wall.

He pinned me there, trying to force the shaft of the spear against my throat to choke me. While that might not have killed me, I knew it could render me unconscious for a precious few seconds. Then it would all be over. He'd clean my head from my body and then be in possession of two medallions.

I snarled at him and snapped my jaws at his neck. I missed, and he twisted his head and bit back, but his teeth only glanced off my helmet for his effort.

I lifted my left leg and planted my foot against the wall, then pushed while I kicked out with my other foot. My heel hit Adisa in his abdomen and knocked him back six feet, freeing me for the moment.

He dug in then rushed at me again, this time aiming the spear point at my left eye. I waited until the last second and dove to my left, rolled to my feet, and jerked a golden spear from the nearest rack.

I'd never used one of these before, but I figured I could manage if Adisa was. Unless he had some kind of special ability bestowed on him by the lion god. In which case, this would be a short fight.

He growled in frustration as his strike missed and smashed into the stone wall. Chunks of it broke free, but the spear didn't appear blunted in the least.

Adisa grunted in frustration, pivoted, and charged me again. His attacks were sloppy, uncoordinated and unplanned, but they were violent enough to compensate.

He stabbed at me again, and this time I spun my spear up, blocking the attack and knocking his blade up and to the left. I followed the defense with a counter of my own, twisting my body sideways while flipping my spear backward and jabbing it at Adisa.

The sharp point caught him on the flank, where his armor revealed a gap. A gash opened in his side, and dark blood spilled out and over the lion's fur.

Adisa roared, jumping back for a moment to regroup. He looked down at the wound, angry at first. But his expression changed as the cut began to heal itself. Then he bared his teeth in a sinister grin.

I waited, holding my weapon out to the side as if inviting him to come in for another taste.

He accepted and rushed at me again. This time, he stopped short and swung his weapon in a broad arch, aiming for my neck. I shifted my feet and blocked the attack. The spear shafts clanked loudly, the sound echoing around the room. The torches danced around us as if cheering on the battle.

Out of my periphery, I saw Asim still in a heap on the floor thirty feet away. I didn't know if he had hit his head or if the pulse of energy from Adisa had knocked him out. Either way, I couldn't tend to him until I dealt with the enemy hell bent on separating my head from my body.

Adisa spun his spear like a baton and then lashed out at my neck again. I ducked then stabbed up with my weapon, catching him again, this time in the abdomen. He howled from the pain as I drove the spear up and through his back, driving him toward the wall. I lifted him off the ground and shoved him until I felt the spear's tip hit stone.

He kicked out his right foot and caught me on the jaw, but I didn't let go. Then he raised his spear over his head, and stabbed down with it, aiming for my neck.

I leaned to the right, narrowly dodging the first attempt, but he swept the blade in a follow-up attack. I felt the sharp edge slice through my neck, cutting deep into the flesh. I instantly let go and fell back, the rush of blood spilling out of the wound. It gushed over my armor, and for a moment, I felt faint.

He'd nearly taken my head off, and I cursed my carelessness. I tried to maintain my balance, but the room spun around me as I stumbled backward. My heel caught on the floor, and I tumbled over onto my back.

Back on his feet, Adisa yanked my spear out of his gut, growling at the pain as the blade slid back through his flesh. He stalked toward me, letting the spear shafts slide down to where he held them both just below the base of the blades.

I retreated, scurrying backward as the wound on my neck began to heal.

"Where are you going?" Adisa sneered.

I started to push myself up off the floor, but he was too fast. Adisa leaped and drove his spear down through my right forearm and into the floor. The tip sank deep into the rock, pinning me there.

Grimacing, I tried to free my arm, but he pounced onto my other, smashing it into the floor with his heavy right foot.

I kicked, desperately attempting to wriggle free, but my brain was still foggy.

"Is this what you see?" Adisa asked. "This white mist that swirls around your enemies?"

I didn't like the sound of that. I could only surmise that if an evil person donned a medallion, they saw the opposite of what I could see. Instead of a red mist, theirs was white.

There was no time to ponder the meaning of it. I pushed hard with my arm, but his strength was equal to mine, and the weight was too much to overcome.

"Now," Adisa said, "I will have the power of two medallions. And no one will be able to stand up to me."

He held out his spear as if it were the Grim Reaper's scythe, ready to finish me. Standing up straight, towering over me, Adisa offered one last satisfied, menacing smile.

Something moved suddenly behind him, and I caught a flash of shiny metal near his neck.

Then Adisa's expression changed in an instant. One moment, he looked triumphant, savoring what he thought was sure to be victory. The next, his lips twisted into a confused frown. His forehead wrinkled. The spear in his hand dropped harmlessly to the floor, the clatter echoing around the chamber.

A thin line of blood appeared around his neck. The life vacated from his eyes a moment before his head toppled off and landed on the floor. His body fell next, landing at my feet. Then a bright white light erupted from the body. The room shook. I shielded my eyes against the glare, but it and the noise only lasted for a few seconds.

As suddenly as it began, the room returned to its previous state —lit only by the torches burning along the walls.

And then I saw him. Standing just behind where Adisa had been, Asim held a sword he'd taken from one of the racks. He breathed heavily, and his eyes bore uncertainty.

The red fog swirled around Adisa's body, consuming it greedily.

The medallion that had been around his neck now hung from Asim's. The amber gem in the center pulsed with radiant light.

"Are you okay?" Asim asked.

I rolled over and jerked the spear out of my arm. "It doesn't feel great, but yeah, I'm good."

I stood up and stared into his eyes. The same light that emanated from the gem also glowed in them.

He looked down at Adisa's body as the mist did its work. "Is... this what you see all the time?"

"The red fog? Yes. It marks the wicked so we will never take the life of an innocent."

He allowed a nod then seemed to be listening to something. "The voice, is that..."

"Apedemak? Yes. His power dwells within you now, Asim."

He shook his head and dropped the sword on the floor. "That cannot be. I am—"

"You are," I cut him off, "a guardian now. You'd better get used to it."

His head twisted around, as if he were searching for a way out of there. "But I am nothing special."

"Nor was I. Personally, I still don't think I am anything special. You have been chosen, Asim. You took action to save my life. You have been brave during this whole ordeal. And I'm pretty sure Amari was preparing you for this role for a while now."

He seemed to consider the statement. "But I am not a warrior."

"I beg to differ. If not for you, we wouldn't have been able to get into Adisa's compound. And last I noticed, you were pretty good with that rifle from a decent distance. Doesn't sound very un-warrior-like to me."

He held up his hands in front of his chest, looking at them as if for the first time.

"You summon the power when you need it," I explained, sensing his next question. "It will always be there for you. And you can't die unless someone does what you did to him."

"That part I remembered from the stories Amari told me. It's why I went for the neck."

I grinned. "Good student."

His confusion turned to concern. "My sister. The others. Where are—"

"Vero took them back to the village. She and a few others drove Adisa's trucks out of Dongola. They're safe."

"I need to see her," he said.

I nodded. "If we hurry, we might be able to get there right around sunrise."

Suddenly, the chamber around us disappeared, blinking into utter blackness. The dark lasted only a second before we found ourselves standing once more in the center of the Temple of Apedemak beneath the stars.

"I don't know if I can get used to this," Asim admitted. He looked as though he might pass out.

"You will," I reassured. "Just give it time."

CHAPTER 36

As the first light of dawn brushed the horizon, the vast expanse of the Sudanese desert transformed into a canvas of soft pinks and golds. The cool night air began to warm, carrying with it the subtle scents of sand and distant acacia blossoms. The rocky hills that cradled the village emerged from the shadows, their rugged silhouettes etched against the glowing sky.

Driving along the beaten path that passed for a road, I felt a profound sense of relief wash over me as the sun peeked over the horizon. The engine's steady hum was a comforting backdrop to the unfolding morning.

Asim and I had talked a little since we left Naga, but I didn't need to explain much. He'd been taught about the legends of the guardians, and their role in the world. Amari had taken him under his wing. The shaman had, no doubt, known Asim's lineage, and a deeply rooted connection to Apedemak and the family of guardians associated with him throughout all of history.

As we crested a small dune, Asim's village came into view—spread out in a natural basin between the hills, its simple structures bathed in the gentle light of sunrise.

At the edge of the village perimeter, Adisa's cargo trucks that Vero had commandeered were parked in a neat line. Their presence was a reassuring sight, signaling that Vero and the young women who had been taken were safely back home. The trucks stood like silent sentinels, their worn exteriors reflecting the first rays of the sun.

I guided the Land Cruiser toward the trucks, the tires leaving faint tracks in the sand. Pulling up beside one of the bulky vehicles, I turned off the engine and sat for a moment, taking in the scene.

Stepping out of the vehicle, I felt the crisp air wrap around me, sending a chill across my skin. It carried the earthy aroma of the desert mingled with hints of wood smoke from the village fires that had started to stir. The sky overhead was a vast expanse, the stars fading as daylight took hold. The gentle breeze brushed against my face, a whisper of the heat that would come later in the day. I stretched, the tension of the past hours easing from my muscles. The quiet was profound, broken only by the distant sounds of the village waking up—the lowing of goats, the muffled voices of early risers, and the soft clatter of pots and pans.

Looking toward the entrance of the village, I saw a group of familiar figures gathered. Vero stood tall and composed, her posture exuding both strength and relief. Her gaze surveyed the surroundings, ever watchful. Beside her was Amari, his sense of calm evident even from a distance. Others milled about, their silhouettes moving gracefully in the dawn light.

As I walked toward them, the warmth of the rising sun began to touch the landscape, casting long shadows and highlighting the rich hues of the sand and stone. The village huts, made of mud and thatch, glowed softly, their simple forms blending seamlessly with the environment. Smoke curled lazily from a few chimneys, carrying the scent of brewing tea and freshly baked bread.

Among the gathering, I spotted Asim's sister. Her features mirrored his—the same determined eyes and quiet strength. She moved with purpose, assisting an elder with a gentle hand. The sight of her safe and engaged in the rhythms of daily life brought a smile to my face.

To my surprise, the old American, Starnes, leaned against one of the cargo trucks. His weathered hat was tipped back, and his eyes surveyed the scene with a mix of weariness and contentment. The lines on his face told stories of years spent navigating landscapes like this one. There was a hint of a grin as he caught my eye, a silent acknowledgment of shared experiences.

Magali was there too, the bartender from Dongola. Her colorful headscarf caught the light, and even in this early hour, she exuded a lively spirit. She chatted animatedly with a group of women, her hands gesturing in wide movements as she spoke. Her presence here, so far from the bustling town where we first met, seemed both surprising and perfectly natural.

The atmosphere was one of quiet celebration. Relief and joy mingled in the air, palpable even without words. Children peeked out from doorways, their curious eyes reflecting the glow of the morning. A few brave ones ventured out, chasing each other with carefree laughter that echoed softly.

I took a deep breath, the cool air filling my lungs. The scent of the desert at dawn was unlike any other—a blend of sand, sparse vegetation, and the faint musk of animals. It was a reminder of the stark beauty of this place, harsh yet profoundly alive.

As we approached, Starnes gave me a wink.

"What are you and Magali doing here?" I asked.

The old American shrugged. "We figured it wouldn't be the right thing to do to let them drive back through the desert on their own. So we rode along with them. Just in case."

Magali smiled, her eyes drawn to Asim. "I'm sorry I left you," she said.

I knew something was up between them, but to what level I had no idea. Maybe it had been a burgeoning romance that was doused by her need for a change of pace or scenery or simply bigger dreams than this desert village could provide.

Whatever it was, Asim walked up to her, wrapped his arms around her, and embraced her tight. She hugged him back, and they held each other for a long moment.

Asim's sister hurried over to them, and joined them. "I was so worried you wouldn't come back," she said.

Then she noticed the medallion hanging from Asim's neck. She took a step back and looked him up and down. "Is that..." Her words faltered.

Asim nodded. "Yes."

"He's officially a guardian now," I said.

Vero joined me by my side, clearly relieved that I'd made it back.

"What happened?" she asked.

"I'll tell you all about it later."

Amari approached us, a warm smile beaming from his weathered face. He stopped close to Asim. Magali and Korisi stepped away to allow the shaman to speak directly to him.

"You have done well," Amari said. "You are the descendant of Apedemak, one of the ancient guardians of Africa, a protector of the people, and warrior against the forces of evil."

He bowed low, and everyone around them did the same.

Asim looked uncomfortable with the honors. "I don't know if I am ready," he confessed.

Amari stood upright again, his smile never wavering. "That is how I know you are. One who believes themselves ready for such a burden would not be. Only a truly humble person, with a pure heart, is capable of this undertaking."

Asim contemplated the statement. "I will do my best."

"I know you will."

Amari turned to me and Vero. "Thank you both. You have given the people of Africa a much-needed gift. But I am sure you both know... your journey is far from over."

He stepped close and put his arms around us, turning us away from the group. "For now, you are needed elsewhere. I sense more trouble is coming, the kind that only guardians can handle."

I let his words sink in. I had no clue how the guy knew what was going on in another part of the world, but I also knew his abilities reached beyond the normal senses of human beings.

"He's not wrong," Xolotl said. "The forces of darkness are getting more desperate by the day. This is only going to get harder. I hope you're okay with that. Not that you have a choice."

I grinned at his snark.

"Amari," Vero said, "a moment ago you said one of the guardians of Africa."

He sensed the second part of her question. "Yes. There are two from this ancient land."

"Who is the other?" I asked.

Amari smiled. "A very powerful one from the lands to the north. You met his uncle in your dream."

After a few seconds, the answer hit me.

"Horus."

CHAPTER 37

After saying our goodbyes to the villagers, and our new friends, Vero and I made the long drive back to Khartoum.

I'd hardly call it civilization, but compared to the remote places we'd been in for the last few days, it felt like a metropolis.

We arrived at our gate in the airport and took a seat near one of the windows.

With decent cell service for the first time in a while, we pulled out our phones and checked up on the latest events going on back across the pond.

I had several missed text messages, all from Jesse and Jack.

They'd tracked down the company that made the frequency emitter that had caused my unseen friend such misery before. According to Jesse, the manufacturer was GenTech, a weapons maker that specialized in next-generation technology, including acoustic and frequency weaponry.

I'd have to research them further, perhaps on the flight back.

Next to me, Vero was scrolling through news reports from

Mexico. I could tell from the concerned look on her face that whatever she was reading wasn't good news.

"What's going on?" I asked.

"It's the cartels," she said. "They've taken control of two towns in the south. They're spreading like a virus. And the government isn't doing anything about it."

I sensed where this was going and peered into her eyes. "Does that mean you have to go back?"

"I think so," she said. "Artemis said we have to. It's our duty, to protect the people."

"I know. Do you want me to come with you?"

"No. I mean, yes, obviously I do. But you have your own problems to deal with back in the States. I'll be okay. I can handle it."

I smiled at her. "I know you can."

I put my phone away and leaned back in the chair, wrapping my arm around her. She pulled close to me and rested her head on my shoulder and neck. Soon, we'd be separated by miles, but our spirits would always be united.

Even though I knew she was extremely powerful, I still worried about her. I'd rather go with her to Mexico to deal with the issues there, but I knew that wasn't an option.

For now, all I could do was enjoy this moment, holding her. The battles to come could wait, at least for a little while.

THANK YOU

Thank you for taking the time to read this story. I hope you enjoyed it. To find out when the next story will be released, and to get updates on new content, join the VIP Reader Club here: https://read erlinks.com/l/3400241

ALSO BY ERNEST DEMPSEY

Sean Wyatt Archaeological Thrillers:

The Secret of the Stones

The Cleric's Vault

The Last Chamber

The Grecian Manifesto

The Norse Directive

Game of Shadows

The Jerusalem Creed

The Samurai Cipher

The Cairo Vendetta

The Uluru Code

The Excalibur Key

The Denali Deception

The Sahara Legacy

The Fourth Prophecy

The Templar Curse

The Forbidden Temple

The Omega Project

The Napoleon Affair

The Second Sign

The Milestone Protocol

Where Horizons End

Poseidon's Fury

The Florentine Pursuit

The Inventor's Tomb

Adriana Villa Adventures:

War of Thieves Box Set

When Shadows Call

Shadows Rising

Shadow Hour

The Relic Runner - A Dak Harper Series:

The Relic Runner Origin Story

The Courier

Two Nights In Mumbai

Country Roads

Heavy Lies the Crown

Moscow Sky

Thief's Honor

Strings of Deception

The Adventure Guild (ALL AGES):

The Caesar Secret: Books 1-3

The Carolina Caper

Beta Force Comedy Thrillers:

Operation Zulu

London Calling

Paranormal Archaeology Division:

Hell's Gate

Where Dead Things Stand

Guardians of Earth:

Emergence: Gideon Wolf Book 1

Righteous Dawn: Gideon Wolf Book 2

Crimson Winter: Gideon Wolf Book 3

ACKNOWLEDGMENTS

As always, I would like to thank my terrific editors, Anne and Jason, for their hard work. What they do makes my stories so much better for readers all over the world. Anne Storer and Jason Whited are the best editorial team a writer could hope for and I appreciate everything they do.

I also want to thank Elena at L1 Graphics for her tremendous work on my book covers and for always overdelivering. Elena definitely rocks.

A big thank you has to go out to my friend James Slater for his proofing work. James has added another layer of quality control to these stories, and I can't thank him enough.

Thanks as well to my friend Allison Valentine who does an amazing job with the Hunters and Runners page on Facebook on top of all the hard work she does for so many authors.

Last but not least, I need to thank all my wonderful fans and especially the advance reader team. Their feedback and reviews are always so helpful and I can't say enough good things about all of them.

Made in the USA
Las Vegas, NV
27 December 2024

15480867R00184